LEE COUNTY LIBRARY
107 HAWKINS AVE.
SANFORD, N. C. 27330

Ringer

ALSO BY DAVID R. SLAVITT

PROSE

Cold Comfort
Jo Stern
King of Hearts
The Killing of the King
The Outer Mongolian
ABCD
Anagrams
Feel Free
Rochelle, or Virtue Rewarded

POETRY

Dozens
Rounding the Horn
Vital Signs: New and Selected Poems
The Eclogues and the Georgics of Virgil
Child's Play
The Eclogues of Virgil
Day Sailing
The Carnivore
Suits for the Dead

RINGER

DAVID R. SLAVITT

E. P. DUTTON, INC. | NEW YORK

Copyright © 1982 by David R. Slavitt

All rights reserved. Printed in the U.S.A.

No part of this publication may be reproduced or transmitted in any form or by any means, electronic or mechanical, including photocopy, recording or any information storage and retrieval system now known or to be invented, without permission in writing from the publisher, except by a reviewer who wishes to quote brief passages in connection with a review written for inclusion in a magazine, newspaper or broadcast.

Published in the United States by
E. P. Dutton, Inc.,
2 Park Avenue,
New York, N.Y. 10016

Library of Congress Cataloging in Publication Data

Slavitt, David R.
Ringer.
I. Title.
PS3569.L3R5   813'.54   82-5103
AACR2

ISBN: 0-525-24139-6

Published simultaneously in Canada by Clarke, Irwin & Company Limited, Toronto and Vancouver

Designed by Nicola Mazzella
10 9 8 7 6 5 4 3 2 1

First Edition

For Janet

ACKNOWLEDGMENTS

Early in 1942, the Abwehr, the German intelligence organization, landed eight saboteurs on American shores. The history of this odd abortive mission has been set forth with admirable clarity and care by Eugene Rachlis in *They Came to Kill* (Random House, 1961), upon which I have relied for background. I have merely extended the truth into what I hope is a plausible and entertaining story. Adolf Hitler's plan, as described in the following pages, is in fact what he proposed.

LEE COUNTY LIBRARY
107 HAWKINS AVE.
SANFORD, N. C. 27330

RINGER

PROLOGUE

Passing by the place, a casual observer wouldn't have been able to tell that it was one of those bars. It wasn't the kind of place that had given Berlin its reputation for stylish naughtiness only a decade before—in the early thirties, say—when there was a garish exuberance to those meat markets where dandies in business suits or evening clothes mixed with toughs wearing work clothes or leather jackets with metal studs. That old flaunting was no longer possible. Indeed, at the bar and at one or two of the tables were women, sitting and decorating the place, giving it the look of an ordinary night spot. The men of the bar joked with them, even bought them drinks from time to time—but didn't go so far as to leave the bar with them. The men left with each other, mostly in couples but occasionally in foursomes.

That casual observer, if he were to look a little more closely, having perhaps nothing better to do as he waited at the bus stop across the street, might even have noted a certain pattern in the comings and goings of the bar's clientele. If he were unlucky enough to have a long wait, he might have been able even to distinguish among the cruisers, some of them circumspect and nervous, some of them loud and mocking, and some of them quite businesslike about what was—almost certainly—a business. In the course of an evening, one of these professionals might wander out of the bar five or six times, always with a different companion, each time spending a short while in a nearby flat before returning, alone, to the dim, smoky bar.

There was, in fact, such an observer. He wasn't a policeman, for no policeman would have bothered so much about being inconspicuous. He wasn't a shy adventurer, trying to work up his nerve to the point of crossing the street and entering the Gaiety Bar, himself. He simply stood there at that bus stop for more than an hour, without having taken either of the buses that passed him.

A hundred feet ahead of him, a young blond man with the barrel chest and slender waist and hips of a swimmer led a slightly older and much less athletic-looking man in a dark brown topcoat around the corner to the entrance of the large Italianate building. It had once been a private home but was now broken up into apartments. The young blond opened the large front door and held it for the older man. It closed slowly, the swath of light from the inside hall fixture diminishing on the sidewalk. Just a little way beyond the light, the man from the bus stop stood, looking a little bored.

Either from greed or from contempt for his guest, the young blond man worked rapidly. Only nine minutes elapsed before the man in the brown topcoat reappeared in the doorway. He walked past the man in the trench coat, who might have been waiting for someone in the building or might have stopped to blow his nose—there was a handkerchief up to his face. The man in brown did not look back or notice the other put his handkerchief into his pocket and move toward the slowly closing door. Even if, for some reason, he'd looked around and had seen this, it wouldn't have registered. He had no reason to care.

Inside, the man in the trench coat climbed the steps of a once elegant spiral staircase. A couple of the balusters were missing and the runner carpet of a dingy gray was worn through in spots. He seemed to know where he was going. At the top of the stairs, he knocked lightly on the door to the left.

"*Ja?*"

"I seem to have left my gloves," the man said, speaking German in a low stage whisper.

The door opened. The blond man looked puzzled. He did not recognize this person at his door. He was certainly not prepared for the explosive push that threw the door wide and pushed him backward, into the room.

"Who are you? What do you want?"

The man didn't answer. The sudden appearance of a knife in the man's hand made no sense at all. The blond swimmer type had never seen this man before, would surely have recognized the cleft chin and the odd eyebrows that made a circumflex over each orbit. He could not understand what ill will the man could bear him. A queer baiter? A repressed homosexual? But those types were vocal and spewed filthy insults along with their violence. This man didn't say a word.

The blond man retreated a step and then another step. There was a table behind him. There was a drawer. There were knives in the drawer . . .

It was as if the man were toying with him, leaving him a little hope up until the end.

"This must be a mistake," the blond man said, not whining, not wheedling, anxious lest he enrage the other man.

There was no show of emotion at all, though, and that was the worst of it. When the arm came up, dropped, avoided the expected parry, and came in underneath and from the side, there was no particular expression on the face at all.

The other man felt a searing under his rib cage. And then nothing.

The killer struck again and again. He was not crazed, felt no frenzy at all. But he wanted to make it look like frenzy, which is a messy business. The long slashes, the gouging of the eyes, the cutting off of the penis and testicles were intended to suggest mania and depravity, the rage of a love that had turned sour and violent.

When he was done with the corpse, he looked through the drawers of the little kidney-shaped desk, the dresser drawers, the cabinets over the sink and stove of the little kitchenette, the medicine cabinet in the bathroom, the laundry hamper in the bathroom . . .

The envelope he'd been looking for was in the hamper. He opened it, looked at the photographs, and put them back in the envelope. He tucked it into his back pocket.

There was a noise.

Quickly he whirled, pulling the knife out, ready for whatever the new danger might be . . . and he relaxed. It was a dog. The bugger's little dog. It had come creeping out from underneath the bed. It was growling.

It wasn't a big dog, wasn't any more than a foot and a half high at the shoulders. And it was too late to do any good. But it was growling, challenging the intruder.

The man smiled, amused by the hopelessness of the dog's belated and insignificant attempt. The man looked about the room at all the blood. The smile faded. The dog was still making the most menacing growl it could manage.

The man challenged the dog, making a sudden movement and stamping his foot, almost the way a matador might have done. The dog barked and charged. The man killed it with one expert swipe of the knife.

He shook his head, cleaned the knife at the sink, then dried it. He took off his trench coat and wrapped it in a shopping bag. He had another raincoat of a very light fabric underneath it.

It was too bad about the dog. On the other hand, the dog would otherwise have starved to death. Or would have eaten his master.

He let himself out of the apartment, went downstairs, and let himself out of the house. He drew off his gloves and put them in the shopping bag. A couple of blocks away, he dropped the bag into a dustbin.

He walked for a couple of miles before he permitted himself to stop at a bar—of altogether a different sort from the Gaiety—and have a schnapps. He was upset about the dog. The damned animal should have known better, should have gone back under the bed when he'd stamped that way.

A cold front had brought a chilly drizzle into Stuttgart. Peter King's hair was wet and his coat had beads of moisture on the sleeves and across the shoulders. He hung the coat up on the elaborate bentwood coatrack in the front hallway of his Uncle Felix's house and went into the parlor for a brandy. There was a tantalus on the table, but Uncle Felix left it unlocked. Peter removed the crosspiece and took out the brandy decanter and poured himself a small quantity. He looked at the tumbler and poured in a little more.

"So? You find her?"

He looked around. Uncle Felix was wearing his soft slippers and Peter hadn't heard him come into the room.

"I see you're celebrating," Felix said.

"No, just fighting off the chill. It's turned nasty out there."

"So, you didn't find her?" Uncle Felix asked.

Peter shook his head. He didn't want to get into any discussion about it, wanted to avoid the fight he could see coming.

"Good," his uncle said, glaring, daring him to disagree.

Peter didn't say anything.

"If you're not celebrating, then I will," Uncle Felix announced. He took the decanter and poured himself a brandy. "To your very good luck," he said, raising the glass. "And to the luck of the family. We did not need to get tied up with such people."

"Her mother and my mother were friends," Peter said, hoping to defuse the discussion. It wasn't a relationship he'd initiated, after all. He'd never even met the girl.

"Your mother should have had better sense. If that friend of hers wanted to throw her life away and marry some Jew . . . your mother should have washed her hands of her."

"What difference does it make?" Peter asked. "I was too late. She's disappeared. Fled, I hope. Or taken away."

"Taken away, I'm sure," Uncle Felix said.

"You sound almost pleased."

"Why not? I'm not displeased, surely. They're vermin. They're a plague!"

Peter didn't say anything. The man was inviting a quarrel, and no doubt he deserved one. But Uncle Felix, his father's brother, deserved at least a degree of deference.

"This was a Jewish house, you know," Uncle Felix told him.

"This?"

Uncle Felix nodded. "They sold it to me. For a song. Everything you see. The furniture. The Turkish carpets. The chandelier above your head. The crystal decanters. The glass in your hand. All for a song. They got out, but they had to leave all this behind. And they were lucky."

He was grinning. He raised his glass again. "To luck, my boy. To luck!"

"You stole all this," Peter said.

"One can only steal from men. One can't steal from vermin. Be sensible. When you pick an apple from a tree, are you stealing? Be serious!"

"I am serious," Peter said. "We seriously differ about these questions."

His Uncle Felix looked at him, took a sip of brandy, and put the glass down on the sideboard. "Then one of us is wrong, no? I'm telling you we don't need any dirty Jews in the Koenig family. I beg your pardon, the King family. If you had told me why you were coming to Germany, I'd have told you to keep away. I'm glad you failed. It was a stupid idea."

The idea had been a marriage of convenience that would get the daughter of Peter's mother's best friend out of Germany and into Switzerland. Peter had been working in Geneva as a trader in a commodities brokerage house. His mother had written him from Cleveland, Ohio, about the plight of her friend's daughter. Peter had asked Uncle Felix to arrange a visa, never stopping to consider that Felix's views might be different from those of the rest of the family, particularly those who had left Germany and were living in the States.

He hadn't mentioned his real purpose to Uncle Felix, either, in the preliminary letters, only because he'd been worried about censors. He'd alluded to a wonderful business opportunity and left it there. Uncle Felix had used his influence to arrange the two-week visa.

As Peter should have realized, the very fact that his uncle had influence was a bad sign. But he'd gone blindly and blithely on, asking his uncle's help in locating Lise Blum. Abruptly the uncle and nephew had understood one another. The two men—who had greeted each other with affectionate embraces—had become sudden enemies. But still, they were family. There were limits beyond which blood kin could not decently go.

Peter watched as his uncle put the decanter back into the tantalus and covered the device with its crosspiece. He locked it this time. It was a mean gesture, Peter thought, a closing down of the last pretense of hospitality, but its meanness was easier to grasp than the other, more serious meanness. That was incomprehensible.

"You didn't inform on her, did you? You didn't turn her in?" he asked.

"It was too late," his uncle replied. "She'd already been taken away. They all had been."

"I see. I'll be leaving, then, Uncle. Say goodbye to Aunt Anna for me."

He went upstairs to pack his bags. He would not spend another night under this man's roof—or under the roof of some poor bastard from whom it had been stolen. Not another hour.

He did not hear his uncle close the door to the wood-paneled study. And he certainly did not hear anything of the telephone call to the Gestapo.

The sun glinted off the water. Down the beach, off toward Montauk, a pair of gulls complained to each other and fought over some bit of edible sea wrack. There was a cold wind coming off the water.

Private Herbert W. Conrad, Jr., was lugging a case of Rheingold beer along the sand. It was heavy going. He was wearing waders. He was carrying a wire basket, the kind they use for digging clams. This one was a little different because he'd rigged it with a top that fastened over it.

When he found the breakwater he'd marked, he walked out into the water, just below the low-water mark. He put the beer into the clam basket, then lowered the basket into the water. He had a length of light Manila line coiled around his waist. He unwound the line and paid it out, walking slowly back toward shore. He secured the end of the line to a small boulder that was a part of the breakwater.

He was attached to the 113th Mobile Infantry Unit of the U.S. Army Coastal Defense Command. The unit's assignment was to patrol a stretch of beach, cooperating with the East Amagansett Coast Guard Station in keeping America safe from invasion.

It was Private Conrad's view that invasion was not very likely. It further occurred to him that his assignment to this unit and this duty was a particularly nasty piece of retribution for a relatively minor infraction. Still, if they wanted to punish him, they could. They'd reduced him to private and they could make him walk the beach and keep an eye peeled for invading armadas or enemy submarines or a flight of zeppelins overhead.

But they couldn't keep him from enjoying himself. It was gorgeous country, bleak and severe now in the dead of winter, but with a curiously soft kind of light that could seem to embrace a naked tree. It was the water, he supposed, or the way the light bounced off the water. Even out of sight of the ocean, in the flat fields that looked like farm country anywhere, there was that odd quality of light. There had been a hurricane a couple of years back and it had left the place clean-looking, swept hard by a stern farm-wife.

Well, okay, if they wanted to punish him by sending him here, he could stand it. It was like Brittany, maybe, or Sardinia . . . or, really, like Cape Cod, except that it was only a couple of hours from New York City. He could stand it and make the best of it, as with the beer, for instance. It would be icy cold but not frozen, and safe as the gold in Fort Knox.

The wind had that wonderful sweet-salt tang to it and the beach was dazzling. Conrad could see for miles, and he was the only moving figure on the beach except for those two fat herring gulls.

He walked back toward the road where he'd left the bicycle. When they sent him out here again, he'd be well fixed. On those long lonely vigils, a man could get thirsty. Walking back and forth, holding off the Germans and the Italians and the Japs single-handedly.

Well, the Germans and the Italians, anyway. There was probably some other poor son of a bitch in Long Beach or Santa Monica looking out at the Pacific and doing the same thing—if he was smart. Burying beer and keeping calm.

He mounted the bicycle and started pedaling. He could hear the cry of the gulls and he could smell the air.

Some punishment.

Germans, for Christ's sake!

ONE

Specialist-Captain Ernest Kirschner rubbed the balls of his finger tips in hard slow circles on his forehead, opened his eyes, stretched and looked across the room at a gaudily colored wall calendar that displayed—for February 1942—a view of the gate at Lubeck. Kirschner remembered visiting Lubeck in '33—or was it '34?—with his children. He remembered the marzipan, a modest but real contribution to civilization. There must have been a dozen shops, each claiming to be direct successors of the inventor of that confection. The children had adored the little vegetables, fruits, and flowers, all with that sweet almondy taste.

The break had taken him no more than half a minute, but he was refreshed, ready to open the next dossier on the table. He glanced at the first page. Another internee. An American citizen, thirty years old, unmarried, father deceased, mother remarried, no siblings . . .

Interesting, this one, if rather isolated and lonely. The captain read further. Evidently, the man had been working in Switzerland as a cocoa trader, had come into Germany, been detained for questioning, and then been caught by the declaration of hostilities. He'd been in an internment camp since then. This one might be possible, but then the captain didn't want to leap to any conclusions. He told his aide to send the man in.

"Peter King?" the captain asked, looking at the file cover.

"That's right," the young man answered. He wasn't defiant but neither did he cringe.

"Sit down, won't you?"

There was a single straight-backed wooden chair. King sat.

"You want to go back to America?"

"Yes."

"Why?"

"I'm an American. Here, I'm in a camp. There, I'd be a free man again. Of course I want to go back."

"And your mother is in America."

"That's right."

"But you have relatives here also."

"That's correct. Still, I am not a combatant. I have been locked up in that camp for two months now, waiting to be repatriated." He would have continued, but the captain held up a palm, like a traffic cop.

"Yes, yes. I know all that. That is why you are here. There have been delays. The repatriation of citizens of countries with which we are at war is not a matter of the highest priority, as you may imagine. The question is whether you might be willing to make yourself useful to the Reich, if a way could be found to make your situation a matter of more than personal importance. You follow me?"

"I'm not sure that I do."

"It is a question of loyalties," Kirschner said. "You are an American citizen, but you are a German also. Of German stock. Of German blood. The struggles of the German people are also your struggles. The question is whether you might wish to volunteer to undertake a mission for the Reich. In the United States."

"May one know what sort of mission?" King asked after a moment's thought.

It was a predictable question. Kirschner had been counting on it. "If I were to tell you, and if you were not to accept the assignment, then your knowledge would be awkward. Even dangerous. Your release would be . . . impossible."

"I see. And if I refuse the mission? I mean, without knowing what it is."

"You would not then be a danger to Germany. But you would be considered more or less hostile. Your plight would not be one to arouse a great deal of concern."

"I might be kept in the internment camp, you mean?"

"That is not the only possibility, or by any means the most unpleasant."

"I haven't done anything. I'm . . ."

"Innocent?" Kirschner asked. "In war, innocent people die all the time. It is regrettable. You appear to be an intelligent young man. Let me put it to you that these are difficult times and that one must choose, one way or another. Innocence and guilt, complicity . . . These are empty categories. One must be realistic and accurate. What you have to consider is whether Germany is likely to win or lose. If you make that judgment accurately, then the rest of what you must decide will be a matter of simple logic. If you are incorrect, that, too, will be a matter of simple logic, and you will be destroyed. We are all called upon to make such choices."

"I see," King said. "And I must decide immediately?"

"You may sleep on it. I should think that would be fair to both of us. You will be kept here, in a cell, I'm afraid, but it's not uncomfortable. You will not be bothered. And tomorrow you can let us have your decision."

"Thank you. I appreciate your letting me have a little time."

Kirschner made a gesture of gracious generosity, describing an arc with his extended hand, palm up. Then he pushed a little button in a Bakelite box on the table. The aide came in.

"I hope you decide sensibly," Kirschner said to the young man.

The aide took Peter King away.

Kirschner had not lied to him. Or to any of them. He knew what his weapons were—the steely hair, the kindly expression, the thoughtful blue eyes, the sincerity. He had used them all fairly. From the old days, in the first war, after he had been wounded, when they assigned him to interviewing prisoners for information, he had found that whatever truthfulness and honesty he could bring to the conversation would be repaid in kind. It was also aesthetically more satisfying than the other methods.

He wondered which way young Mr. King would decide. Some of the candidates, he was sure, would volunteer. Whether they would be better off than the ones who didn't was an unanswerable question. The odds were extremely long against this undertaking.

He took off his steel-rimmed spectacles, held them up to the light, polished the lenses with a linen handkerchief, and put them on again. Not only was it a risky undertaking, it was bizarre. Crazy.

The kitchen clock showed that it was a few minutes past four in the morning. The dead of night. After five, it wasn't so bad. One could tell oneself that one was up early, have breakfast, wait for the sun to rise, and then go to the office. And before three, one could tell oneself that there was only the problem of getting to sleep, but still one could look forward to a few good hours.

Between three and five, though, there was the naked truth of insomnia, the result of the pressures of the job and the cause for grave concern that one would be less well equipped to do the work that was impossible to begin with.

The cocoa was as much out of habit as it was to help him sleep. And the dachshunds liked it. What he didn't finish, he poured into their bowl. It had happened often enough so that they sat at his feet, their heads cocked alertly, their silky tails waving back and forth. These were the long-haired dachshunds, as good as the short-haired dogs for ratting but with a little elegance, a little style. Tristan and Parsifal, his companions of the small hours, his confidants, his friends, had the advantage over most of his associates in that they never talked nonsense. They did not ask stupid questions. And they were loyal. There were not many of his people in the Abwehr of whom he could say so much.

He mixed the cocoa, the sugar, and the hot milk in the pan. He was wearing a sweater over his pajamas and a maroon flannel robe over that, but he was still cold. He was always cold. He raised the shawl collar around his neck.

"Well, boys, what do we do now?" he asked, speaking softly because his wife was asleep upstairs. But he did speak aloud, as if the dogs could understand him, as if the look of attentiveness on their faces signified the intelligence it so closely resembled. "How far can we rely upon the Americans' contempt?"

He swirled the milk in the pan. He wanted it to be just at the boiling point but not yet boiled. It took patience and attention, like so many other things in life.

"A group of amateurs comes wading ashore to perform an absurd task. Will the Americans believe it? Will they not suppose that the group has another purpose? Let us imagine an interrogation that may include torture . . . And none of them reveals any further information. Will the FBI be fooled? Would I be fooled?"

He turned off the flame. "The trick," he said, "is to use the amateurishness of the amateurs, to turn the weakness of our recruits into an advantage."

The dachshunds did not disagree with him.

He poured himself the cocoa and held the hot mug in his hands, getting the heat from it with his palms. "The trick is to have only amateurs captured. There could be, among them, one professional, about whom the rest knew nothing, and who might have some other objective in mind, some more immediately useful purpose than the one specified in the Führer's order. A secret from the Americans and a secret from Hitler. And from the Gestapo too." He laughed, then took a sip of the hot cocoa. It was hot in his throat, but the rest of his body was not much warmed by it.

He stood there for some minutes, thinking, drinking the cocoa, considering the various possibilities and dangers. When the beverage had passed its optimal temperature and had begun to cool down toward the condition of disagreeable sweet muck, he poured it into the dish the dogs shared.

On the way to his bedroom, he stopped in the study where there was a direct telephone to Abwehr headquarters. He picked up the instrument. The man on switchboard duty answered immediately. "Yes, admiral?"

"Put me through to Colonel Piekenbrock, please."

He waited a moment. He heard the ringing of the phone in Hans Piekenbrock's house. Two. Three. The poor man was asleep. Four . . .

"Yes?"

"Hans. Canaris here."

"Yes, excellency."

"On that project we were talking about this afternoon, the one with the amateurs . . . You remember?"

"Yes, of course, excellency."

"Think about putting in a ringer. A professional. To accomplish some other purpose."

"Not related to the purpose of the others?"

"Not necessarily, no," Canaris said.

There was a pause. Then Colonel Piekenbrock said, "It's dangerous, of course."

"You mean for the man we send? Or for us?"

"For both," Piekenbrock said.

"Yes, but give it some thought," Canaris said. "Sleep on it."

"I'll certainly try," Piekenbrock promised.

Canaris replaced the phone in its cradle. He patted the dogs, turned out the study light, and went back upstairs to lie in bed for a while and hope for a little sleep himself. But as he lay in the dark, his eyes wide open and his pulse sounding in the inner ear against the pillow, he found himself remembering the scene from that afternoon nine days earlier, in Keitel's office at the Oberkommando der Wehrmacht. Auntie Keitel, he was sometimes called. Canaris was uncomfortable with that kind of disrespect, but he could understand how Keitel had come by the nickname. A smallish man, he looked even smaller behind the huge desk in the lofty room with its churchly echoes and resonances. Keitel spoke softly, and most of his visitors took the cue and responded in the same hushed tones.

"I am afraid I have some unpleasant news," Keitel had said, fingering the official folder that was the small island on the great sea of empty blotter. "The Führer has ordered an operation in which we are to land a small number of English-speaking men in America. They are to blow up the Jewish department stores of New York."

"You're joking, surely," Canaris had protested.

"I'm afraid not. It is the Führer's order. It is his own plan."

"What possible good would that do us?" Canaris had asked.

"From the military point of view? None at all. But this is a political question. Or one of psychological warfare. The American declaration of war . . . The Führer has said it was too easy and that it cost them nothing. Let them see that it will have its costs."

"He doesn't expect them to change their minds, does he?"

"My dear admiral, I have no idea what he expects. It is not up to me to argue with the Führer when he gives me a direct order."

That was why they called him Auntie, of course. He tended to agree too easily with superiors, and he kept his desk and office and mind clear of the messiness of the real world. Canaris might have a disagreeable moment sending "a small number" of men to their deaths in a useless and absurd mission, but for General Keitel it was just a dossier, handed from higher up for him to hand on down the chain of command.

"You said you had bad news for me," Canaris had reminded

him, grasping at that straw. "I take it that you have your reservations about the mission?"

"No, none. I do what I'm told to do. That bad news is the fact that Reichsführer Himmler was in the room at the time. He knew about it already. So . . ."

The general leaned forward as if to be confidential. It was a ridiculous gesture, reducing the distance between them from ten feet to nine feet and three-quarters. He lowered his voice still further, but that did no good either. "It occurred to me that your enthusiasm for the assignment might be limited, at best. That you might try to postpone the operation, delaying it or even improving upon it. It crossed my mind that you might try to resist the order. But Himmler is watching us. He is watching you. It could be the occasion for which he has been waiting, his opportunity to assume control of the Abwehr's operations, merging them into his Gestapo. You must obey the order and you must contrive to make the operation a success. You understand?"

"Yes, general, I understand," Canaris had said.

And lying in bed, his lips were pressed together as they had been back in the OKW office, when he had kept back the complaint: *Why did you not argue? Why did you not resist?* He was right to have suppressed those insubordinate and useless questions, if only because he knew the answers to them.

It was beginning to get light. Had he slept, even for a little bit? Had he drowsed off for a few precious minutes? There was no way to be certain—which was a mercy. He could at least imagine that he'd had a little sleep.

Quietly, he got out of bed and went to the bathroom to shave.

In the admiral's office a few hours later, Canaris and Piekenbrock discussed the situation over coffee. "If anything is to be done," Canaris suggested, "it must be done now, at this early stage. Later on, any irregularity would be obvious."

"Yes, excellency, I agree," Piekenbrock said.

Hans Piekenbrock was a courtly man with rather prominent jug ears, a man with a sense of humor, or a sense of irony—which was more important these days. His habit of addressing the admiral as "excellency," for instance, was a way of referring to the good old days when, under the Kaiser, all general officers were entitled to be addressed that way. It was also a reflection of the change in the times, the deterioration of the manners and the men around them. So there was something a little mocking as well.

"The difficulty," Canaris said, "is that our colleagues will be watching us. We have been warned. They'll be on the lookout for any improvement we try to make in the plan as it has been proposed."

"It hardly seems as if we could disimprove on it much," Piekenbrock remarked.

Canaris gave him a cold stare. It was possible to go too far, even when what one was saying was irrefutably true. Most of the time, Piekenbrock knew what to leave unsaid.

"I am sorry, excellency. I was only thinking that this is such an awkward problem, one might almost wonder whether the Reichsführer hadn't suggested it to Hitler . . ."

"If that's so," Canaris replied, rocking slightly in his large leather chair, "then there's no point in struggling. What it comes down to in the end is a question of influence. If they can tell the Führer what to do, as you've suggested, then they've already won. But I'm not sure it's come to that."

"But what can we do? What answer is there?"

"Something brilliant. Something that improves upon this plan without appearing to do so . . . Something for which we can take credit without the risk of offending the Führer."

"Not so easy," Piekenbrock said. He didn't have to have the details spelled out. Heydrich and Himmler would be looking over Canaris's shoulder and would go immediately to Hitler like tattletales in the schoolyard running to the teacher. The rivalry was deep and long-standing, coming from the fact that the Gestapo was a part of the Nazi party while the Abwehr was a part of the old army. Mutual distrust was built into them from the very beginning.

"You spoke last night of a ringer," Piekenbrock said. "A saboteur or an assassin?"

"I was thinking assassination," Canaris said. "That would be more dramatic. And perhaps even more useful. The Americans are so rich that they can rebuild whatever we destroy. People are not so easily replaceable. But whom would it be to our advantage to kill?"

"Roosevelt?"

"No, no. If we kill him, Wallace becomes president. Not a

communist, but a sympathizer. Worse for us than Roosevelt himself."

"You have someone else in mind, then, excellency?"

"I've thought of a man, yes."

The colonel waited. It was not quite proper for him to ask the admiral a direct question at this point. He knew that Canaris would either tell him or not—and that putting the question would do nothing to influence that decision.

"I'd just as soon not tell you that just now," the white-haired admiral said, taking a last sip of his coffee. "I'd rather have you draw up your own list. There might be three names, perhaps. Or one, if you have a particularly strong candidate. You could perhaps do better than I've done. Take a day or two. Then, when you have your nominee, I'll tell you mine."

"Of course, excellency."

"Meanwhile, we must find our killer, almost immediately. The Gestapo is rounding up people for us, and we're interviewing for the mission already. There's nothing to prevent us from putting our own protégés into the pool. At this stage, nobody would notice. In a couple of weeks, it would be awkward."

"Yes, I see that," Piekenbrock said. "I'll get on it right away, sir."

"Very good of you. More coffee?"

It was not a real offer. Piekenbrock never accepted more coffee when the admiral's own cup was empty.

The Zeiss mansion in Charlottenburg looked to be late eighteenth or early nineteenth century. Piekenbrock supposed it was a country place once. The city had no doubt grown out to absorb Charlottenburg and urbanize its once rural retreats. The rise and fall of civilizations was a mystery, but the rise and fall of a city's neighborhoods was just as mysterious. This area suddenly prospers and that one dies, while another—the one through which the car now moved—remains fashionable for years, for generations. There were some principles that could be glimpsed—the western parts of most cities flourish better than those in the east, because of the preference of the rich for the afternoon sunshine—but they were too general to be reliable. The East Side of New York, for instance, was the fashionable side.

The car turned into the gate and slowed to a stop beneath an elaborate porte cochere. The driver opened the door for the colonel, who got out, rang the bell of the elaborately carved door, and waited. An elderly butler opened. The colonel showed his credentials and asked to see Karl Roeder. The butler invited him inside and offered to take his coat.

"No, thank you. I'll keep it."

"As you prefer," the butler said and he went to fetch Herr Roeder, leaving the colonel to study the dark oil paintings in their gilt frames and the imposing Chinese porcelain jars on either side of the double doors that led into the main salon.

Roeder appeared. He was rather more frail-looking than the colonel might have expected. He was wearing an elegant dinner jacket with wide lapels and a watered-silk vest. He had a deeply cleft chin and odd eyebrows, like gables or circumflexes. His lank hair kept falling down over his eyes, and the languorous carriage somehow seemed to go with the hair. He moved like a reptile, Piekenbrock decided. Which was as effective for a thug as any other zoo creature.

"You wanted to see me, colonel?"

"To have a few words with you, yes. If you please."

"No trouble, I hope?"

"No, no. But if you could spare me half an hour?"

"There must be some unoccupied sitting room. Erich?"

"The conservatory, sir?" the butler suggested. Piekenbrock wasn't sure whether the "sir" was for Roeder or for himself. Was the man a servant or did he sit with the family? "I have my car," he said. "We can talk outside."

Roeder got his coat from a capacious closet. The butler held the door for them.

When the car had begun to move, Piekenbrock asked Roeder whether he would be interested in performing an important service for the Reich.

"I thought I was performing an important service," the young man answered.

"As Herr Zeiss's Doberman?"

"As his bodyguard," Roeder said. "As his companion."

"If I were a magnate in my sixties, I'm not sure I'd want a twenty-nine-year-old killer as a companion, although I can see that it might be useful to have one around as a kind of pet."

It wasn't a question. Piekenbrock did not expect any comment from the young man.

"I'm making you an offer," Piekenbrock reminded the fellow, keeping him off balance, or trying to.

"Go ahead. Make it," the young man said.

"Before I do, I think we ought to get straight what your present situation is. We ought to understand one another. You should realize that I know how Herr Zeiss has been kind enough to get you out of certain legal difficulties. I understand that you have performed certain services for Herr Zeiss in return."

"So?"

"So it ought to be fair and equal, oughtn't it? A favor for a favor? But it isn't. He can turn you over to the Kriminalpolizei at any time, should you happen to displease him. But you can do very little to hurt him. You are in his power and are likely to remain there for the rest of your life. I am able to offer you a chance to wipe the slate clean. To put all that behind you. You can start fresh."

"How nice."

"It's not an opportunity that often comes along to a professional killer," Piekenbrock said dryly, looking out of the window.

After a moment's consideration, Roeder said, "You've gone to a lot of trouble, haven't you?"

"Some. I have the impression that you are the right man for this job. It could be worth your while. You'd be free of Kripo attention and of Herr Zeiss as well."

"If you can get Herr Zeiss to agree, then I accept."

"I'm delighted. I congratulate you. It will be a greater challenge to your talents than you have had until now. But what else is talent for, eh?"

Piekenbrock instructed the driver to take them back to the Zeiss mansion.

The silly ass was grinning, his vanity having been gratified. Piekenbrock was not smiling. He was no longer amused by that old joke that was still going around and still getting a reaction. The old joke was flattery—the oldest joke in the world.

They had put King in a cell down in a basement. It was worse than the Dulag in which he'd been kept for the previous couple of months—which might or might not have been deliberate on their part. Probably not, he decided. It was only temporary, to let him consider what he wanted to do.

Of course, the Dulag was temporary, too. That was supposed to be a brief stay until they decided whether to release him to a neutral country or intern him in a Stalag for the remainder of the war. But that temporary arrangement had stretched out from day to day and from week to week.

Here, King had his appointment with the captain, to let the captain know he was joining up. As he had, of course, decided to do. Let them send him back to the U.S.A., and then let them send him angry letters about his failure to do whatever it was that they'd told him. He thought he had done well to conceal his delight when the captain had first made the offer. He'd considered accepting then and there but he was worried that he might sound too eager and that they might not believe him. So, when the captain offered him time to think about it, he'd figured that it would look better if he took that time, made it look as though he'd deliberated and worried about it, and showed as much sincerity as he could manage to fake.

He'd been led down to a basement and put in a cell with a sink, a toilet, and two bunks. He'd waited for a few hours. Then, the guard had brought in a large metal container of stew with a hard roll and a smaller container of coffee. As the guard had passed the dinner into the cell, King had been able to see the cart from which the guard had served him. There were a half dozen other dinners on the cart. For the first time, he began to worry. It could be some kind of competition. He had no idea how many applicants there might be or how many places there were. It could come down to a contest in which each of them tried to outdo the others in protestations of Aryan loyalty and fervor.

The stew wasn't anywhere near so bad as what King had expected. It was a lot better than what they'd been getting at the Dulag. He ate it all, sopping up the last of the gravy with what was left of the roll.

He was surprised when they brought him a cell mate, a man a little older than King, sandy-haired, and with a nervous kind of blink that wasn't a twitch yet but might get there, King thought. The door closed behind him. They stared at each other.

"How do you do?" King asked. In English.

"How do you do?"

"I'm Peter King."

"Gerhard," the man said. Peter never did find out whether it was Gerhard something or something Gerhard.

For a moment or so, there was a difficult silence. King was torn between suspicion of the other man and the sense that the two of them were in the same boat. As the other man was too, no doubt. Either could be some kind of plant, an informer for the Nazis, at least as far as the other was able to tell.

"American?" the man asked at last.

King nodded.

"You?"

The man nodded.

There was another moment of silence. Then the other man made his move. "They give you the pitch?" he asked.

"I beg your pardon?"

"The ticket home! They give you the proposition?"

"Yes," King said.

"Me too," the man said. Then there was another pause.

"I don't trust it," the man said. "There's got to be some kind of a catch to it. There has to be a trick."

"You think so?" King asked, more suspicious than ever.

Gerhard nodded. "Figure it this way. Your first thought—or mine, anyway—was that whatever the game was, it was a way to get home. Go along, and then get dropped or landed or whatever, but get back to the States, right? And then cut out."

King didn't say anything.

"Come on. It had to have crossed your mind."

"So?"

"So, it had to have crossed their minds too. They're crazy but they're not stupid. They must have thought it out that far."

King sat down on one of the slab bunks. He couldn't figure the man out. An *agent provocateur?* But he was so terribly obvious. On the other hand, that could be the subtlety of it. "So?" he asked again.

"So they have to have figured a way of dealing with that. Like . . . it can't be alone."

"What can't be alone?"

"I don't know. Whatever it is. The mission. The caper. It can't be something that one person is doing. It's got to be a team, and everybody on the team will be watching everybody else. Everybody will think that everyone else could be some kind of watchdog. And the beauty of it is that everybody will be right. There'd have to be at least one."

"Possibly," King agreed. But to himself, he wondered what the choice was. Freedom or captivity? Get killed in this thing or get killed trying to escape from one of the internment camps? Which way were the odds better?

As if the other man had figured out what he was thinking, Gerhard said, "It's a crummy deal. You hold out, and sooner or later they let you go. They've got to. But this way, if you go along, then you wind up as a traitor to one side or the other. And that's a hell of a dangerous thing to be in these times."

"Why should I listen to you?" King asked.

"Don't. Just think about it, yourself. Never mind me."

"Why are you telling me these things?" King asked.

"That's a more interesting question," the other man said, running his fingers through his hair. "Either you're one of them or you're not, right?"

"That figures."

"If you're not, then you and I are in the same fix. It's as much good to me as it is to you to talk about our mutual problems. On the other hand . . ."

King didn't say anything. He just waited.

"On the other hand, if you're a stooge, if you've been planted . . ."

"Yes?"

"Then I'm telling you now what I'm going to tell them, anyway, to their faces. So it doesn't matter. You see? I'm no worse off, even if you're one of them. I've got nothing to lose."

For a moment, King felt tempted. Still, he remembered those meals on the trays on that cart. How many men were there, trying for how many places? And if this man wasn't going to try—especially if he wasn't going to try—friendship was a luxury.

"Maybe," he said, and he lay down on his bunk to stare at the ceiling and wait for them to call him. There was a grille covering some kind of heating duct, way up near the ceiling in one corner. He wondered whether there was some microphone arrangement.

Would they bother, at this stage? If they were listening, then . . . What had he said to Gerhard? Not much.

He wondered whether he should point to that grille, show the other man that it was there. But if anyone was listening, Gerhard had done the damage already. A nice fellow, earnest and engaging, but a man for other and better times, King thought. Right now, he told himself, he owed the man nothing. He had enough on his hands, looking out for himself.

It was after midnight when Colonel Piekenbrock appeared in the radio room of the Abwehr HQ, way up on the fifth floor. It was unusual for so important a man to show up at so late an hour, but nobody dreamed of questioning him. He took the big log book to a small table, turned the gooseneck lamp on, and looked through the book, going backward as he scanned the pages from bottom to top. From time to time, he made a small notation in his little leather-bound notebook.

He returned the log book to the operator's desk and went to the file where the communications of the current week were kept—the bottom copy on flimsy paper, at any rate. He was looking for three particular flimsies, each authorized WC for Wilhelm Canaris. He read one, replaced it, and found the next. He read that one.

"New York to obtain all published schedules of official activities of Institute for Advanced Studies, Princeton, N.J. Reply within 96 hours."

Not half bad, Piekenbrock thought. Not bad at all.

Simply from thoroughness, he looked at the third message. He closed the file, locked it with his own key, and went downstairs, tired but satisfied.

On Canaris's game, he'd cheated a little, but he'd won.

On the real assignment, he hadn't cheated at all. And he'd done pretty well. Canaris would be pleased.

The lock in the door made a rattle. The door opened. A guard—SS, this time with the black and silver uniform—called for "Herr Koenig." It took King a moment before he realized it was him they wanted.

The guard brought him back up to the captain's room. There was light outside. The captain looked as thought he had been working all night. He had stubble on his cheeks and his tunic was opened at the collar. There was an ashtray on the table at his elbow, half full of small butts.

"You have made up your mind?" the captain asked. He was weary. He hardly seemed to care what answer Peter King gave. It was almost certainly the result of the captain's fatigue. On the other hand, it crossed King's mind that their positions had now changed. He was the hopeful one now. Would the captain take him? Would the offer be withdrawn?

"Yes," he said. "I'm willing."

"I hoped you would see it that way," the captain told him, "and I wish you the best of luck."

"Can you tell me what I'll be doing?"

"What the mission is? No, I can't. What will happen is that you and some others will be taken to a training school, run through a quick but useful course, and then—I assume—the selection will be made and those who are chosen will be told what they need to know. You have had any combat training?"

"No."

"Engineering training? Electronics? Explosives?"

"No, I'm afraid not."

"Well, no matter. They can teach you what you need to know."

"I hope so," King said.

The captain managed a weary smile. "You will be willing to swear the oath of loyalty to the Führer?"

"Yes," King said, because there was no choice. *What do oaths mean, anyway?* he asked himself.

"Very good. Good luck to you, then." The captain pushed the button on his desk. The guard came to escort King back to his cell.

He wondered whether he'd find Gerhard there. Not that it mattered a whole lot, one way or the other.

They went back downstairs, the same corridors and the same doors. At the cell door, King waited while the guard unlocked and then held the door wide. King went in and . . .

"Oh, my God!"

"What?" the guard asked.

"Look!"

Carefully, as if he were worried that King might be trying to trick him, the guard stuck his head into the cell. King pointed.

Gerhard was hanging from the grating of that vent up in the corner. Even from a distance and at first glance, the man was obviously dead. It had been a slow hanging. His neck hadn't broken. Instead, he'd asphyxiated and his face was bluish. His eyes were bugged out and his lips swollen into an expression of rage.

"He has killed himself," the guard said. There was a note of contempt in his voice, as if he thought that suicide was the coward's way out.

The guard called other guards. A ladder was fetched and one of the men climbed up and cut the rope.

Rope?

It registered in a slow, nasty way. Where had Gerhard managed to get hold of a length of rope? And how had he managed to get up there to reach the grillwork?

He couldn't have hanged himself.

The guards carried Gerhard out, closed the door, and left King to get over the shock as best he could.

If they had killed the man, he asked himself later on that night, why hadn't they cut him down? Why had they left him up there to be discovered?

But that had to be the point of it, to get the message through to King and those he'd be joining in the training program.

But which message? That they should keep their noses clean? Or that some of the things Gerhard had talked about were true, accurate enough to make the Nazis uncomfortable?

He lay there on the bunk, looking up at the little grille. He closed his eyes, but he could still see it.

The admiral sent for Piekenbrock first thing. The girl hadn't come in yet and so there was no coffee. It was all business.

"You've found someone?" the admiral asked.

Piekenbrock told him about Karl Roeder, whom he'd found through the conscription office of the OKW. He'd looked for odd deferments. This one had been arranged by Herr Zeiss, personally. "And Roeder's files at Kriminalpolizei have been cleaned out too, which must have been expensive."

"You were able to discover what was in them?"

"Some. He's a strong arm who occasionally kills. There was a story one of the detectives told me of a homosexual who tried to blackmail Zeiss's nephew not long ago. The blackmailer was killed, perhaps by some other enraged homosexual, or perhaps not. Nobody knows. But the guess is Roeder."

"Is he good? Or just lucky?" Canaris asked.

"One never knows."

"Stable, at least?"

"Oh, yes."

"How is his English?"

"Good. He has something of an accent, but that isn't uncommon in America. He spent some years there when his father—who also worked for Zeiss—was installing planetarium machines. That was what I liked best about him. The language."

"Any others?"

"None as promising as this. There was so little time. They assemble at the Munich training center tomorrow night. Anyone we try to add later on is likely to draw attention . . ."

"We'll have to make do, then," Canaris said. "We'll see how it goes. We can always change our minds, if we have to."

"Of course," Piekenbrock agreed.

"Have you thought of a target for him?"

"I've thought of one, excellency. Perhaps Albert Einstein?"

"The very man I'd thought of."

"A good choice," Piekenbrock said.

"You sound like a wine steward," the admiral said, a suggestion of a smile playing about his thin lips.

"He was German trained," Piekenbrock said. "German science and education made him what he is. There is no reason the Americans should have the benefit of his intelligence. And as for shock value, he'd be as good as Macy's surely."

The admiral nodded. "I am told," he said, "that there is a kind of energy that can be derived from the splitting of the atom, an energy so intense as to be all but unimaginable. It could end the war. Whoever had such a weapon could simply drop one as a demonstration and demand the capitulation of all enemy powers. Of all countries anywhere in the world. And Einstein knows more about atomic physics than anyone alive. That's the reason."

"I see," Piekenbrock said.

The girl had arrived. She brought in the coffee things. Piekenbrock wasn't sure whether to remain or not, now that their business was done.

"You'll stay for a moment and have coffee," Canaris insisted.

"To celebrate. I think you've done very well, considering how little time there was. Very well indeed."

"Thank you, excellency."

There were stag heads and boar heads up on the wall and sets of antlers over each of the doorways. Almost certainly, it had been a hunting lodge, donated or commandeered for the course. Outside, there were woods, a steep declivity, and a fair-sized river that described a lazy loop around the property. It was an attractive piece of country, but Peter King was not certain which piece it might be. He had been kept in a series of holding cells, hospital rooms, barracks, and transit centers, where he had been examined and X-rayed but told nothing. He had worried all the time about being sent back to the Dulag or assigned to some worse and more permanent Stalag. Then there had been a long ride in the back of a closed truck. Alone with one guard, he'd wondered if it wasn't a dare or some kind of test. Was he supposed to jump the guard?

Apparently not. Nor had he been rejected. They'd brought him to this house, put him in a room up under the roof in what had been the servants' quarters, and left him to listen to footsteps on stairs, the flushing of a toilet, the ringing of a phone. He had assumed, as night fell, that he was supposed to sleep. He had been lying on top of the bed, still fully clothed except for his shoes, which he'd slipped off mostly from habit, when there was a sharp double knock at the door. Almost immediately, he heard the sound of the lock turning. The door opened wide.

An army sergeant ordered him to come along. "And no talking, mind you."

No talking? To whom could he talk?

Only then, in a kind of gradual and subtle way, like the coming of the light at dawn, did it occur to him that there would be other people he wasn't supposed to talk to. And that the training was to begin.

There were others in the room, some in uniform, some not. There was a group in the middle of the room, all silent, all presumably having been given the same instruction as he'd received. There were others, seated on the great leather-covered sofas at the edges of the room, some of them whispering. They, presumably, were officials. Or instructors. Or supervisors in some capacity or other.

In the middle of the room there were . . . ten, eleven. Counting himself, twelve. One of them was a woman. The other eleven were men. All of them youngish. Twenties or very early thirties . . .

"Your attention!"

King looked around. In front of the fireplace there was an army captain, tall, a little fleshy, with grizzled hair *en brosse,* and a dueling scar. All he needed was the monocle, and he could put on one of those old-fashioned spiked helmets to play a comedy kraut, King thought. But there was nothing funny in what he was saying.

"A few words of warning, before we begin, madam, gentlemen. You already know that you are candidates for an operation in which you are to be landed in the United States. It is not impossible to contemplate the capture of one or more of you. In order to protect those who have not been captured—and you will realize that this is to your own benefit, each and every one of you—it is vital that you not divulge information about yourselves now that could lead to your own capture later. No last names, ever! No information about family, birthplace, current residence, education, anything that could trace back to your identity. You have to assume that there will be a strenuous manhunt for you, and that your anonymity is your first and best protection. While you are together, you are each other's companions in arms, perhaps rivals, perhaps allies. But over there, if you are separated, you immediately must assume that those whom you cannot see may be your deadly enemies, willing to betray you to save themselves some inconvenience, whether it be imprisonment, torture, or even death. You understand that?"

King could not help looking around him at the others. They were looking around, also. Appraising, guessing, wondering. It was a lot worse than that awful moment at the Last Supper where there was only the one bad apple. The girl? Pretty enough, but that was hardly any guarantee of her character. The men? Most of them looked fit, healthy, perfectly reasonable-looking types . . . But that meant nothing.

Having enjoyed the dramatic effect of his pause, the captain resumed his address.

"Each of you has volunteered. Some of you are citizens of Germany. Some are citizens of the United States. Or of other nations. But all of you have volunteered to be a part of the German People. We wipe the slate clean and we start afresh, with the oath. You will all raise your right hands and repeat after me. 'I swear by God this holy oath—' "

The twelve of them repeated the words. King pronounced them too, thinking, *They're only words. It's just a ritual. It doesn't mean anything.*

". . . that I will render to Adolf Hitler . . ."

". . . that I will render to Adolf Hitler . . ."

". . . Führer of the German Reich and People . . ."

"Führer of the German Reich and People," they repeated.

". . . Supreme Commander of the Armed Forces . . ."

". . . Supreme Commander of the Armed Forces . . ."

". . . unconditional obedience . . ." The captain came down hard on those words. The words weren't meaningless to him.

". . . unconditional obedience . . ."

". . . and that I am ready as a brave soldier . . ."

". . . and that I am ready as a brave soldier . . ."

". . . to risk my life at any time for this oath."

". . . to risk my life at any time for this oath."

The captain looked out at them, smiled, and said, "It is an oath which you will fulfill willingly or unwillingly. And the less willing you are, the more likely it is that you will be called upon to fulfill it. So . . . I bid you all a pleasant night's sleep. Your training will commence before breakfast tomorrow morning. At six o'clock. You will be called. Heil Hitler!"

TWO

After the swill he'd been living on in the internment camp, Peter was delighted by the hearty breakfasts, the feasts at dinnertime with green vegetables and fresh fruits. He understood that they were fattening him up for the slaughter, but that didn't diminish his enjoyment of the meals. The training was strenuous, with classes, calisthenics, lab session, and then trivia games in the evenings when they drilled each other on the names of movie stars and ball players. Obviously, they were being trained to blow something up. Or, as they learned, down. The demolitions expert explained to them how beautiful a thing it was to blow a building and see it collapse down into itself, its tall chimneys retracting like the necks of turtles, as the bricks and stones returned to the embrace of mother earth. A poetic Thuringian, he loved his trade.

It was a grim, competitive business. It wasn't clear how many of the dozen candidates would qualify. And the work pitted man against man—or woman—as they practiced unarmed combat or matched wits trying to tail one another. Much of what they were learning seemed more applicable to Germany than to the States. King hoped it was true that the counterespionage services of America were as vigilant as the lecturers warned. He knew that in Germany all the devices of opened mail, tapped phones, watched train stations, paid informers, and all the rest of it were anything but imaginary. There were practice sessions, both in the woods and in Munich, in the use of buses and stores and restaurants to elude someone trying to follow them. In the woods, they learned how to confuse tracking dogs. How to turn the tables from pursued fugitive to pursuing attacker, doubling around. In some of these exercises, it was necessary that the trainees be associated in pairs or teams of four, but the combinations always varied. King remembered the prediction of the hanged man that it wouldn't be a solo operation. There would be a team. Of course . . .

They used first names. The tall one was Rudi. The fat one was Willi. Karl was the skinny one. Horst had the carrot-colored hair. Gunther was fair with hair so light that it looked white, even though he couldn't have been much more than twenty-five. Kurt had big ears. Max had a broken nose that veered off to the left. Johann had a mustache. Reinhart was the shortest. Ulrich had the tattoo of the sea serpent on his left forearm. Elfreda was easy, being the only girl. Peter supposed there was some physical characteristic they picked out to connect with his name—maybe his big feet.

There was competitiveness, but there was suspicion and fear too. More likely than not, some of them were informers—and everyone was aware of that possibility. Nobody was safe. Kurt's German wasn't all that easy; he preferred to speak English, which he did idiomatically and well. But it wouldn't be hard to pretend to speak German badly. Johann came on like a sales manager or a camp counselor, talking about teamwork, but there was nothing mutually exclusive about being a team player and a Nazi. Elfreda was maybe the least likely to be an informer because she was the only woman and therefore very conspicuous—but then her unlikeliness made her as good a candidate as anyone.

Late at night, alone in his room, he turned these thoughts over and over, calculating and recalculating what he should do, what the odds were, whom he might trust, whom he should fear . . . There had been some reference to an examination exercise, a test problem of some kind. Peter had seen it as his opportunity to fail, if that was what he wanted to do.

Of course, what the penalties might be for failure were as difficult to imagine as the risks that would accompany success. In the meanwhile, he had to assume that she and the rest of them were thinking the same thoughts that were going around in his own mind, were making the same calculations, and were coming up with the same conclusions.

Roeder's instructions had been to follow orders and do what the rest of them did, not distinguishing himself in any way. And he had been careful to keep to the middle of all the classes and competitions, showing himself as neither the best nor the worst. He liked to think that he could, with a little effort, excel, but his earlier life had not been distinguished by the expenditure of effort. His excellence had been more a private conviction than a public, vulgarly demonstrated thing. And he was never more convinced than now. He knew the great difference between himself and the rest of the trainees. The rest of them were decoys, cannon fodder. Kurt was flabby and could barely get through the physical training sessions. Horst was more than a little slow. Peter was introspective and calculating. Elfreda he could hardly take seriously. This was an unwomanly thing to be doing—so she was probably a lesbian or a whore. Willi was a decent enough fellow, but Karl was reluctant to get too friendly with him or with anyone. The time might come when he'd be forced to sacrifice one of them in order to keep free himself and able to operate.

He had no idea yet what his target was to be. But he knew it would be an assassination. The training with rifles, with small arms, with knives, and in unarmed combat was primarily for his benefit. The work with demolitions was for them. But he kept his place in the middle of the group in all the activities. He did what he'd been told.

He was enjoying himself. Never before in his life had he found a situation that so closely approximated his inmost feelings of difference, of being mysteriously special and superior, of having a particular destiny before him. And it was because he was having a good time that he resented the approach that was made to him one afternoon on an urban exercise in Munich, where he had been given a destination and a tail to elude. He had just cut through a restaurant, going out the back door past the vegetable cooks, and through an alley that was used for truck deliveries, when he heard his name.

"Herr Roeder! Very well done! You have the knack, it seems."

His last name? He was immediately alert to the irregularity of it, and therefore to the danger. The man was in his early forties, wore a dark trench coat and a soft velour hat. He had steel-rimmed glasses shaped like aviator goggles but with untinted lenses.

"Thanks," Roeder said. "It wasn't hard. Who are you? An instructor?"

"No. I am from the Gestapo. Captain Jost. You will come with me." It wasn't a question.

"I think you've got the wrong boy, captain."

"No, no. You're the one we want. I have no doubt. The car is waiting."

At the end of the block, where the alley was interrupted by a real street, a black Mercedes was waiting with its motor idling, a driver standing at the curb to hold the door open. Roeder hesitated, looked at the captain, at the driver, at the empty street. Where was his tail, now that he needed one?

He got into the car. The Gestapo captain climbed in after him. The driver slid behind the wheel and roared off.

"I'll come right to the point," the captain said. "We want your cooperation."

"Oh?"

"You're being trained for a mission. We know that. We want to know who your target is."

"You do?"

"And in exchange, we'll see to it that your records with the Kripo are destroyed."

"That's the deal I've already been offered from the Abwehr."

"It doesn't mean much if you get square with the Kripo and have the Gestapo on your back, instead."

"Why don't you just ask the Führer?" Roeder inquired. He looked away, considering the long row of anonymous four-story flats they were passing.

"Herr Roeder, we're asking you."

"I don't like being threatened. And to tell you the truth, I don't think there is anything much you can do to me. So my guess is that it's an empty threat, which is the worst kind."

"You're a fool, Roeder."

"One of us probably is," he agreed.

"My impression is that it's you rather than me. You're the one who is unable to see the consequences of his actions."

"Is that so?" Roeder asked. "If you could make an official inquiry, you'd do that. It's a lot easier that way. But you're doing it the hard way and my guess is that you don't want a whole lot of people to know about it. Which means there's not much you can do to me."

"Not today," Captain Jost said.

"Well, I never worry about tomorrow. That's what makes me a free man. And there aren't a lot of us left in Germany, are there?"

There was a long pause. Jost was fighting his anger. At length, he asked, "Where would you like to be dropped off?"

"Near the lodge," Roeder said, not only because that was convenient for him but to find out whether they knew where the lodge was. Apparently, they knew.

The flats gave way to individual houses, at first simple and unimposing, and then larger. Then the estates started, the high walls and the elaborate landscaping hiding the fanciful structures that were set well back from the winding road. Roeder was waiting for the other shoe to drop. It was inconceivable for it not to do so. They passed the gate of the lodge and went another thousand yards to a place where the road widened a little and the driver could turn around.

"I wouldn't mention this conversation to anyone, if I were you," Captain Jost suggested, the importance of the suggestion in no way diminished by his attempt at offhandedness.

"Oh?" Roeder asked.

"It would not be a question of worrying about tomorrow. You wouldn't last five minutes."

"Unless you're bluffing. And I think you are. In fact, I think you're full of shit."

"We'll be talking again one day, I'm sure."

"Thanks for the lift," Roeder said. He got out of the car. It roared back down the road toward Munich.

It was two nights later, when Roeder was on his way upstairs after a pointless evening session about American sports, with all the nonsense about baseball and the names of the teams and which teams were in which league, drearily transmogrified into facts to be memorized and recited. He was weary of it and irritable. Still, there were certain things he had trained himself to do out of habit, things it just didn't feel right to omit. Therefore, he opened his door just a few inches and snaked into the room. He closed it behind him. He looked down. The little pebble had been moved. It was several inches off its small chalked mark—and that meant that someone had entered the room while he'd been out of it.

He covered the room slowly and methodically, going over every square centimeter of the place, knowing that the only possible reason for someone to come into the room was to take something, or leave something, or try to learn something by looking around. What had been moved? What had been touched? There were a number of odd little traps he'd devised since his ride with the Gestapo captain. He went through the dresser drawers and saw no evidence of anyone's having looked into them. He saw no sign of his toilet kit having been touched. He examined his shoes. He looked at the electric light fixture overhead. He counted the floorboards . . .

The bed? Somebody had moved the bed. Why? What sense did that make?

Still, he remembered the Gestapo captain's threat. "You wouldn't last five minutes," he'd said. That had to mean that there was a Gestapo man planted in the training camp.

It couldn't be a coincidence. There was a Gestapo plant, but someone else had happened into his room—no, the odds against that were too long. So he had to assume it was the Gestapo man who'd been in here and had moved the bed. Why?

In a single sudden motion, he whipped the covers off. Nothing. No bomb. No viper or scorpion. Nothing he could see. He took one of the drawers from the dresser and delicately poked the mattress. Then harder. Nothing that was detonated by pressure. He flipped the mattress over. He flipped the iron bedstead over. Had the man bumped the bed on the way to something else in the room? But what sense would that make? Why would the Gestapo have an oaf. . . ?

It was possible, but he couldn't rely on it. The bed, then.

He felt the mattress, examined it for small tears or cuts. He looked into the pipe bedstead.

There it was. A small packet. Or not so small, after all. A long tube. Carefully, delicately, he extracted it. He touched it. It gave when he squeezed it. Inside the long paper tube, there was a rolled glassine envelope containing a white powder. It wasn't an explosive. He opened the envelope and touched a little of the powder to the tip of his tongue.

Cocaine.

Someone had planted cocaine on him. Obviously, the idea was

to get him thrown out of the training program and the Abwehr's protection.

He smiled. He put the glassine envelope back into the paper tube and replaced it in the bed's hollow leg. He remade the bed, adjusting it carefully into its original position. He replaced his little pebble on the faint chalk mark just inside the door and eased out of the room, closing the door behind him.

They were in the gym, all twelve of them, doing their morning exercises with Klaus, the oldest of the drill instructors. Klaus was a grizzled veteran of the First World War, something of a martinet. He even carried a swagger stick with which he corrected defects in the sit-ups and push-ups. He was in the habit of poking the error, indicating that the knees should be kept straight or the butt down. It was a perfectly traditional if not altogether pleasant way of proceeding. He was obviously not used to training women. He was not comfortable when the categories were blurred. It was not clear whether these people were trainees or prisoners, enemies or allies. And Elfreda was the most problematic of them all, being female. She was not an equal—that seemed clear.

She was having difficulty, that morning, with her push-ups, as beginners often do. Her ass kept sticking into the air. Whenever this happened, Klaus poked the offending area with the swagger stick.

She tried it again, but the straight line was hard to maintain and she broke again. He poked her again, only this time it was more a light blow. "Again," he ordered, and it was his choked tone that alerted the rest of them that something wasn't right.

The transaction was no longer one between Klaus and Elfreda. What happened to those two would affect the rest of them. They all knew this and they looked at one another. Peter was the one who stood up. Ordinarily, this would have diverted the instructor's attention and anger, but he was oblivious to anything except the woman down on the floor near his feet. "Again!" he ordered, yelling now. And this time, when he hit her, it was with enough force to make her cry out.

"That's enough. Just hold it, right there," Peter said. He was quiet, hardly speaking above a whisper in fact.

"Silence, you. Back to your place," the instructor ordered. His face turned a deeper crimson. His eyes were bugging out.

"Just leave the woman alone," Peter told him, his subdued tone intended to soothe the man back to reasonableness.

"You'll pay for this," Klaus yelled.

"All of us?" Peter asked. He looked around.

The ten men hesitated and exchanged looks. Willi was the one to stand up first. Then Johann. And Karl. Then the others. It was now all of them, all twelve—if one counted Elfreda who remained lying prone on the floor—against the instructor.

"You want me to call the commandant?" Peter asked.

"No," Klaus said. He wasn't yelling now.

"Touch her one more time, or even look at her cross-eyed, and we all go to the commandant. All of us together," Peter said.

The instructor nodded.

Peter stood there, as if he could not decide whether to push further or leave it where it was. He looked back at the other men, then returned to his place, got down on the floor, and waited for the instructor to order them to continue. The others returned to their places.

Klaus led them in their knee bends and then dismissed the class, somewhat earlier than usual.

On the way upstairs, Elfreda came up to Peter to say, "I want to thank you for what you did."

"It was my pleasure," he told her. "I know that sounds like . . . like what one is supposed to say. But I really enjoyed it. I'm only sorry he was beastly to you."

"I've endured worse."

"Haven't we all?"

"Still, thanks," she repeated. She seemed about to say more, but she couldn't quite make up her mind. She turned and continued up the stairs.

Elfreda had not taken Klaus's grubby little fanny swatting particularly seriously. She expected such behavior from a good little Nazi. They were all toadies to superiors and bullies to people they thought of as inferiors. No news there at all. The people who were training with her weren't a whole lot better. All she wanted was to get back to America and extricate herself from this madness. It was possible that some of the others had the same thought she did, but she had to assume that most of them were dedicated Germans, willing to do what the Fatherland wanted of them. Kurt, she thought, was a faggot. Horst was a borderline moron. Karl was a true weirdo, a man likely to explode at any moment. Peter was pleasant enough, but she assumed he had some ulterior purpose in mind, sexual or otherwise. She did not want to get friendly with any of these people because she hoped to betray them all.

Her presence at the lodge as a member of the training group had been the result of a lucky accident. The adjutant at her internment camp just had not read the memorandum very carefully and had stopped at the first paragraph. The request had been for volunteers of English-speaking Germans who might be able to undertake action behind enemy lines. Only later on had he noticed in the body of the third paragraph, on the second page, that the candidates were to be in good physical condition, able to swim, preferably were to have knowledge of demolition techniques, and were to be of the male sex. He had apologized and had been about to send her back to her barracks, but she asked him to inquire why a woman would be excluded as useless. There had been a vague suggestion of some sexual reward—upon which she might have been willing to make good if it had been absolutely necessary. He had made the inquiry. Some bureaucrat or official somewhere had then read the inquiry and had decided that there might be some possible advantage in having a woman.

That afternoon there was a scheduled field exercise, a kind of game the instructors had devised to develop their ability to move in open country without being seen. There was a man with a pair of field glasses stationed on a small rise at the end of a long meadow. The twelve trainees were all placed at the far end of the meadow and were all supposed to advance toward him, taking what cover they could from the topography, the high grass, an occasional shrub or low bush. The man or woman to get closest to the knoll would be the winner of the game.

Peter and Elfreda happened to be placed close to each other. Perhaps he had contrived it. She couldn't tell. But she heard him whispering what seemed to be a reasonable suggestion. "What we've got to do is move off that way and into the trees. Then we can circle around, get beyond him, and come back."

It wasn't committing either of them to anything, and she wanted to do well for the same reason that they all wanted to do well. She wanted to be a member of the group that was going to land in America. So she nodded and, keeping low, wriggled along the ground after him, out of the meadow and into the second- or third-growth timber to their left. They worked their way a little deeper into the wood and at last were able to stand up and talk normally.

"Thanks, again," she said.

"I don't know that thanks are in order. Who can be sure it's such a good idea to win at this kind of game?"

"It's usually better to win than to lose."

"Usually. But it depends on what the prize is, doesn't it?"

"Going home. That's not such a bad prize," she said.

"I hope not. But what if they've got some way to force us to do whatever the job turns out to be? Figure they have some kind of a scheme—blackmail or God knows what. And once you've done it, you're theirs forever. They can keep you on their string and jiggle it whenever they like."

"Maybe," she said. "But it's a big country. They've got to find you to jiggle your string." And then, after a pause, she asked him, "Why are you telling me these things?"

"Why not?"

"You're testing me?"

"Maybe. I figured that we might work together in a limited kind of way. We could be allies."

"How do you mean?"

"I don't know exactly. We don't know what the setup really is. We don't know how many people will get to go or what they'll have to do. Or what will happen to them. But it's better to have a friend than not. In emergencies. Besides, it's the only thing they're not set up for."

"Maybe," she said, cautiously. "It's possible."

"Look, I understand that you can't trust me completely. I've got more reason to trust you . . ."

"Why?"

"If you were some kind of a plant, then Klaus wouldn't have been bothering you that way, would he?"

She shrugged.

"But you don't know what I'm really thinking. It's a little like being out on a date with the high school football captain. You can't trust him either." Peter laughed.

"I can trust a little," she said. "*They* don't laugh."

39

The demolitions instruction was tedious, particularly if one had no intention of blowing anything up. Peter's only object was to pass the course, performing well enough on the various projects not to get flunked out of the training program. His other objective—no less important—was to keep from getting blown up. That demanded that he pay attention and use common sense. This was made clear to him the afternoon he was sent out with Max and Ulrich to force an entry into a large metal tool shed with a big padlock on it. The three men were supplied with explosives and fuse caps, and that was it. No further instructions. They had to work out among themselves who would do what, how they were to organize themselves—which was, Peter assumed, a part of the exercise.

They trotted out across the rolling meadow in the middle of which this little shed had been set up. When they got there, they found a spade that had been left out in back of the shed, leaning against the galvanized wall.

"I think we're supposed to use the spade," Peter said. "Either to pull the hasp off the door or to shovel a way in under the wall. There isn't a floor to a building like this."

"Then why did they give us the explosives?" Max asked. He sounded sneering and sarcastic, but he sounded that way at breakfast when he asked someone to pass the sugar.

Ulrich thought that shoveling in under the bottom was too much work. And there was a cold drizzle, so it would be unpleasant. The three of them stood there, arguing. Finally, Max said he was fed up, tired of talking, and was going to blow the door.

"Go ahead," Peter said, and he walked off to take cover.

"Not only will I blow the door, I will also report that you were uncooperative and disobeyed orders."

"Go ahead," Peter said, convinced that Max was some kind of informer. He certainly seemed like one.

But then it was difficult to be sure. Max went around to the front of the building, and either he used too large a charge or too short a fuse, or the fuse was defective and blew too soon, for clearly something had gone wrong. There was an enormous boom that caused Peter's ears to ring—and he was fifty yards away behind a tree.

It blew Max apart. One of the pieces of the shed, which turned into instant shrapnel, caught Ulrich in the shoulder and cut him badly. He hadn't run from the blast site but had walked in a dignified way.

Ulrich wasn't sure whether to be angry at Max, or at Peter, or at the demolitions instructor, but he was angry at someone. When he heard that they were supposed to use the shovel, that it had been left there for them to use if they wanted to, and that Peter had been correct, he was beside himself with rage. There was blood still oozing from the back of his windbreaker. He must have been in considerable pain. He lunged at the instructor, the poetic Thuringian, yelling "You bastards . . ."

The Thuringian—his name was Ludwig, like Beethoven's—extended a palm in what appeared to be a policeman's "halt" gesture. But the fleshy part of the palm caught Ulrich's nose and broke it.

"The second lesson," Ludwig explained, "is that you should know your limitations. Don't pick fights you aren't sure you can win. The first lesson was to use the least dangerous means of accomplishing your ends—a shovel instead of explosives, for example. Class is dismissed."

He walked away, leaving the rest of them staring down at Ulrich who lay on the ground, writhing, blood streaming from his nose. Ulrich was taken off to the hospital that afternoon and he never returned.

Captain Koepke was the officer in charge of the training facility. He was a red-faced, beefy man who was always dieting, never successfully. He looked up when his adjutant announced that Gunther Munch was asking for an interview.

"Very well. Send him in," Koepke said. He removed his spectacles and polished them with a linen handkerchief he kept just for that purpose in his tunic pocket.

Munch came in. He was the white-haired one, almost albino.

For a moment, Koepke was able to entertain the hope—however faint—that there might be some other business, some other reason for the interview. He was a good officer and a good training commander because he liked the men and wanted them to do well. This kind of situation was, therefore, especially disagreeable.

When he heard Munch mention Karl, though, he knew that this had to be the man. The traitor. The infiltrator. The plant.

He listened while Munch completed the tiresome recitation—how Karl had approached him with the offer of a little cocaine to help pass the time. There was a nicely worked bit about how Munch weighed his dislike of carrying tales against his concern for his fellows and for the mission. His regretful decision was to bring the matter to the commandant's attention.

"Yes, of course," Captain Koepke said. "I understand. I really do understand . . ."

"I'm grateful to the captain," Munch said, obviously relieved.

Koepke picked up his telephone. "Ask Karl Roeder to come in here, would you?"

"No, no, captain, you can't do that!"

"Why not? I am obliged to hear his side of the story, am I not? Isn't that the fair thing to do?"

"But I'm here in the room. He'll know I am the informer."

"Yes, of course. A man is entitled to confront his accuser, isn't he?"

"He'll . . . he'll kill me."

"Do you think so?" the captain asked.

"Without your protection, I'm sure he will . . ."

There was a knock. Then, without waiting, the adjutant opened the door. Karl entered. He looked at Gunther, then at the commandant behind the desk.

"Gunther tells me that you've offered him a sniff or two of cocaine. Is that true?"

"It's a lie, as the captain already knows," Karl said. "I came to you two days ago to report the fact that someone had entered my room and planted the cocaine in the leg of my bedstead. I told the captain at that time that I believed someone would try to inform on me for drug use . . . And that it was my belief that the informer would be a Gestapo plant."

"Is the last part true? Is that why you've tried to do this?" the captain asked.

Gunther Munch looked from the captain to Karl Roeder and back to the captain. It crossed his mind that the captain had used Karl Roeder's last name, violating one of the strictest rules of the training program. But then, there was no possibility that the two men would both be going on the mission now.

"There's no way out, I'm afraid. You might just as well tell the truth, you know," Karl said, rather gently.

"It's true. It was for my uncle. He's in jail for smuggling. They said that it could go easy for him or very hard, depending on whether I cooperated or not."

"Understandable," the commandant said.

"And your next contact? How were you to let them know what happened?"

"There's a tree near the edge of the compound. It has a hollow place. I leave notes there. They leave answers."

"Show me," Karl said.

Gunther looked at the commandant. The commandant nodded.

"Now, if you please?" Karl asked. It had the intonation, at least, of a request.

Gunther left the office and walked through the front hall of the lodge. He led the way out through the front door and across the drive to the large lawn alongside the house and then into the woods, along a more or less clearly defined path, just inside the chain-linked fence. After a while, Gunther stopped. There was a large beech tree that had its lower limbs jutting over the fence. One could reach through the fence to the trunk of the beech tree.

"That's it," Gunther said.

"I see."

"Now what?" Gunther asked.

"What do you think?"

"I don't know," Gunther said, but there was fear in his eyes. "I only did what they told me to do. They forced me. It wasn't anything personal."

"No, of course not. Neither is this. But you know, they wanted to get at me, those friends of yours. And what they wanted to do to me wouldn't have been very pleasant.

"I'm sorry."

"Yes, I think you probably are," Roeder said. He produced a switchblade knife and clicked it open. Gunther took a reflex step backward but the chain-link fence stopped him. He made a quiet grunt as Roeder buried the knife under his rib cage, thrusting in and upward.

The really difficult part was lifting him up and heaving him over the fence so that he'd be found at the base of that beech tree. Roeder had to raise him up, bracing him against the fence, and roll over the top of the fence what was, in every sense, dead weight.

"And?"

Colonel Erwin Lahousen, director of Abteilung II, the sabotage and special duties section of the Abwehr, and Colonel Piekenbrock were dining with Captain Koepke in the gatehouse of the lodge. Koepke had been telling them the story, or what he knew of it. Answering Lahousen's question, he shrugged, held up his palms, and said, "And nothing. In the morning, the body was gone."

"Splendid," Piekenbrock said quietly, gazing into his large crystal snifter.

"It was gratifying," the captain agreed. "And I am not questioning my instructions. But still, isn't it likely to infuriate the Gestapo?"

"Oh, yes," Piekenbrock agreed. "Very likely."

"That's the point, Koepke," Lahousen explained. "The idea is to get them so angry that they make mistakes. That they do something foolish. It's the admiral's own decision."

"It will no doubt have occurred to you that this mission is absurd on its face," Piekenbrock said quietly. "The Gestapo is waiting to see what we do with it. If we bungle it, they'd be delighted. If we exceed our instructions and try to turn the mission into something more—shall we say more reasonable?—they'll be ready to pounce. That's what they're trying to find out. What are our intentions?"

"I see," Captain Koepke said. He did not ask what the Abwehr's intentions were. He didn't want to know.

"Tell me," Lahousen prompted, changing the subject, "how do they seem, these trainees?"

"Considering the very short time we had for recruiting and the abbreviation of the training course, we could have done much worse," Koepke said. "With luck, they may do reasonably well."

"They're beginners," Lahousen said. "They're supposed to have beginner's luck."

"Or, it may be," Piekenbrock speculated, "that the beginner's great asset is his ignorance of what can go wrong. His confidence hasn't been shattered."

"Quite true, colonel," Koepke said. Not that they were all beginners. That seemed quite clear to the captain. But he didn't want to go into that either. "More brandy?" he offered.

THREE

They were in a truck, nine of them, bouncing along in the dark. The back windows had been blacked out. They were to be dropped somewhere, without papers, without a pfennig, equipped only with their wits and training. They were to make their way back to the lodge near Munich. But how far the truck would go and in what direction, and how far apart the drop-off places would be, were all unanswered questions. All they knew was that it was a qualifying exercise, a kind of final exam.

Gunther was gone. Two days ago, he'd just disappeared. They had looked around at breakfast and noticed nine places at the long table instead of ten. There hadn't been any announcement from the Abwehr officials, but each of them had wondered. Had Gunther tried to escape? Had he made it? Or had he been the plant, the man listening for subversives and malcontents among the trainees? Was his disappearance a good thing or a bad thing? There was just no way to know.

It was too dark for Peter to see the hands of his watch. They had left a little after seven, but he had no idea how fast they'd been going. And the product of the rate and the time wouldn't necessarily equal the distance anyway, because they might have been circling around, taking some indirect, misleading route. All he could do was guess at a maximum distance, which was better than absolute ignorance.

They'd be dropped in groups of three—they'd been told that—but what they did after that was apparently up to them. It was part of the exercise, each group having to decide whether to stick together or split up. And if they stuck together, obviously they would have to decide about leadership. Pick a leader? Or vote on every decision as they went along? Peter supposed that part of the plan was to find out who had leadership abilities. But this was a peculiar way to go about it. He wondered about the Abwehr's own leadership sometimes. Why should they have to improvise that way, dropped out of a truck in a field somewhere?

But that's how it was going to be. They'd been told, that evening, about the exercise. They'd been made to empty out their pockets. And they'd been hustled into the truck. Since then, they'd been going along at what seemed to be a brisk clip—if he could judge by the whine of the tires and the truck's swaying. Once he was out and on the ground, he'd be able to check the time and figure a maximum distance. But how in hell was he going to find out what direction they'd gone?

The truck slowed, turned, drove for a while, slowed again, and stopped. A door slammed up in front. The back door opened. It was one of the instructors. He consulted a piece of paper he had in his hand. "Elfreda, Peter, and Karl, out. The rest of you, stay where you are."

Peter jumped down and turned to help Elfreda. Karl was the last out, bounding down with an easy grace.

"Where are we?" Karl asked the guard, not quite in a whisper but not so anyone in front would be able to hear either.

"Sorry. Can't tell you," the guard said. "Good luck all."

He trotted around to the cab, climbed up, and slammed the door as the truck moved off.

Peter looked around. They were on a secondary road. There were fields. There were hulking shapes of farm buildings. He looked at his watch. By the faint light of the stars, he could make out that it was a little after ten in the evening. Figure three hours and maybe fifty miles an hour. Call it a hundred fifty miles, tops. Maybe two hundred fifty kilometers. Maybe a little less.

"What now?" Elfreda asked.

"I don't know," Peter said. "I guess the choice is going to ground here or moving out."

"We ought to move," Karl said. He sounded very sure of himself.

"Why?" Peter asked.

"If they dropped us here, then they know where we are as long as we stay here. If we move, even a mile or two, they don't know our location anymore. Who knows what was following the truck? Or what the orders were?"

"It figures, I suppose," Peter said.

Elfreda nodded. "Which way?" she asked.

"If they were following the truck, then we'd be safer going in the same direction as the truck was going. It'd give us a few more minutes," Karl said. And he turned and started walking along the left side of the road.

Peter and Elfreda exchanged a brief look. Neither of them had any better ideas. Or any objections. They followed along. Sooner or later, there'd have to be a crossroad, maybe even signs saying the name of a nearby city or directions to various cities. How many kilometers to Munich, for instance.

They walked along that secondary road for ten minutes or so. The truck that had dropped them off was long gone. The only sound was the gentle sough of wind in the trees. Still, Karl stopped every now and again, listening. Peter listened too. But there was nothing. They reached a *T* intersection, but there was neither signpost nor marker. Left or right? Or stop here and wait for sunrise? Karl didn't even pause. He turned to the right and kept on going, not even pausing to look behind him to see whether the others were following him. Peter had no clear reason for not following. Neither did Elfreda. They took the same turn and hurried a little to keep up with Karl's brisk pace.

Abruptly, Karl stopped again. "Listen," he said. "You hear something?"

"I think there's a brook," Elfreda said.

"I know there's a brook. But besides that. You hear it?"

Peter strained to hear. Was there another noise or was he only imagining it? Karl resumed his walking, or almost jogging. He hurried down the road another hundred and fifty yards, stopped again, and listened again.

"Yes," Elfreda said. "I hear it. An engine, I think."

"More than one," Karl said.

"It could be," Peter agreed. "So?"

Karl looked at Peter as though he were a moron. "So we had better get off the road, don't you think?"

There was the brook on one side, down below the level of the road in a gully. Peter assumed they'd cross the road and go into the fields. But Karl struck out for the brook.

"We'll get our feet wet," Elfreda said.

"And hope they won't want to," Karl said. He didn't waste time looking for the best place to cross. He just waded in and over and out.

"I'm afraid he's probably right," Peter said. He helped Elfreda down the incline. They waded in. The water was very cold. They clambered up the other side of the gully and climbed the gentle incline of a meadow.

Peter paused, listening. There was no question now but that there were several engines. A convoy of trucks perhaps? It was impossible to tell. The terrain was uneven and the curves and hills of the road hid the lights of the vehicles.

"Over here, this way," Karl called.

Peter and Elfreda hurried in the direction Karl had indicated.

"Thanks," Peter said.

"Don't be an ass! If they find you, they'll look for me."

"Still . . ." But there was no time to argue.

Peter followed along after Karl who seemed to know what he was doing, if not where he was going. The important thing was to move and to keep an eye out for whatever hiding place presented itself. Place or places. What if they found a place that wasn't large enough for three? Who would stay and who would keep on going, either to find another place or to serve as a decoy? There was no sense in worrying about any of that, not yet anyway. Peter wasn't even sure that those trucks had anything to do with him and Elfreda and Karl.

"Up there," Karl said.

"What's there?"

"Trees. An orchard. Apple trees, I think. If we can climb up into the trees . . ."

"All right," Elfreda agreed.

It was a reasonable thing to try. To get below or above or behind the people who were looking for you was basic procedure.

They climbed over a low stone wall and walked into the aisles of old gnarled trees.

The sounds of the engines were much louder now. And the lights of the convoy of three trucks had come into view. Or, no, there was a fourth. And a fifth.

"They can't be looking for us. It doesn't make any sense," Peter said.

"Doesn't it?" Karl asked.

"Of course not. It's just an exercise," Peter told him.

"For the Abwehr."

"And who are they?" Elfreda asked, nodding down toward the road.

"Gestapo, I'd guess," Karl said.

"Why would they be after us?" Elfreda asked, pushing.

"After me," Karl said. "But they may not be particular. You're in danger too, I'm afraid."

Peter didn't ask whether his danger and Elfreda's was from the Gestapo only or from Karl as well. Judging from the size of the search party, the stakes were pretty high—on both sides. Peter was annoyed that Karl hadn't warned them before, but then he checked himself. Karl hadn't known which partners he was going to get.

Did the Abwehr know? It was utterly stupid for Peter to be caught this way, in the crossfire of some absolutely irrelevant quarrel. This had nothing to do with him. Or with Elfreda. But to whom could he complain?

The trucks had stopped. Then they began to move again. It was all a false alarm. Just a convoy of trucks and they'd stopped for a moment . . .

"Up. Into one of the trees," Karl said.

Peter looked down at the road. The first three trucks had moved on, but the last two were still there. There was a reasonable possibility that men from those trucks were fanning out to search the fields on both sides of the road.

"Up! Now!" Karl said.

Elfreda went to one of the trees and Peter looked up at another, planning his climb.

"No, no. All of us in one tree," Karl said. "Quick. Up!"

Peter climbed up after Elfreda. There was no time to argue.

The fact that it was Karl's ass they were after gave him a certain authority, and he wasn't at all shy about exercising it. It made a certain sense. The Gestapo—or whoever it was down there—would have three times as good odds at finding them if they were in three different trees. And this way, at least he and Elfreda and Karl would know where the other two were.

That was it. Karl would know where Peter and Elfreda were. And perhaps be able to keep some sort of control over them, should they think of selling him out, betraying him with a shout.

Had Gunther anything to do with this? Peter remembered the odd-looking man with the lank platinum-blond hair and the cold blue eyes.

"Higher!"

"It's not easy in the dark," Elfreda said.

"Do it. Go higher. You, too," Karl said. "What can you see?"

"Lights," Elfreda said, and, sure enough, from the direction of the road, looking like huge fireflies, there were lights moving and flashing.

The three of them clung to the branches of the tree. Peter was actually seated on a large branch as it emerged from the trunk. He felt like a possum or a raccoon, trapped up a tree . . . The thought of those coon hunts suggested coonhounds, which in turn suggested dogs. Could these people have dogs with them? Peter regretted that they'd waded straight across the stream. They ought to have traveled in the stream for a cold, wet hundred yards or so . . .

"Do you hear any barking?" he whispered.

"No, do you?" Elfreda asked.

"No. If we're lucky, maybe there won't be any," Karl said. "They have an endless supply of men, but only a few trained dogs."

"I hope," Peter said.

They waited. It was agonizing to watch the progress of the lights. Most of them, when they'd crossed the meadow, kept on going into a plowed field that was behind it. But two or three of the pursuers climbed over the fence and into the orchard. It was a matter of their patience and thoroughness and there was no way to gauge that. And their whim. Peter tried to deflect the closest of the soldiers with sheer psychic force. But if it worked at all it worked the wrong way. One man, drawn irresistibly closer, was coming straight into the trees as if he knew where they were.

And then he stopped, opened his fly, and started to urinate against the base of one of the trees. That was what had drawn him into the trees. And when he was finished, he'd leave, go on back to the meadow, and resume his search.

And he might well have done just that, except for a wind that swept through the orchard and rustled the leaves of the apple trees, not just the tree in which Peter and Elfreda and Karl were hiding, but all of them. Still, it caught the attention of the soldier, who took his flashlight from where he'd tucked it under his armpit and shone it upward into the tree he'd peed on. And the tree next to it. And the next. He would be reaching their tree in a matter of seconds.

Peter was paralyzed with fear. And yet there was nothing he could do, nothing but hold his breath and hope. The man could trip. His batteries could give out. He could have a heart attack . . .

He'd reached the tree. He shone the light upward, and its beam clearly picked out the large dark shape of the falling body. Karl had jumped, had landed heavily upon the soldier . . .

There was a grunt and a sharp crack.

Peter looked down and was amazed to see that it was Karl who picked up the torch. He held it so as to illuminate his own face. He held his index finger to his lips. Then he flashed the light at the soldier in the Gestapo uniform. Then he flashed it back to light his own head as he made a horizontal motion across his neck with that same finger. Meaning *dead*.

And then he moved off, shining the torch back and forth as if he were looking for someone, as if he were that dead soldier.

Brilliant! All he had to do now was work his way across the orchard, get to the periphery of the search area, switch off the light, and then keep going. By the time they realized that one of their own men was missing, he'd be long gone.

He would. But Peter and Elfreda wouldn't.

"We can't stay here," he whispered. "They'll come looking for him. And when they find him down there, we can't be up here."

As quietly as he could, he climbed down to the lowest branch, the one from which Karl had jumped. When Peter jumped, though, he was hoping to avoid the body down below. He hit firm ground. He groped around and found the body. He pulled it a little away from the tree.

"Okay."

He heard the impact as Elfreda hit the ground.

He felt the body, patting it as he searched. Karl had taken the man's sidearm. And the flashlight, of course. But what else was there that could be of use? There was a scabbard at the belt. He worked that off and took it with its knife. He patted the buttocks. A wallet in the hip pocket—that Karl had been too hurried to bother with. Or that he wouldn't have deigned to take. Peter took it.

"Let's go," Elfreda said, drawing out the last vowel for emphasis.

They walked as briskly as they could, given the fact that it was quite dark and the ground was sometimes rough. There was no sense in trying to hurry if it meant risking the twisting of an ankle, Elfreda thought. Her pace was what she found comfortable, and either Peter matched it or he was accommodating himself to her. She remembered the other trucks that had moved on up the road. There was no point in making such wonderful progress in fleeing the searchers behind them if it brought them into another search area.

Ahead, there were the hulking shapes of the outbuildings of a farm. It was cool. Elfreda was wearing walking shoes, a dark wool skirt, a sweater, and a light cloth coat. She wondered about the wisdom of approaching those farm buildings too closely. All they needed, now, was to have a watchdog wake up and start to bark. Peter stopped ahead of her. She stopped also. She could hear the sounds of the trucks in the distance as they drove away, behind them and way off to the right. Those trucks or other trucks. Reinforcements? It was possible. Anything was possible. If they'd found the body of the man Karl had killed, they'd be out in real force now.

"There's a dirt road here. Maybe it leads to some other road," Peter whispered, explaining the reason for his left turn.

She didn't say anything. She followed along. It was just as well to follow him as to strike out on her own. She wasn't married to him or even committed to him from moment to moment. She supposed that, all things considered, she'd have preferred to be with Karl—who was in greater danger perhaps but had demonstrated impressive resourcefulness. Not that Peter had done anything stupid, but the way Karl had broken the man's neck, killing him with hardly a sound . . . that had been awesome.

But Peter was right about the dirt road. It eventually reached another blacktop road that led, in turn, to a wider roadway with houses along it at irregular intervals.

Peter stopped again.

"What now?" Elfreda asked.

"Those look like gardens, don't they?"

They did, indeed, look like gardens. There were several of them, too small to be farmers' fields. Villagers' plots, perhaps, like the Victory gardens back home. The gardeners evidently came out here in the evenings or on weekends to tend their vegetable patches. And there was a small shed where they kept their tools. Nobody was gardening now, in the middle of the night.

"The shed?" she asked.

He nodded. They took a closer look at the shed. It had a simple hasp and padlock. The wood was soft. Peter was able to pry the hasp off the door frame with the knife he'd taken from the Gestapo man. Inside, there were spades, hoes, cultivators, and a couple of piles of burlap sacks that had once contained fertilizer and could be used later for carrying back turnips or potatoes or whatever. They were dirty and musty but not verminous, so far as she could tell.

"We might as well hide in here for a while, until sunrise anyway," Peter suggested. The tentative quality of the "might as well" seemed to be an invitation for discussion.

"And then?" she asked.

"I guess we find a large town or a city. And we steal a car and head back to Munich."

"Sounds all right to me," she said.

"Meanwhile, we ought to get some sleep. We'll need it," he said.

Now? If he was going to make any moves, she supposed that this would be the time. And he had the knife. She was cold and frightened and tired and more than a little sorry for herself. She hoped he'd just go to sleep.

She was relieved, then, when she heard him say "Good night" from the pile of burlap sacks on the other side of the shed. She lay down, listening, allowing herself little by little to believe in her good fortune—for this one night and with this one man. It was a luxury not to be assaulted. But then, any variation from her long sequence of bad luck was welcome.

She had been orphaned at the age of six when a runaway truck had killed her mother and baby brother on a Leipzig street corner. She had been sent to her Aunt Edith and Uncle Rupert in America, while her elder half sister, Hilda, had been sent to a cousin in Mannheim. Elfreda's Aunt Edith was a mousy woman who lived in Troy, New York, and was married to Uncle Rupert, the brewmaster in a small brewery. His joke was that whatever beer he worked for was Rupert's beer. He brought home a fair amount of the product and drank it up, and on a good night he fell asleep. At other times, he'd yell at Aunt Edith or their two sons or at Elfreda. It was unpleasant but tolerable—until the transformations of puberty left Elfreda more vulnerable to the remarks and advances of her two cousins and her uncle.

When she was sixteen, she ran away, having taken sixty-two dollars of her aunt's household money as back pay owed on a million hours of dishwashing, ironing, floor scrubbing, and bedmaking. She went to New York where she got a job as a waitress in a coffee shop. And found a place to stay. And began to build a life for herself.

The news from Europe was bad, though, and it had been getting worse. She tried to reach her sister by letter. They were returned, addressee unknown. She tried the Department of State, but even though she was a United States citizen, her half sister wasn't. She tried a private detective agency, but their fees were so high she thought she'd do just as well coming over herself.

It would have been better if she'd never come here to Germany, she thought. Better for herself of course, but better for Hilda, too. Terrible, terrible.

She could still see the angry face with the tears running down Hilda's cheeks as she shouted over and over, "I'm dead, don't you understand? I'm like a dead person. Now go away and leave me alone. I'm dead."

She wasn't dead. She was a stripper in a Berlin dive, a parttime prostitute, a morphine addict, but not dead, except in spirit. Wounded, but not dead. Elfreda had stayed in Berlin, hoping to help, or at least to do what she could. She was still in Berlin when the war broke out.

She heard Peter moving. Now it comes, she thought. It always does.

"You awake?" he asked.

"Yes," she said coldly.

"Just going outside to pee. Sorry."

For Karl Roeder, the night had been easier, although the first few minutes after he'd jumped down and killed the Gestapo corporal had been strenuous. He'd picked up the flashlight, worked his way across the orchard, switched the light off, and then set out at a run. He had passed the boundary of the orchard and then the farmhouse and its barn and chicken house. He'd cut back to the road, crossed it, cut across fields on the other side of the road, and kept on going until he came to a sizable river—the Rednitz, but he didn't know that. He followed along the riverbank looking for a bridge, found one in a couple of kilometers, and crossed, keeping on that road until he came to a small village that announced itself as Kornburg. He still had no idea where he was. It was a little after eleven at night.

There wasn't much to Kornburg. The little town had a couple of stores on its main street, a post office, a municipal building, and a small inn, in which there was a restaurant and a little taproom. The bartender of the taproom had just closed up and had cleaned the bar, washing the last of the glasses and mugs and putting them in the rack to dry. He had locked up at a quarter past eleven and had gone out to his car, an aging Taunus, to drive home.

Karl saw him, approached, and said, "Excuse me, but can you tell me where I am?"

"Kornburg," the bartender said.

"Kornburg? Where is that?"

"A few kilometers from Nuremberg," the bartender said, puzzled now more than anything. Why didn't the man know where he was?

"Then I'm far from Munich?"

"Oh, yes," the bartender said. "It's a two-hour drive at least."

"Take me to Munich."

"What?" the bartender asked.

"This is a gun. I am prepared to use it if you are stupid or stubborn enough to force me. But I'd rather you just drove me to Munich and asked no questions. Understood?"

"What are you, crazy?"

"Yes. I am a lunatic. Does that make you feel better? I am a homicidal maniac. Try me!"

The bartender took a moment to think about it. Call out? Try to run? Try to take the gun away from the man?

"All right," the man said. "I'll drive you. Wherever you want to go."

"Get in on this side. Leave the door open and slide over."

A maniac, maybe, but not stupid. The bartender did what Karl ordered.

FOUR

The town Peter and Elfreda found themselves approaching that morning was Schwabach, a little village just a few kilometers from Nuremberg. They were in no particular hurry. Indeed, their plan was to wait until dark and then steal a car. Their chances, they agreed, would be better after dark. And the vigilance of the police might by then have waned just a little. There were almost certain to be roadblocks around the area where the Gestapo corporal had been killed. It would be easier to melt into the crowd of a city for the day, then make their move later on.

They had a few Reichsmarks with which to get coffee and a couple of rolls. They walked on to Nuremberg and spent a great part of the morning inspecting the walls, gates, towers, and battlements just as any tourists would have done. In fact, they felt a little like tourists. They looked at the churches, the St. Lorenzkirche and the Marienkirche. And they shared a hot sausage from a man with a little cart on the sidewalk. They killed the afternoon in a movie. When they came out of the theater, it was almost dusk. The time had come to pick out an automobile. Near the St. Lorenzkirche there was the Old Nurnberger Hofbrau Haus with a row of cars in the open plaza between the beer hall and the looming bulk of the Gothic church. There were half a dozen cars. Peter tried the door of each of them, working down the row, driver's side, passenger's side, driver's side, and so on. The driver's door of the third car was not locked. He was able to get in, lean across, open the passenger's door, and invite Elfreda into the car. The hotwiring took a little longer than he'd expected. For one thing, it was dark and the car was unfamiliar. He'd worked on a BMW and an elderly Daimler back at the training school. This was a Fiat. But more important, there was the pressure, the need for haste or—even better—efficiency. At any moment, the owner of the automobile could materialize, could summon police, could turn out to be a party member himself, armed and happy to have an excuse to shoot someone . . .

None of that, Peter told himself. There wasn't any use in worrying. It'd just slow him up even further. The ideal thing was not to think about any of it at all, to put out of his mind all the risks they were running. But the next best thing was to project himself way up and out, so that he was looking down at the fumbling figure in the car with an amused indifference, as if he were watching a not very good movie and wondering how the scene was going to come out.

He found them, at last, the damned wires. The right ones? He yanked, felt them give, then touched them together. He got the spark, felt the engine cough, catch, go.

"You've got it," Elfreda said, her voice tight with the tension.

"Yeah," he answered. "I do, don't I?" He released the brake, put the car into reverse, backed out of the parking place, put it into first, and moved forward.

"Which way?" she asked.

"Beats me," he said. "The only thing is that we don't cross the river. We're south of the river now. Munich is south of us. So . . ."

"That figures," she said. "But there's a bridge up ahead."

"So there is," he said. He slowed, stopped, looked behind him, executed a deft U-turn with the little Fiat, and drove back in the direction from which they had come. They repassed the St. Lorenzkirche, continued through the Frauenthor, passed the railroad station, and headed south.

There was a signpost with the names of cities and arrows. Neumarkt, Regensburg, Ingolstadt, and Munich were dead ahead.

"That's encouraging," he said, for her sake as much as for his own. She'd been blessedly quiet, even during those tough moments with the ignition wires and his ten numb thumbs.

"So far, so good," she said, either agreeing with him or warning him not to get too confident.

They had passed Neumarkt without incident and were through the little village of Seubersdorf when the tire blew out. The car swerved sharply to the left. Peter fought it, got it back in the right lane, but oversteered. The car skidded, veered crazily, and floated off the road into a culvert.

"You all right?" he asked.

"I think so. I held on . . . I braced myself on the dashboard."

"I had the steering wheel to hold onto," he said. "Too bad about the car."

"He should have paid attention to his tires."

"Hard to get rubber, I expect," Peter said.

They got out of the automobile, Elfreda having to slide over to the driver's side because her door was jammed. "Back to that last little town?" she asked. It was a sensible idea. He nodded.

Seubersdorf was only a few minutes behind them by car. On foot, it was a lot more strenuous. The terrain was hilly and the road steep, rising and then declining sharply. They could see the little village below them and to the left. There were a few houses. There was a store, a municipal building, a small church, a garage. And then, as the road started to rise again, there were more orchards and woods with an occasional house or barn.

It was late enough so that there was little traffic. A truck passed them noisily. A car roared past. But these were interruptions in syrupy silence. They descended toward the village.

"I wish there were more cars," Peter said. "It'd make it easier to steal one. The sound of the engine starting . . ."

"There's the hill," Elfreda suggested. "We could coast a bit maybe, and improve our chances."

"It's a thought," he acknowledged. He imagined the owner looking out of his bedroom window and recognizing the sound of his own engine. She'd worried about that too. She hadn't criticized him for the way he'd handled the blowout either, even though Peter had reproached himself. If he'd been a little more skillful, he might have kept out of the ditch. They could have changed the tire and gone on. But it was too late for that now.

She was thinking ahead. He owed it to her to do as much.

"Halt!"

They were still a little above the village, next to a fallow field that separated two houses. They hadn't even begun to worry about being spotted. But when they turned around, there was the man on a bicycle, shining his electric torch on them. He got off the bicycle.

"Your papers?"

"We don't have them," Peter said. "They're back in the car. We had a blowout."

"Yes? What kind of car?"

"A Fiat. It's in the ditch down the road."

The beam of the flashlight did not waver, but with his other hand the policeman took an automatic pistol from its holster. "You will march, please. I shall be behind you. We will go to the Seubersdorf post. That way."

He laid the bicycle on the ground. Peter's impulse was to run. This was as good a moment as he was likely to get. But if he made it, Elfreda wouldn't—and there was no way to signal her without alerting the policeman. He was torn. What if there was some way to connect them to the killing of the Gestapo man the night before? Would the Abwehr have the clout to rescue him and Elfreda from the clutches of the Gestapo? Would they be inclined to try, particularly if it meant swapping Karl for the two of them?

These thoughts flashed by, terribly quickly. And then the moment was over. The bicycle was on the ground. The policeman was ready to take them to the station. Still, Peter figured there would be no harm in trying another tack. "We could go back to the car. It's just down the road a little. I can get the papers for you. They're in the front seat. We went into a ditch and came to get help . . ."

It was impossible to see the face of their captor. The flashlight was pointed at Peter and Elfreda and behind it there was nothing but a halo of white hair and sharp chiaroscuro of features that produced a caricature or a primitive mask.

"It won't take five minutes," Peter said cheerfully.

"That car has been reported as stolen," the policeman said, as if he were delivering the punch line of a bad joke. "Now, you will walk slowly toward the police substation in Seubersdorf."

Peter and Elfreda exchanged one quick, helpless glance.

"Now!"

They marched. At the bottom of the hill, there was a small stone bridge across which the road turned a little to the left and into the village. The police substation was a part of the municipal building, a squat square structure with fancy pediments over its tall windows. The police entrance was around to the side and down half a flight of stone steps. Inside, there was a tiny substation—a man at a desk, essentially, with a couple of cells in a corridor behind him. The architecture was different but it looked more or less like the sheriff's office in any low-budget Western. The policeman who had brought them in exchanged a few hushed words with the man at the desk. The desk man produced a large key ring from somewhere behind him—the ring was big enough to fit around a man's head—and handed it over.

"Back through there," the policeman said.

There were just the two cells. Elfreda went into the first and Peter into the second. The policeman locked the door and went back to the front room.

"It isn't exactly a fortress," Peter remarked, in English.

"It doesn't have to be," she answered, also in English.

Then, after a long pause, she observed, "They seem to have put a great deal of effort into finding a stolen car."

"It's just the famous German efficiency, I hope. Otherwise . . ." He didn't have to continue. They were both thinking the same thing, wondering whether they were doomed merely to failure or to death.

They waited for more than an hour. Elfreda actually curled up on the slat bench in her cell and dozed off. Peter began to hope that it was simply a police matter, that they'd be held until morning and brought before some kind of magistrate . . . To be booked? To be formally charged? He had no idea how the German system of justice worked, or what forms it observed before it did what it damned well pleased. If they got into a courtroom, they could explain about being on an Abwehr exercise. That wouldn't necessarily tie them to Karl and the Gestapo man he'd killed. Except for that, the only thing to worry about was the prospect of a term in jail for stealing the car, which wasn't a whole lot worse than incarceration in an internment camp for enemy aliens. Maybe it was meant to be this way, Peter thought. It was providence, keeping him from a mission about which he'd never been altogether enthusiastic.

He had loosened his shoelaces and stretched out on his slat bunk, was turning these matters over in his mind, trying to figure the odds and yet not to hope too much or to fear too much, when he heard them coming.

The man from the desk was leading the way. He had that big key ring. Behind him were two men in light trench coats and dark fedoras.

"Up. Out," the man with the key ring ordered.

The men in the trench coats didn't say anything. One of them produced a pair of handcuffs, however. He snapped them on Peter's wrists, behind his back. Then he frisked Peter. He found the knife, still in its scabbard.

"So? You take no measures for security here?" the other one asked.

"I assumed he'd searched them already, when he brought them in. I'll speak to him. I'm very sorry, inspector," the deskman said. What worried Peter was the man's look of fear.

"Let me see it," the inspector commanded.

The other one handed it over.

"A Gestapo knife. Where did this come from, I wonder?" He smiled. It wasn't clear whether he was asking Peter a question or not.

Still, it seemed to Peter that this was as good a chance to try to work out a story that Elfreda wouldn't contradict later on. She was in the next cell and could hear everything. "They issued those knives to us back in Munich . . ."

"Silence," the inspector said. "You will speak only when addressed. I wasn't addressing you." He looked at Peter with icy contempt.

"I lost mine," Elfreda volunteered. It was risky, but she was letting Peter know she had heard and would go along.

"Silence!" the inspector said. "Put the cuffs on her, too."

The other one produced another pair of handcuffs and obeyed the order. The two men hustled their prisoners back out into the little courtyard on the side of the building. There, looming up like a great metal beast, a sleek black Mercedes was poised on the cobblestones. The younger one drove. The inspector sat in front, a gun in his lap. Peter and Elfreda were in the back. The car pulled out of the courtyard and turned onto the road. It was headed back toward Nuremberg—as Peter had more or less expected.

Just past Neumarkt, the senior man in front gave an instruction to the driver. "Up ahead, on the left."

Peter had no idea what was coming up ahead on the left. They weren't anywhere near Nuremberg yet. Was it another Abwehr post? Would they be brought back to Munich after all? Unlikely. Had that been the case, there wouldn't have been the need for handcuffs. There wouldn't have been the flat refusal to talk or to listen to anything that Peter or Elfreda might say. That was a distancing maneuver, a way of denying that their prisoners were human beings. So there was no reasonable ground for hope of any gentle treatment.

But instead of a grim Gestapo interrogation center, there was a farmhouse. An attractive, typically Bavarian farmhouse. Stucco with dark beams, and carved decorations at the corners of the roof.

"You wait. You watch them," the senior man said to the junior man, and he went inside the farmhouse.

The junior man lit a cigarette and took a deep drag. Peter realized that this was as good an opportunity as they were likely to get. Somehow, if he could contrive a way to distract the fellow, to divert his attention . . .

Peter shifted his position. Elfreda glanced at him. He mouthed the words, slowly, very clearly, but with no voice, "You. Go. Pee." And he made a slight indication with his head in the direction of the woods outside.

"Excuse me," Elfreda said, aloud and in German. "I have to urinate."

The man in the front seat looked back, smiled as if she'd told him a dirty joke, and shook his head.

"I don't have any choice about it," she said. "In here or out there. But I have to go!"

"Damn!" the man said, to himself more than to them.

"You're not afraid of me, are you?" Elfreda asked. "You have a gun, after all."

He opened the front door. He flipped his cigarette in a high arc. He opened the back door for Elfreda. As the door opened, the dome light went on, showing the man's face in an amused smirk. The dirty joke was getting better.

This was what Peter was banking on, the distraction, the inattention, the loss of mental balance. Feeling alert and calm, his mind racing so that the real world seemed to be in slow motion, Peter watched for the moment when Elfreda was almost out of the car. Then out. Then, bracing himself against the back of the seat, he kicked at the door with both feet, getting the strength of his back and thighs into it. The door shot open, and the man was knocked to the ground. The rest was up to Elfreda.

He watched her turn, shift her weight to her left foot, bring her right leg back, and kick smartly, hitting the side of the man's head with the ball of her foot. She smiled the way an athlete sometimes does at a moment of perfect performance.

It wasn't rape. Detective-Inspector Kappe had no moral objections to rape, but he thought the inert and unresponsive lump of female flesh was unaesthetic. It was far better to have the woman's cooperation, her collaboration. The knowledge that the woman's soul was in rebellion, that her spirit hated every moment even as her body performed with enthusiasm and energy, was like a hot condiment in an exotic dish. To lie in bed with Frau Wildner, to nuzzle his head between her pillowing breasts and hear her heart pound as she simulated lust, was altogether pleasing. In a moment, he'd rouse himself, put his uniform on again, and go down to the car, perhaps waiting there a while to let Corporal Heitz give her a tumble.

What was most exhilarating was the sense of power. The survival of the fittest. Wildner's husband was in a concentration camp, a left-wing dreamer and an enemy of the state. As long as Frau Wildner remained attached to her husband, she would continue to be unfaithful to him—in order to ensure that he got good treatment, extra food, whatever advantages she could contrive for him. And Kappe's cousin ran the camp in which Herr Wildner was detained. So whenever he was in the neighborhood, he could come by to be entertained with an ardor that was as fervent as it was fake.

It was a shame Kappe couldn't linger more. But he had to get those two car thieves back to Nuremberg. A little treat for Heitz was all he had time for. (Outside, as he sat in the car, he could imagine it and then, later on, he'd hear Heitz's description, blow by blow.)

"I must be going, I'm afraid."

"So soon?" she asked, pretending desolation.

"Duty calls. I really shouldn't have stopped at all. But you are so enjoyable."

"You are too kind," she said. He could hear her heart banging in her chest. It said *liar, liar, liar*. He was flattered.

He sat on the bed and she held the boot while he thrust his foot into it. Her breasts swayed back and forth like cowbells. He got into the one boot and then, after a little struggle, the other.

"A tight fit," she said.

"Like you," he said, and gave her a playful swat on her bare buttock.

"I'll think of you," she said.

He was sure that was true. Especially while Heitz was fucking her. He gave her a tender kiss on the cheek and went down the dark carved staircase to let himself out.

The car? Where in hell was the car? And Heitz? Where was he?

"Fool!" the detective-inspector said aloud. It was not clear whether he meant Heitz or himself.

They had cut down past little towns like Pollanten and Berching, heading for Ingolstadt. At Beilngreis they reached the Altmühl and Peter decided to turn right and head westward, along the river. He was looking for the right configuration of road and riverbank and when he found it, he stopped, pulled the body of the Gestapo driver out of the back seat, and lugged it to the escarpment. Elfreda helped him, holding onto the feet while he took the hands. It was like throwing a waterfront counselor off the dock at summer camp, one, two, three and letting go. The body made a satisfactory splash as it hit the water.

It was a relief to be rid of the corpse. More particularly, it was an opportunity to inhale, to shift gears from the moment-to-moment existence at the edge of panic to something else, the beginning of confidence. There was, for both of them, at least a hope of success. As long as the dead man had been in the back seat of the car, it had been obscene to think about their own chances of survival. Now it was possible to do that.

Peter was puzzled, though, by other kinds of feelings, quite giddy and strange, that came to him unbidden and would not go away. He had never killed anyone before. Now that he'd done it— and with his bare hands—he was surprised to find that it felt good. To kill this particular man, this Nazi, this Gestapo functionary, had been quite thrilling—like sinking a basketball into the hoop from way outside the key. He had come bounding out of the car, had fumbled for the keys, lying on top of the unconscious man, and had worked to try to get Elfreda's cuffs open. It had been very difficult getting the damned key into the damned hole. But they'd managed. She'd freed herself, then freed him. And he'd been the one to find the rock and bash the unconscious Gestapo man's head with it.

So they were as good as Karl. Or as effective. As deadly, anyway. They had managed to fight back for the absurd and outrageous behavior of the Reich toward them and toward the world. No matter what happened to them, now, they had made their contribution. It was that as much as their complicity in the killing that prompted in Peter the new thought—that he could trust Elfreda. Or, that if he couldn't trust her now, then he couldn't trust anyone, ever. She was tired and a little bedraggled. Her hair was falling over her face. She looked wonderful. She was, he realized, the kind of woman who looks terrific on a horse. Big definite features, and a broad brow and smooth skin.

"You're staring at me," she said.

"Am I? I guess I am."

"Yes."

"I'm just feeling good," he said, grinning.

"We're not out of it yet," she reminded him.

"No, probably not."

"We'd better get moving."

They got back into the car. Before he switched on the ignition, he looked at her and said, "I don't know. It isn't right to thank you. But it isn't right not to thank you."

"I know."

"I'm happy we're together."

"You make me blush," she said.

"Good," he said, and he switched on the motor.

They drove for a while, crossing the river at Kinding and then heading south. They went perhaps twenty minutes without speaking. Then, when they passed a road sign indicating Ingolstadt as being sixteen kilometers ahead, he wondered aloud, "We could go back to the lodge and get on with this. Or we could make a break for it . . ."

"Make a break for what?"

"From Munich to the Swiss border. What can it be? Sixty miles? Probably less. We could make a run for it."

"We'd never get across the border. They'd spot the car. We have no papers."

"You think?"

"I don't know what to think," she said. "I'm afraid of them."

"They don't seem to be absolutely sure about what they're doing," Peter said. "The Gestapo and the Abwehr haven't got this too well coordinated."

"But it'd be Gestapo at the border," Elfreda said. She wasn't happy about it. She was staring ahead as if there might be some flaw in her reasoning that she hoped to see in the road ahead of her.

"Back to the lodge then?"

"Not in this car," she said. "But . . . yes. All we need now is to steal one more car and we've got a good chance. And if we get back to the lodge, they'll get us back to the States. What more can we ask for?"

"What more, indeed?"

They were on the Autobahn, heading south now. He'd decided to risk the main road, bargaining for the distance they'd make in the safest hours in the dark of the night just after their escape. He'd hoped to make it past Ingolstadt and then to cut off to one of the smaller roads that cross through the Dachauer Moos to Munich. But she was right about the car. They had to ditch it and find another.

They took the turnoff for Pornbach, then cut south to Pfaffenhofen an der Ilm, Elfreda navigating by means of the maps that were in the glove compartment, Peter driving. At Pfaffenhofen she suggested they swap cars. "It's getting light," she said. "It'll be riskier in an hour."

"All right," he agreed.

He had to slow down because of the narrow streets. In the middle of the town there was a large square with a parking area at one end with a number of cars. Peter pulled up into one of the empty slots. "This time, we'll look at the tires," he said.

She chuckled.

They were back at square one, repeating what they'd done at Nuremberg. But this time it went more smoothly. He found a light-blue BMW with good tires and its windows rolled partway down.

He could reach in and unlock the door. He could jump the wires and start it. Elfreda had the map from the Gestapo car. Peter waited for her to climb in and then pulled away. The entire operation couldn't have taken more than two minutes.

Just beyond Hohenkammer, Elfreda suggested that they find a place to stop.

"What for?"

"We're not far from Munich. I think we've got it within reach now. But we ought to play it as safe as possible. There'll be more traffic later on, when people are going to work. Now, we're conspicuous. If they're looking for us, we're the only fish in the tank."

"Not a bad thought," he agreed. "Besides, I'm tired. I've been driving forever."

He slowed down so they could look for a place to turn off. He took his side, and she looked to the right. She was the one who found the naked chimney. The house that had stood around it had burned down some time ago, but there was still a rutted track that led from the road into what had perhaps been the front yard. There were bushes along the road, and they could cut into the yard and turn, following the track, so that the car was concealed behind the old hedge that was now overgrown and easily ten feet high.

"Perfect," he said, praising the place and praising her for having found it.

"We've been in worse places," she said.

"Haven't we?"

He shivered, partly from the cold—the temperature had fallen during the night and there was a damp chill in the air—but partly from fatigue. Or the delayed impact of the experiences they'd had. All that self-control he'd needed in order to function, all that rationality and efficiency he'd managed to find within himself, receded now that they were, at least for the moment, safe. He shuddered like a man with a chill.

"You're not getting sick, are you?" she asked.

"No, I don't think so. Just cold and tired. It's . . ."

". . . perfectly understandable," she said. "I'm cold too. It's cold." She slid over and they huddled together for warmth, their arms about each other. They sat that way for some time until his shivers subsided. Then she ran her fingertips down his stubbly cheek.

"I haven't had a chance to shave," he said.

"I know," she said quietly. And then she added, "It's all right."

He felt better for a moment. Then he began to realize—gradually, but with a growing certainty—that the all-rightness included not only the condition of his unshaved cheek but their condition together, their being together in the car, their holding each other. It was a sexual assent and more than that. It was an acknowledgment of the odd kind of alliance he'd felt, himself, when they'd flung the body into the river.

She was, in the most feminine and womanly way, endorsing the real world, accepting it, contriving even to enjoy it. If he might have preferred a grand luxe hotel with embroidered pillow slips and champagne in ice buckets at the bedside, she was willing to swap such easy dreams for the here-and-now, the front seat of the car, the ghostly chimney, the scraggly hedge, just as long as they were together. It was, indeed, all right. All of it was right.

He'd turned his head toward her, pulled her head just a little toward him, and kissed her, gently, as married couples kiss if they are lucky enough still to be in love. This was why she had suggested that they pull off the road and wait for the morning traffic into Munich! Of course, of course, of course.

They kissed and touched and held each other, not wanting to rush things, enjoying each step of the lovely way. But eventually it was too good to restrain in the cramped front seat. "The back seat would be better," she said.

"We're like a couple of teenagers."

"They're not so stupid, those teenagers, are they?"

"I guess not," he said, and then he couldn't talk anymore.

For a little while, they slept, sprawled across the back seat. Perhaps it was a quarter of an hour or maybe a little longer. But when he awoke, his arm was stiff. Otherwise, he felt refreshed, restored as if he had slept all night. He moved carefully, so as not to wake her. He went off into the woods to pee. When he came back, she was gone. He waited for her. She had gone on the same business and returned, combing her hair with her fingers.

"What I wouldn't give for coffee," she said.

"An hour from now, if we have any luck at all, we'll be back at the lodge. There'll be coffee there. And eggs. And hot water."

"Hot water?"

"To shave in. To wash in."

"I rather like your beard," she teased.

"Oh, so that's it. I was trying to figure out the difference between last night and tonight. You like beards."

"No," she said. "It's you that I like. That I could trust you. That you didn't force yourself upon me."

"Why would I have done that?"

"Because you could have. Because you had the knife."

He was saddened to think what kind of life she'd had, what kind of men she'd known who had treated her badly. Perhaps, one day, if they ever got through this, there might be the luxury of finding out such things. Even of putting them right—of making it up to her. Now, there was other work at hand.

He started the car's engine, put it into gear, and backed out onto the road. He shifted into forward gear and headed south. They crossed the Amper, joined an increasing number of automobiles and trucks already on the road, and were in Munich by seven-fifteen. Twenty minutes later, they drove through the gates of the lodge. They signed in at the gatehouse and went on up to the main house where there was a team of instructors ready to welcome them and hear their reports.

They were surprised to learn that they were nearly the last to straggle in. Even fat Willi and dumb Horst had made it back before them. Willi had simply waited for the instructor to go back up front to climb into the cab and he had jumped right back into the rear of the truck—it was going back to the lodge, so why not hitch a ride? Reinhart and Horst had followed along. They'd all jumped out of the truck in Munich and had walked up the hill to the lodge, the first to come in, much to everyone's surprise.

There were other stories going around. Johann had broken into the poor box of a church, stolen enough money to take a bus back to Munich, and had sauntered in at midday. Kurt had sat by the side of the road where he, Johann, and Rudi had been dropped, and had fallen asleep. In the morning, he stuck out his thumb and was lucky. A farmer with a truckload full of hops had given him a ride almost to Munich.

Only Rudi was still out. And he showed up soon after Peter and Elfreda. His story was the most curious of all, for he had presented himself at a police station in Zirndorf, saying he'd been robbed, his money and papers taken. He'd given his name as Liebert, the demolitions instructor's name and the lodge as his address. The Abwehr duty officer had confirmed that there was a Liebert at this address. The Zirndorf police sergeant had advanced Rudi enough money for him to get back to Munich.

Nobody talked about Karl's experiences. He was back. He'd made it. But he hadn't said much to his fellow trainees. Peter wondered whether Captain Koepke knew what had happened, until the captain brought it up himself. "We have heard about the unfortunate incident in the apple orchard," he said at the start of their private interview. "Indeed, we have been concerned since that news reached us about your welfare and Elfreda's. What happened?"

Peter hesitated.

"Would you rather that I talked with the two of you together? I am not trying to trip you up. There is a certain lack of harmony between the Abwehr and the Gestapo, which has nothing to do with you. But it is vital that we know the truth. I promise you, there will be no punishment."

He decided to risk it. He told the captain about stealing the car in Nuremberg, about the flat tire, and about their capture. "What made it especially bad was that I still had the man's knife," he explained. "I just hadn't thought to get rid of it. And those police who locked us up never searched me. So I was afraid that the Gestapo would connect us to the killing. That they'd blame us for it. So, when they took us back toward Nuremberg and the opportunity presented itself . . ."

He explained how he and Elfreda had killed the Gestapo driver and had escaped.

"You did well," Koepke said. "I congratulate you. And you have my word that there will be nothing more you have to fear for what you've done. It was their fault, in a number of ways—not least for being stupid enough to fall for such a trick." He laughed and offered Peter a schnapps.

After Peter had left the room, Captain Koepke put in a telephone call to Berlin on a secure line. He spoke for twenty minutes, hung up, waited, heard the phone ring, answered it, and spoke again—this time to Admiral Canaris himself. They were on the telephone for a little more than half an hour.

That afternoon, the captain sent for Karl Roeder to let him know the substance of that conversation. First, he told Roeder about the death of the Gestapo driver. "Which means," the captain explained, "that either they're very lucky or very good. I've discussed it with Berlin, and the decision has been made to put you all together in one group. If anyone here is likely to be useful to you, Peter and Elfreda are the best candidates. Similarly, if there's anyone here who might be a danger to you, it's still those two you have to look out for. So they might as well be directly under your nose."

"Yes, that's true enough."

"I take it, then, that you've no objections?"

"None at all," Roeder said. "In fact, I think I ought to congratulate them. Why not? They did well, for amateurs."

"Don't underestimate them," the commandant warned. "Remember, the man they killed is just as dead as if a professional had killed him."

That evening, there was a banquet to celebrate the graduation of all nine of the trainees and there was an announcement from Captain Koepke at the end of the dinner, with glasses of champagne poured out for everyone: "Tomorrow morning, you will be leaving here. Your transport has been arranged. Your first destination will be Paris, where you will have a three-day pass."

Those last words produced a cheer from the table. Captain Koepke acknowledged it as if it had been meant for him personally.

When the table was quiet, he continued, "On the expiration of that three days, you will report to the Office of the Commandant of Paris for transport to the coast and to your submarine. You will be landed in America, on the coast of Long Island. You will make your way to New York City. Your targets will be the Jewish department stores of New York. Following the personal order of the Führer, you will blow up Macy's, Gimbels, Saks, Bergdorf-Goodman, Bonwit-Teller, Best's, Bloomingdale's, and Abraham and Straus. You will be provided with papers, money, necessary equipment, and contacts in America for further orders as well as for aid. You have already received the necessary training. To that, I can only add my personal wishes for the best of luck. Heil Hitler!"

They all drank. Peter looked around the room. The others were looking around too. Everyone was trying to conceal the obvious and inescapable shock.

It wasn't just the news of what the targets were. It was the realization—the absolute certainty—that they were out of their fucking minds.

Captain Koepke, having drained his wine, flung the goblet into the stone fireplace. The rest of them followed suit. It felt good to break something.

Canaris and Piekenbrock accepted the chairs that had been held for them by the rather too showy aides, but they declined General Heydrich's offer of coffee.

"None for me, then," Heydrich said. "That will be all."

The aides snapped to attention and saluted. Heydrich nodded. They retreated, marching in unison, and closed the huge double doors together. It had been choreographed and was either impressive or depressing, according to the observer's frame of mind. Piekenbrock glanced at the admiral, whose face showed nothing at all.

"Two Gestapo agents have been killed by your Abwehr trainees," Heydrich began. "It was a waste. Inexcusable."

"I quite agree," the admiral said, as if Heydrich had been commenting about the weather.

"The responsibility for such a blunder must be fixed!" Heydrich continued, emphasizing his words by tapping with his fingertip upon the polished surface of the conference table.

"As you think best," Canaris said, "but I should expect that your service wouldn't be eager to compound the mess any further. You can certainly handle it internally, can you not?"

"Internally? Internally? Are you denying that it was your men who killed the Gestapo agents? Are you denying that it was your exercise? Your responsibility?"

"My responsibility?" Admiral Canaris asked, as if he were genuinely mystified. "Your people knew we were having an exercise. Or did all those trucks and all those men just happen to be on patrol outside Nuremberg that night? You were after our people, hounding them for reasons that are too devious for me to guess at. And you were clumsy about it. None of our people was armed. And the Abwehr trainees were outnumbered by your armed agents by at least ten to one. No verbal command was ever issued. No show of legitimate authority was ever made. And still your people contrived to get themselves killed . . . It seems very clumsy and unprofessional to me. But if you want a full-dress inquiry, I shall naturally be willing to cooperate."

"Detective-Inspector Kappe has been disciplined," Heydrich said.

"I should expect so. But that is internal, is it not? What further do you want of me?"

"I want to know what your plans are for Karl Roeder."

"He's just another member of the team."

"He has another target. I know it!" Heydrich shouted.

"You don't know any such thing," Canaris returned calmly. "If you really did know it, you wouldn't be shouting, would you?"

Piekenbrock took out his handkerchief and blew his nose. He didn't want anyone to see him smiling. He certainly didn't want to take it upon himself to enrage Heydrich any further than his chief felt like doing.

"A trained killer?" Heydrich sputtered.

"We trained them all, or tried to, in the short time that we had available."

"You do not need assassins to blow up department stores," Heydrich said.

"No, but it is useful for our people to be able to defend themselves. And there is the possibility that, once the primary mission has been accomplished, there will be other uses for these agents whom we'll have in place."

"But which is the primary mission and which is the secondary?" Heydrich wanted to know.

"How can one ask that? You have read the Führer's order."

"You cannot take that order seriously."

"I take all orders from the Führer most seriously," Canaris intoned gravely.

Piekenbrock watched the pulsations in the little vein that meandered across the upper-left part of Heydrich's forehead, wondering how much more agitation would be required for it to pop.

Canaris had won. Piekenbrock could see it in the way his chief sat back in his chair. "I take them seriously and I earnestly suggest to you that you should do the same," the admiral said, his face the very picture of the wise old adviser.

Heydrich wouldn't give it up, though. He was silent for a very long time, staring at his reflection in the highly polished surface of the conference table. "It still goes back to the fundamental question," he said. "Why were we not officially informed of this exercise?"

He was, Piekenbrock thought, like a novice bridge player who cannot believe the ace is no good anymore, the opponent having all trumps in his hand.

"For two reasons, general," Canaris replied, patiently going over the ground again. "One, we did not want to make it too easy for our trainees. We wanted to have them experience the position of the fugitive, of the outsider, with only his own wits to rely on. Two, we knew you were aware of our training facility and had agents reporting on it all the time, following our people, interviewing them, trying to infiltrate . . ."

"I see," Heydrich said.

"If that is all, general? I have a very full schedule of appointments this afternoon. Colonel Piekenbrock?"

Piekenbrock got up. The admiral rose. The SS general drew himself to attention, clicked his heels, and gave the party salute. Canaris and Piekenbrock returned it and marched out of Gestapo Headquarters, their heels resounding on the marble floors of the grandiose hallways.

When they were in the back of the admiral's limousine, Canaris made a curious circular motion with his right hand. The colonel cranked up the window that separated their compartment from the driver's in front. When they were sealed off, Canaris said, "He thought he had me. And he very nearly did. One reason he never found out about Roeder's target is that Roeder doesn't know it yet. None of them down there knows it."

The admiral looked out of the window at a darkening sky. It would rain soon.

"That's risky for Roeder, isn't it, excellency?" Piekenbrock asked after a pause.

"There were risks either way," the admiral told him. "The question was whether Roeder should run them or . . . or I should. And I chose him."

He was tired. He lounged back in the plush of the seat and closed his eyes, signaling the end of the conversation.

In Paris, Peter was surprised when Karl invited him to a grand dinner at Maxim's. "Just you and me, and of course Elfreda. You must come," he said. "We owe ourselves a party, the three of us."

Presumably it was also a gesture of reparation, even though Karl never alluded to that. But Peter had had some time to consider how Karl had been the one the Gestapo had been after. That had explained his need to escape at any cost. That was why he'd killed the Gestapo man. But his flight had left Peter and Elfreda in a difficult predicament. Had they not managed to get away themselves, the Gestapo would presumably have been less than gentle with them. It had been because of their connection with Karl that Peter and Elfreda had been forced to kill the driver the next night.

Peter's regrets about that killing were qualified at best. After all, the man had been a Gestapo agent and a legitimate enemy. Still, Peter had never before been forced to kill a human being. There was a chasm he had irretrievably crossed. And that crossing was not an occasion for rejoicing.

He accepted, nevertheless, because he did not want to be rude—not to Karl who could be dangerous, or to Elfreda either. It was no great sacrifice to make, after all, to endure dinner at Maxim's, even if it came with Karl's congratulations and jokes. Peter supposed that he and Elfreda together could keep Karl's odd high spirits in check.

Actually, it was something to wonder about. Karl was usually an undemonstrative kind of fellow, very much in control of himself. But he seemed to have been transformed somehow, excited either by the City of Light or by the prospect of their mission to the United States. Peter's curiosity was aroused.

There was champagne waiting for them. And Elfreda looked wonderful. She had spent the afternoon at the Galleries Lafayette where she'd been able to find a simple black dress off the rack. And she'd had her hair done differently—swept up and pulled into a chignon—so that she looked as if she dropped into Maxim's twice a week. The famous pink lights warmed and flattered, but she accepted their compliment as if it were her due. Peter and Karl looked much more like people who were stepping up in class for a special occasion.

The sommelier poured the champagne. Karl proposed a toast. "There is some African tribe—I forget which—that believes you aren't a man until you've fathered a man and killed a man. I drink," he said, "to maturity."

His speech was perfectly normal, neither slurred nor too carefully enunciated. Peter nevertheless had a very clear impression that this glass of champagne was not Karl's first drink of the evening.

"To staying alive," Peter said. "It's another way of getting to be mature."

"I take it," Elfreda said to Karl, "that you were already mature?"

"More than that, I'd say," Karl answered. "Venerable. Old before my time." He laughed and drained his glass.

Peter didn't see how it was all that funny but he smiled politely, sipped his wine, and waited, his appetite for enlightenment now as much whetted as his physical appetite. Karl was not himself tonight. Why? More important, could there be some advantage in it for Peter?

The meal was wonderful, starting off with quenelles of fish with a delicate sauce that had white truffles in it. Then there were sweetbreads in a rich wine sauce and a fine Bonnes Mares. Karl had laid it all on in advance, or had had the good sense to let the maître d'hôtel pick what was good. It was an impressive meal, but Peter thought Karl's eating was automatic. He wasn't enjoying it enough.

"A lovely dinner," Elfreda said over the crepes.

"Was it?" Karl asked, as if he hadn't noticed. "The least we deserve. The very least . . ." He ordered another bottle of champagne. It was a perfectly appropriate wine for dessert, but Peter was now sure that Karl was swilling. He'd been treating the meal as if he were on an expense account of a company he hated. That explained the invitation, too—he'd included Peter and Elfreda because the three of them together could eat more than Karl could by himself.

"You seem upset about something," Peter said. He didn't want to seem to pry, but there had to be a way of drawing Karl out a little. "You want to talk about it?" he asked, figuring that the straightforward question was as likely to work as anything more indirect.

Karl shook his head. But he said, "It's very sad. Very sad, my friends. They are throwing us away. They are taking people with real talent, with spirit, and they are . . . wasting us."

"You too?"

77

"I got more or less what I might have expected. It is a joke, really." He stopped to drink some of the champagne.

"A joke?" Peter prompted.

"Two birds with one stone," he said. He laughed.

"I don't get it," Peter admitted.

"It's just as well. Better you should forget about it entirely. Better for your health."

Peter waited. He glanced at Elfreda, but she was absorbed in cutting off a dainty piece of crepe with the side of her fork.

"Excuse me," Karl said. He got up and went off toward the men's room.

"You think I should follow him?"

"No," Elfreda said. "You don't want to spook him any more than he already is. If he's going to tell us, then he will tell us on his own. There's not much you can do," she said.

"You think he will?" Peter asked.

She shook her head no.

"It's strange," Peter said.

"For a man like that, very strange," she agreed.

Karl returned to the table. He had washed his face in cold water and combed his hair. He sat down at the table, smiled, cleared his throat, and asked, "Now, where were we? Your plans for the evening?"

"I thought of going for a walk down the Champs Elysées and then going back to the hotel," Elfreda said.

"And you, Peter?" Karl asked. "Something a little more lively perhaps? The late show at the Casino de Paris?"

"No, I'm afraid I'm a little tired. And I've had a good deal to drink," Peter said.

"A shame, though, to waste an evening in Paris," Karl said. "But perhaps you'll put it to good use after all." He flashed a smile. It wasn't a leer, Peter decided. Then Karl called for the check. "Have another coffee if you like," he suggested. "Dawdle. It's a nice place. I'm off to the bright lights and dark shadows. One last time. My thanks."

He put a tip under his napkin, stood, and was gone.

The waiter refilled Elfreda's cup and then Peter's.

It should have been altogether a pleasure to linger with a beautiful woman in one of the great restaurants of Paris. But Peter kept thinking of Karl and what he had been on the verge of telling them. Was it healthier not to know? Clearly, the knowledge had been weighing heavily upon Karl.

A complicated fellow, Peter thought, and worrisome.

Elfreda had finished her coffee. "That walk sounds like a fine idea," Peter said to her.

"I was hoping you'd like it," she said.

"I love it. Shall we go?"

In fact, none of them followed the programs they had announced for themselves. Peter and Elfreda went for the shortest possible walk on a route that took them directly back to their hotel and Elfreda's bedroom. Karl, on the other hand, ignored the blandishments of the Casino de Paris. Instead, he walked past the church of the Madeleine and into the Place de la Concorde. He sauntered, looking about in search of the right configuration of novelty and familiarity. It wasn't altogether a conscious search. What he wanted was a way to sign the city, to claim it. The way a bough of a tree crossed a lit window, or the dance of a couple of moths around the globe of an Art Nouveau streetlight . . . Those were satisfactions, his own discoveries, his Paris.

The overwhelming probability, after all, was that he'd never return. Whatever his experience was in these few hours in Paris would be his Paris forever. His life, in fact, was now a collection of these quick and quickened perceptions. The news he'd had from Colonel Piekenbrock had not, of itself, sharpened his vision and his hearing; that process or refinement of the senses and the attention was up to him. But the outcome was clear enough. He wasn't likely to survive the mission. He had not really expected to. But the length of the odds against him was clearer now. And he was also a little bit surprised by the kind of man they'd nominated as his victim. Not a politician or a military figure, but a famous scientist. Professor Einstein, no less. It was a curious choice. Because he was a Jew? Or because his knowledge could be turned into a weapon that could be used against the Reich? It did not much matter to Karl Roeder what the reason was. The result remained the same—that his fate and Einstein's were now intertwined. And because of Einstein's fame, Karl, too, would become famous. Notorious, anyway. The police would never give up. They'd pursue him with the kind of determination they summon up only rarely, when they feel challenged, when the crime raises general questions about everyone's safety and becomes a matter of the policemen's own honor. Indeed, there'd probably be some detective who'd be quite happy to have his name braided into the skein, getting what glory he could from apprehending Einstein's killer.

Karl's mood had improved a little. He was more than half inclined to revive his original plan and look for a whore. It wasn't so much that he felt actively lecherous. It was like the dinner. He felt that he was entitled to the entertainment.

At L'Orient, everything fell apart. For one thing, Reinhart came down with the clap. His spree in Paris had taken him out. He couldn't possibly go in a submarine in that condition. So the teams had to be reorganized. Instead of three teams of three, there were now going to be two teams of four each, with Peter, Elfreda, and Johann in Karl's group and Kurt, Horst, and Rudi in Willi's group. For another thing, the money wasn't right. There were papers, draft cards, driver's licenses, and Social Security cards for all of them, and there were packets of money—three thousand dollars in U.S. currency for each of them with extra packets of reserve cash for the two team leaders. "But what's this?" Willi wanted to know.

They were in a hotel room, waiting for the Kriegsmarine officer to escort them to the U-boat base.

"What's what?" the flustered Abwehr lieutenant wanted to know. Enough had gone wrong already so that he was irritable. Their boarding time had been postponed for six hours at least.

"This. This isn't what American money looks like," Willi said. He held up a bill. He was right. None of them had seen anything that looked like it.

"That's right," Johann said. "I've never seen them like that."

Kurt knew what they were, though. "Those are gold certificates. They've been out of circulation for years. They're no good."

"How many of them are there?" Rudi asked.

"Somebody fucked up," Willi observed.

They all went through the money they'd been given and threw the gold certificates onto the bed, making a pile that came to just over three thousand dollars.

"I'll call for instructions," the Abwehr lieutenant said.

"Meanwhile, let's pool the good money and redistribute it," Johann suggested. It was a reasonable idea. There wasn't likely to be any large store of American currency available any closer than Paris. And if they redistributed the money, there'd still be about twenty-five hundred for each of them.

Peter didn't have much to say about it. But all things considered, he was more pleased than not. He saw the screw-up as evidence that there were imperfections in the famous German efficiency. He was counting on some lapse somewhere by which he could disengage from this madness. With Elfreda or alone.

The only one he was worried about was Karl—whom he had learned to respect and even fear, if not admire. But from what Peter had gathered at Maxim's, Karl might have other fish to fry.

They had traveled all night, arriving at L'Orient a little after five in the morning. They'd been put into this little hotel, the Jour de Rêve, not far from the port, where they'd been told they'd be embarking after breakfast. They'd been called at eight in the morning. At ten the papers had arrived and the money. By noon, they had worked out the redistribution of the good bills. They spent most of the afternoon in a little bar down the street from the hotel, drinking vin ordinaire. It was almost five-thirty and was beginning to get dark when the messenger from the Kriegsmarine came roaring up on a motorcycle with word that the departure was to be in fifteen minutes. Everyone was to be ready with seabag and equipment standing by for the bus.

They ordered a quick final round and drank. "To success," Karl proposed.

They drank to that, whatever each of them thought it was.

FIVE

Private Conrad was back on the beach.

The truth of it was that Conrad was, as the topkick had put it, a "fuck-up," and a "royal asshole." He was perfectly willing to agree to that description. But he'd started thinking, even as the sergeant was chewing him out, wondering why a royal asshole was any more of an asshole than any commoner's asshole. In what way? Was it inferior or smellier?

A bad mistake. You don't think in the army, especially when you're getting chewed out. A man's thoughts are his own business, maybe, but his facial expression is right out there for all the world to see—even the sergeant. So, when Conrad made the connection with poker, figuring out that royal flushes were better than regular flushes, and that by analogy royal assholes were better than regular assholes, he'd felt a degree of satisfaction that had brought on the smile. But it wasn't even that simple. He knew not to smile, was trying not to smile, and the realization that here he was, trying not to grin while this old army sergeant was chewing him out, struck him as very funny. Irresistibly funny. He broke and smiled.

"What are you smiling about, soldier?"

"Nothing, sergeant."

"You're a liar, Conrad. You're a liar and an asshole. An imperial asshole!"

Imperial? It was extended from royal but losing its connection to poker. It was an original formulation, a bit baroque but not at all bad. He constrained his grin, bringing it down to a tight smirk.

"All right, Conrad. You better speak up and let me have it. Now!" The sergeant's voice was quiet, his face only a few inches from Conrad's. It was an ominous combination of signals.

"I was admiring your style of invective, sergeant," Conrad said finally. It was the blandest way to put it that he could think of.

"I'm glad you like it, Conrad. I can't tell you how really swell it makes me feel. And I'm sure you'll spend a lot of time out there on the beaches, walking back and forth on the sand, remembering what a terrific style of invective I have. Isn't that right, Conrad?"

"Yes, sergeant," he'd said, and the damndest part of it was that he more or less did admire Sergeant Garrett's style, even out on the beach, even on a weekend. That he'd pulled a month of weekend guard duty wasn't surprising. If it hadn't been for the grin or the indifferently made bed that had triggered the incident, then it would have been something else. Or someone else. He didn't even hold it against Sergeant Garrett personally, just as he hardly felt himself to be personally involved. His body had to march up and down on the beach. Inside, the real Conrad smirked and joked, untouched and untouchable.

On the other hand, as long as he was out here on the deserted Amagansett beach, he had no objection to comfort. And he'd had enough experience to know how to make his tour of duty as comfortable as possible. There was a thermos of hot coffee laced with brandy. And there was the basket of submerged beer waiting for him. The beer was twice as refreshing for being absolutely illegal, even though it was safe enough. The chances of an officer coming by to check on the weekend guards on the Long Island beaches were infinitesimal.

So, anything to help pass the time. The beauties of nature were only good for a little while. Who was it—Matthew Arnold? Or Ruskin?—who said that even the most glorious sunset palls after a few minutes?

He pulled on the length of clothesline that was tied to the clamming basket. It was heavy, because there were rocks in there for ballast, but he got it up, got the top off, and extracted a bottle of Rheingold. He refastened the basket lid and lowered the improvised beer chest back into the cold black water. He used his old

Boy Scout knife that he carried with him to open the bottle. Slowly, he swigged the beer, feeling its bite. It was really cold.

Great! Better than some blonde Miss Rheingold with her come-on wink. An absurd ad campaign. Miss Rheingold looked like she preferred pink ladies or screwdrivers. Beer could stand on its own as one of the good things in life. One didn't need sex to sell beer.

It was then that he must have seen something. Something must have registered, because he was staring down the beach, looking at where the black of the water met the black of the beach, trying to see if whatever had shone or glinted or flashed would do so again. It was perhaps a half a mile down, or maybe a little less. It was tough to tell in the dark. And there was nothing on the landward side to line it up by.

Private Conrad stood there, the beer bottle still in his hand, but his eyes were fixed in the direction that had somehow caught his notice. And he thought he saw something again—a metallic shine just for an instant.

It was probably nothing. A kid with a Zippo, surf-fishing or standing by the water's edge, maybe with a girl. It wasn't really worth dragging his ass all the way down there to check it out. On the other hand, that was what he was supposed to be doing. Guarding the beach. So it was a question of Private Conrad's own dignity. To admit that there was no purpose whatever to his standing here on the Long Island beach or his walking up and down the sand with his eyes more or less peeled would be to give in to the army way of doing things. In order to keep his own private sense of what his life was about and what his proper role in the army was, he had at least to pretend to be guarding something or guarding against something. For personal honor, then, more than anything else, he started down the beach, walking on the smooth sand just below the high-water mark and holding the beer bottle in one hand, a part of him knowing perfectly well that what he was doing was ridiculous.

He didn't run. He wasn't even walking especially fast. The feeling of ridiculousness slowed him down like a sixty-pound pack. Still, he moved. And there was a kind of inertia to the movement so that he couldn't very well turn back once he'd set out. He had the beer bottle in his hand and he stopped now and then to peer down the beach and also to take a small swig every now and then, but he couldn't just give it up and turn around. From time to time, he had to choose whether to climb over the rocks of another breakwater or make a detour around on the sand, and each time he chose the sand because it would be quieter and he'd be less easily seen. If there was something hostile down there, the right thing to do would be to go around the rocks and up on the sand. On the other hand, each time he did this he felt like an imperial asshole.

He drained the beer and flung the empty bottle up into a patch of marsh grass. He plodded on, wondering as he did so what the hell he was going to do when he got there. He had no rifle. And even with a rifle, there wasn't much he could do against any kind of force. No machine gun. No backup. All he could do was observe and report back. That made sense. But he was thinking—which was a dangerous thing to do in the army.

He walked about a quarter of a mile. He'd been looking at the same spot—he was fairly sure of that—which he'd been able to fix by reference to the wind direction, onshore for the past hour or so and steady on his right cheek. The beach had a kind of point, he knew, and then cut back, so that whatever he'd seen would have to be closer than that change in angle. He was breathing through his mouth so that he could hear better, so that the sound of his own breath wouldn't cover any faint sound from down there, a chink of metal perhaps to go with that glint of light.

And if it turned out that he had actually seen something and—supposing the worst case—that it turned out to be spies? Was he likely to hit them on the head with his flashlight? Could he expect them to stand there patiently waiting, while he ran back to the watchtower to call in for help from the post? More and more, he was overwhelmed by the impossibility of his assignment.

On the other hand, it would be stupid to be scared. It would be stupid to suppose there was anything really there. If there had been any kind of actual risk, he was the last man the army would want to put out here. Sergeant Garrett and Lieutenant Mull wouldn't have permitted it. He had to assume that they weren't altogether incompetent. Or were they? Maybe they were the ones who ought to be out here . . .

He was nearly at the point. The angle of beach was obtuse but still enough of an angle so that to continue in a straight line would be to slice into the surf. It had to be around here, or even back a little bit. He stood still, listening. He couldn't hear anything but the sound of the waves breaking and the hiss of the foam on the sand. He could hear the wind. But that was all. His skin felt prickly, maybe because of the salt air.

As if to demonstrate to himself how foolish he'd been, he switched on the torch and swept the beam back and forth in arcs of ten or a dozen feet. Seaweed, of course, and an occasional shell of a defunct razor clam. A few yards farther down, a pop bottle.

He flashed the light up toward the dune grass and the road beyond. Nothing. He shone the light out toward the sea. There was a kind of mist out there, the warmer air and the cold water combining together. And on the beach? Nothing, nothing. But . . .

There were odd marks on the sand. Footsteps? It was impossible to be sure. There was a fairly deep furrow. Something of moderate size and considerable weight had been dragged up from the sea or down into it, making a deep track as it went. Someone had been here. Those kinds of marks weren't natural. He followed them from the water's edge up the beach and inland, keeping clear of them himself but shining his light upon them. He followed them up into the grass, peering. It wasn't a joke. It was clear that the grass had been pressed down and hadn't yet recovered.

He almost tripped over the paddle. Somebody had discarded a paddle. You could deflate a rubber raft, maybe, but paddles were made out of wood and hard to get rid of. They'd thrown it away, not pausing to bury it because they were in a hurry, eager to get off the beach. Or they'd dropped it in their scurry ashore. It was plausible, either way. He picked up the paddle. It was marked down near the blade: KM.

KM? Kraut marauders? Kraut marines?

But it wasn't possible! *Kriegsmarine!*

They nearly drowned. All that training back at the lodge had been worse than useless. It hadn't prepared them for what they'd have to deal with. They had played with rubber rafts down on the river, where there had been a slow steady current, but nothing like this, no breakers, no undertow, no tossing about. Horst could hardly swim, and his panic had communicated itself to the rest of them. Naturally, Kurt had lost a paddle so the other three had had harder going than they otherwise would have. The two crates of explosives were awkwardly large and kept slipping around, threatening to slice through the bottom of the raft. The undertow got Johann, pulling his feet out from under him so that he was soaking. But they made it ashore. It had been uncomfortable and dangerous, but there they were. The relief was compounded with a feeling of gratitude at being on dry land again. There was also a feeling—for Peter at any rate—of being home. The worst of it was over.

They dragged the boxes ashore, then left them near the water while they carried the raft up the sand. The valve was stuck. It wouldn't deflate. Johann had a knife and managed to slash it a couple of times and stamp it flat. They went back for the boxes of explosives and hauled them up the beach too.

Willi lit a cigarette.

"Put that fucking thing out, will you?" Karl asked. Or ordered. "Somebody will see us."

Willi held onto it, put it to his mouth, puffed.

All they needed was to get caught on the beach with the box of explosives. All of them together, like this, and they'd be lucky to get life in some federal prison. "Put it out," Peter said, seconding the motion.

Willi took one more defiant puff, then flicked the cigarette into the water.

They looked for a landmark, something to come back to. There was a solitary sea pine, a little bit to the left of a small clump of beach roses. And there was nice sandy soil at its base. Johann used his knife to make a small blaze on the tree. They went back for the boxes and the raft, and then they went after the paddles. They needed the paddles to dig the hole. But there were only two. One had been lost coming ashore, but the other?

There was no time to waste looking for the paddle. They took turns using the two that remained, and dug a hole big enough and deep enough to take both of the boxes. They used the remains of the raft as a tarp to cover them, even though they were waterproof. They were filling in the hole when they heard the voice call out, "Okay, guys, I've found it! It's pretty good. You had me going there . . ."

There was a soldier down on the beach near the water. And he had a flashlight that he was shining up toward them. They all lay hugging the ground as the light played around them erratically.

Peter's first reaction was fear. He didn't want to be discovered with the rest of them, with the explosives . . . But were they all bright enough to understand that? Would Horst be able to figure it out?

What if Horst got up, called out, and betrayed them? Would one or two of the others try to kill him?

Peter picked his head up. The others were looking as well. Should he run for it? Would the others? The soldier appeared to be alone. Would one of his teammates, desperate enough or crazy enough, try to attack the soldier?

He was down on the beach where they had come ashore. He would find the marks they must have made in the sand. He would follow them up here. They couldn't possibly escape. There would have to be a confrontation.

He was approaching. And then, suddenly, blessedly, he turned and ran off.

"We're saved, for the moment," Peter said in a whisper.

"But only for the moment," Elfreda answered.

"He found the paddle," Karl said. "I think he had it in his hand."

"Who in hell dropped the paddle?" Johann wanted to know.

"What difference does it make now?" Rudi asked. "The important thing is to get the hell out of here."

"The hole," Willi said. "First we have to finish filling in the hole. Then we can go."

There was a lot in what he said. Either in order to have the explosives to come back to later, or just to keep them from being found, they had to finish filling in the hole. Fast.

They all worked together, two of them with the paddles, the rest with their bare hands.

"Now, we split up. Eight is too many together," Karl said. "The two groups of four."

"In opposite directions," Willi said, agreeing and improving.

It made sense. There was, in any case, no time to argue.

They didn't believe him, not at first anyway. Lieutenant Siemens who was on duty at the time, a reasonable enough fellow for an officer, took it to be a joke and even came out and said that Sergeant Garrett had told him to watch out for Conrad.

"Yes, sir."

"Yes, sir, what? You mean it *is* a joke?"

"No, sir. I meant that I wasn't surprised at what the sergeant told you. I can see how he'd feel that way."

"And you still want me to come out there?" the lieutenant asked.

"Yes, sir."

"If this turns out to be a wild-goose chase, you'll be doing KP for the next hundred years."

"Yes, sir," Conrad said. He was up in the watchtower, looking out over the black water and the black sand. He had the terrible feeling that the oar had been planted, that somebody had taken a wood-burning kit and had written *KM* on the paddle . . . But he couldn't pull out now. "I think you'd better get down here, sir," he said.

"All right, soldier, but it's your ass. Just remember that."

"Yes, sir," he said. Remember it? He'd been thinking about it all the time. The lieutenant had hung up. Private Conrad looked at the receiver and put it back on the hook gently. Right or wrong, he'd committed himself. He didn't even know exactly what to hope for. A false alarm, but one that would take the heat off him, personally. But he couldn't imagine what the hell that could be. He looked at his watch. He waited. He climbed down the tower then back up. They were taking their sweet time. Ten minutes. Fifteen. He looked out toward the place where he'd found the marks in the sand but he saw nothing. He looked back toward the road for the lights of the lieutenant's car. Still nothing. After twenty-five minutes?

It was enough to make a fellow wonder what the point was of having guards out there on the beaches. On the other hand, it was difficult to remember the brief moment when he'd thought there might be a real emergency. The paddle was some kind of crazy stunt. What real Germans would be so clumsy and dumb as to leave a marked paddle around like that? It couldn't possibly be real.

It was half an hour before he saw the lights of the two jeeps approaching from the base. By then he'd figured out that it had been some kind of exercise. Some Pentagon desk jockey could have devised that kind of thing to keep the outfit busy on a Sunday night. And they might even leave paddles around to test the disposition of sentries and the penetrability of the defenses. He sure hoped so. And he figured that Lieutenant Siemens might now let him in on the thing.

But the lieutenant's reaction was dead serious and not like anything one would expect in a drill. "When did you find this?" he asked, studying the paddle.

Conrad told him about seeing the glimmer of light. And how he went down to look and found these . . . "Items," he called them. "Things," didn't sound military enough.

"How far down the beach? Where?"

"Maybe half a mile that way, sir," Conrad told him, pointing.

"Show me."

They took the jeep because it was faster and they bounced along the sand, getting stuck once but getting out of it in four-wheel drive. "It's just before the turn in the beach," Conrad said.

The jeep slowed and then, when he said, "Here, I think," it stopped. The four of them got out, the lieutenant, the corporal who was his driver, a sergeant whom Conrad didn't remember having seen before, and Conrad himself. He showed them the place where something had been dragged out of the water and up into the grass.

"And you found the paddle where?" the lieutenant asked.

Conrad showed him.

The lieutenant walked back and forth, looking at the ground and shining his flashlight in swaths as if he were mowing grass with its beam. Finally he said, "You did right, soldier. You did absolutely right."

He told the driver to get them back to the watchtower so that he could call in his confirmation and order an alert.

As they bounced along, Conrad realized that he was off the hook. But mixed in with that terrific relief was a kind of shock as the realization began to form that there were actual goddamn German spies. Here on actual goddamn Long Island, for Christ's sake!

They were cold and wet. Peter could barely feel his toes. He could hear them though. There was a soft squish every time he took a step, his shoes and socks sea-logged from the landing. They had split up into two groups of four. Willi, Horst, Rudi, and Kurt had headed for town and its railroad station. Peter, Elfreda, Johann, and Karl had headed eastward, toward Montauk. They were looking for a place to hide until morning. Then they'd work their way into New York, not using the train. There was no way to know which route was more dangerous, or more uncomfortable for that matter. They could all swap stories when they reunited at the Thirty-fourth Street Automat at three o'clock in the afternoon.

Assuming that there wasn't a chance of cutting out before then. Peter knew what he wanted to do, and what he supposed Elfreda planned on doing. And how many others were there?

They had been on a narrow blacktop road, a road in urgent need of repair after the winter's depradations. It reached a larger road that ran east and west, and that was where they'd split up. Peter wondered whether there might not be some chance of their splitting up yet again into two groups of two. He and Elfreda would be home free. Literally, home and free.

The main thing was patience, the patience to wait for the right moment, the right configuration of opportunity and inattention on the part of one or both of the other men.

"It's no good here in the road. A car could pass at any time, and we're all dead ducks. How do we explain ourselves?" Karl wanted to know.

"We were fishing," Peter suggested. "Our boat went aground."

"In this weather? At this time of night?" Elfreda asked.

"It's possible. People do dumb things . . ."

"I don't like it," Karl said. "We're safer off the road."

"I agree. We should get off the road," Elfreda said.

It was flat country, and there were fields around them, plowed and planted, but not yet producing anything. Elfreda was right. This was no time to get captured. That sentry on the beach would have gone for help, which might well be on the way. And this would be the road on which it would come.

They left the pavement and marched diagonally across the field to their left, in single file, keeping close together. They were cold, wet, and uncomfortable, and had only a general idea of where they were and no particular notion of where they were going. But Peter was feeling good. This was obviously more cautious than the other group's direct attempt at the Amagansett train station. All they had to do was hold out until it got light, and then . . .

And then? He realized he was thinking about Nuremberg and the trip from there to Munich. Would it be dangerous to try to stay with Elfreda?

"Wait, wait," somebody up ahead was saying. Johann, most likely. "There's a building."

A house? Or a barn? Danger? Opportunity?

"I'll go look," Karl said. "Stay here. I'll be back as soon as I can."

He moved off, crouching low and keeping quiet. In a matter of seconds, he had disappeared.

Why couldn't I have done that? was the question in Peter's mind. And then, almost immediately, he realized that he and Elfreda were together, and that it was, for the moment, the two of them against Johann. Make their move now?

From behind, there came a low rumble of trucks moving along the Montauk Highway.

They had got the generator going and the arc lights were blazing, making the stretch of beach look like a movie set. There were twenty-five or thirty Coast Guardsmen sweeping back and forth over the beach, looking for whatever else there might be in the way of spoor from the landing. Another half dozen or so were digging, in parties of two. There were also a score or so of soldiers from the Mobile Infantry Unit, which had been a little short-handed because it was a weekend. That was why Captain Connolly had called on the Coast Guard station to help out. He'd also called the New York headquarters of the Federal Bureau of Investigation.

Lieutenant Siemens was back on the beach, wearing a sidearm now although it was extremely unlikely that the people who had landed would be anywhere near the beach. Still, with the Coast Guard looking on, he figured it would be safer to keep up appearances. Siemens's opposite number, a coast guard lieutenant named Morrison, seemed to be interested in the same objectives—looking good and not screwing up. There was an old guy, a petty officer, who had been in the Coast Guard from back in Prohibition days and seemed to have some idea of what he was doing. He was the one who had organized the digging crews, and he'd sent the others on great long sweeps of the beach looking for anything at all.

Private Conrad was looking very glum, as if all this strenuous activity were his fault. It was almost as if he expected to be presented with the bill. The lieutenant had other matters on his mind, though. For one thing, he was concerned that the men not do anything to destroy what evidence they did manage to turn up. It wasn't exactly a scientific investigating team out there, walking back and forth over the sand. Siemens was not worried about footprints that the wind and the tide would mostly wipe out. But he was uneasy about the digging crews. What if they found something! Would it be booby-trapped? Would there be fingerprints that inexperienced people might obliterate?

Captain Connolly had said he'd already called the FBI. Siemens didn't imagine that they'd be able to get out here much before dawn. There wouldn't be anything left. Not that that was his problem, particularly.

His first reaction, then, was concern when he saw the two Coast Guardsmen trotting up to their lieutenant to report that they'd found something. Morrison invited him to come along, which was decent of him. Siemens accepted, naturally. The Coast Guardsmen led the way back down toward the water.

On the far side of one of the breakwaters, there was a piece of line that had been made fast around one of the boulders and that led into the surf. Three Coast Guardsmen were pulling on the line slowly while two others were shining their torches into the water.

Oddly, eerily, one of the Coast Guardsmen began to laugh. It was the old petty officer. "Haul away, boys," he said. "It's nothing to worry about."

"What is it?" Lieutenant Morrison asked.

"Beer," the petty officer replied. "You've found somebody's stash."

Siemens's first thought was of Private Conrad. Conrad's eyes were closed. His face was ashen, although that was possibly the effect of the arc lights.

"Shall we put it back?" one of the Coast Guardsmen asked.

"Better keep it. The lab people will want to analyze it, I'd be willing to bet," Morrison said.

A reasonable fellow, Siemens thought. He was covering his ass too.

Poor Conrad. He'd picked the wrong beach to hide beer on.

It was then that somebody came to report that they'd found the remains of a rubber raft and a couple of boxes.

"Tell them not to touch anything," Lieutenant Morrison ordered. "We'll be right there."

SIX

Rudi Muller was cold and wet, but otherwise his feelings about being back in America were difficult even for him to discover. He had started out in Chicago, where he had lived with his parents in an old but still decently kept-up apartment house. Across the hall and down one flight, Gerda had an apartment. Gerda was older than Rudi, thirty (she said—but she might have been shaving a couple of years from the true figure), and a widow. And his first mistake had been to help her carry in the big bags of groceries. Or, having done that, he should have declined her invitation for him to cool off and have a beer. But by then it had been too late. The reason he had offered to help with the groceries was that he wanted exactly such an invitation, had imagined her offering him some form or other of her hospitality, food or a drink first, and then those big boobs and that hair that looked alive, as if there were electricity coming out of her head from generators that were running hot under her flowered housedress. She had seen him staring at her, ogling. And she had imagined giving the kid a thrill, not necessarily taking him to bed maybe, but getting him going.

One thing led to another, and they moved from the kitchen to the living room and on into the bedroom. They didn't have a great deal to say to each other, but she figured out that she could bake cakes for him—he adored chocolate cake—and after they made love she could give him a piece of cake and watch him eat. He was as greedy with the cake as with her body, and she loved the way he'd gather up the crumbs that were left on the plate, mashing them together with the tines of the fork.

She was, she thought, mistress of the situation. And he was perfectly willing to leave to her the making of the arrangements, the setting forth of the rules. He liked having sex put before him as if it were a plate of nourishing food. The convenience of it also pleased him—no strenuous adventuring downtown, no expenditure for movies or meals. It was all on the house and in the house, down the steps and across the hall.

And then the terrible announcement—that she'd come up pregnant.

He was afraid to tell his parents. He was afraid she'd force him to marry her. He had nightmares of confinement, not hers but his own. He was either in some prison cell or in some smaller, darker space, like a closet or a trunk, tied or even chained. He was reduced to the helplessness of a four-year-old being punished for some bad behavior. (He had, in fact, been locked in his room, although not his closet, for deliberately breaking a lamp in his parents' parlor, one of a pair they had received as a wedding gift from an uncle in Augsburg.)

What the dreams came from was less important than what they were telling him—which was to get out, to flee, to put as much space as possible between him and Gerda, him and his parents, him and the little monster that was growing in Gerda's belly. And yet, even with all of that, he might not have done anything, if Herbert Koch hadn't been fired that week at the dental lab where they both worked, making crowns and bridges from casts.

Rudi could not remember exactly why Herbert got fired. It hardly made any difference. Herbert invited Rudi to come along on a trip—to Mexico. He was going to drive down to Mexico City, and then just see what there was to see. On a hundred and ten dollars?

They could get work in Mexico City. And they could see the sights, and come home in six months or a year . . .

It was a crazy idea, but it was a way of escaping from Gerda and her sticky predicament. The unplanned, unimagined quality of the adventure had its own appeal. It was as if he were a character in an exciting story and he had no idea what was on the next page. *Sure, why not?*

A few shirts, some socks, some underwear, and he was almost ready to go. A brief note to his parents. A couple of attempts at a note to Gerda . . . but he gave them up. There was nothing to add to what his departure itself would say.

A crazy trip, not so much fun as he'd expected, and much more uncomfortable—they slept in the car in order to stretch out their meager funds and they ate cheese and fruit from grocery stores instead of restaurant meals—it brought them to Mexico City and the distressing news that one could not simply walk in off the street and get a job. First, you had to have a work permit. And in order to get a work permit, you needed a job. That was the crazy part. In order to get a work permit, they would have had to go back up to the States, arrange for a job by mail, apply for a work permit by mail, and then, with the permit in hand, return.

So, it was hard times. They tried to pick up small sums of money carrying luggage at the airport or shining shoes on the big *avenidas* near the large hotels, but some of the native competitors intimated that there might be physical danger if they persisted in these efforts.

Flat broke, Herbert sold the car for a hundred and five dollars. They lived on that for a while, splurging on a decent dinner from time to time, but watching even that sizable sum dwindle down.

Rudi had no idea what they were going to do. It was Herbert's suggestion that they go to the German embassy. They were, both of them, American citizens, albeit of German descent. The German embassy was closer maybe? Or Herbert just knew where it was? At any event, that was where he went. And Rudi tagged along. There was a sympathetic man in the commercial section who was able to offer them work in a German experimental vineyard—in Japan. There would be free passage for them to Japan, and they would be given room and board and a small wage as they worked under the German vintners who were trying to show the Japanese how to grow grapes and make wine.

It sounded strange, but there was passage to Japan. Rudi knew that things were always darkest before the dawn. He had been subjected to these disappointments and frustrations only to be rescued, as heroes are always rescued, and sent on to the next chapter. He hardly hesitated. He had to encourage Herbert, but Herbert too agreed that it might be interesting to see the Orient.

In a week, they were crossing the Pacific on a Japanese freighter bound for Yokohama. By the end of the month, they were at the vineyard in Honshu, surprised to find themselves not so much the recipients of the German embassy's kindness as the desperate last-minute substitutes for the peons the vintners had actually requested. Not even the peons had been eager to set out for so strange and so distant a situation—and Rudi and Herbert immediately realized what a mistake they'd made. Twelve- and fourteen-hour days in the hot sun, tending the vines and weeding and pruning and watering. Meager food, and hovels to sleep in. They refused to work such hours and the overseer told them the choice was clear: work or get out.

It had been intended as a kind of dare. The overseer hadn't expected them to quit, but they did. Which left the Germans in an embarrassing position: they had guaranteed the two young men as employed and unlikely to become charges of the state. They were both American citizens, but they were an embarrassment to the firm and to its sponsor, the German government. There were some hasty conferences and telephone calls. The resident manager came out to offer them work as deckhands on a German liner currently at Kobe and bound for Bremen.

Another chapter! Why not?

Rudi arrived in Bremen on December 11, 1941—and was arrested as he came off the gangway and onto the pier. He had no idea what they were talking about, because he'd been at sea. He hadn't seen any newspapers or heard the radio programs, and he didn't know that the Japanese had bombed Pearl Harbor four days before, or that the United States had declared war on Japan. Or that Germany had declared war—only two hours ago—on the United States.

Rudi and Herbert were interned as enemy aliens. Rudi supposed that his luck had finally run out, that there would be no more twists and turns in his story. But there was an offer to join an expedition to the United States. Herbert didn't like the sound of it and he declined. Rudi saw it as yet another escape, another rescue from the precipice. He accepted. They let him visit his great-aunt in Augsburg and sent him on down to Munich for training.

Now he had circumnavigated the globe—or nearly. All he had yet to do to close the circle was get from Amagansett to Chicago.

97

It never occurred to him to worry about any of his teammates on the expedition. They were no more real to him than the vintners in Japan or the bullying second mate on the freighter to Bremen. Like the cold and the dampness, they'd soon be forgotten.

The four men walked from the beach into the center of Amagansett without being challenged. There was a railroad station. They waited on the platform benches. Eventually, the sun would come up. Someone would come to unlock the little station and open the ticket window. A train would appear. They would get on it and ride away into safety.

Not for a minute did Rudi doubt that there would be a happy ending. There were always happy endings.

By the time Major John Trumbull arrived at the beach, Special Agent Donald Dunbar of the New York City office of the Federal Bureau of Investigation was already on the scene. Not that Major Trumbull really cared one way or the other about who got there first. He was willing enough to cooperate with the FBI, as long as the Bureau was willing to reciprocate. But you could never tell with those guys. They were, as a class, nuts. And Special Agent Dunbar looked to be fairly typical. His hair was a barely discernible fuzz halating from the long thin skull. He was shorn as closely as a marine recruit.

It didn't necessarily follow that the internal shortage—in the brains, where it mattered—would match the tonsure. But it was a good bet. And the G-2 major figured he'd take it easy for a while. Let the FBI man show his hand first. The trouble was that the question of jurisdiction was delicate—until they knew who the people were who'd landed, and how they were dressed. Spies in civilian uniforms would be FBI quarry. An assault team in uniform would be—at least technically—a military problem, and military intelligence would be responsible for identifying and locating the enemy force.

He introduced himself to Special Agent Dunbar. Dunbar didn't say anything. Lieutenant Siemens saved what might otherwise have been an instant's awkwardness by introducing Dunbar to the major.

"What's going on?" Trumbull asked, not quite curtly.

"We've got it all under control," Dunbar replied, not quite rudely.

"You want to go into a little more detail?" Trumbull asked. It was close to a challenge.

"There are two boxes I've got the bomb squad working on. There are men combing the beach, although the army and the Coast Guard have both been over it and there isn't a lot left to work with . . ."

"If there ever was anything," Trumbull threw in.

"Oh, yes. We've got an oar with markings from the German navy."

"I know about that. Anything new, though?"

The FBI man shook his head.

"Any idea of where to go from here?"

"We've been thinking of sealing off Long Island," Dunbar said. It was perfectly calm and reasonable, as if he were thinking of putting out an all-points bulletin on some license plate.

The major stared at him for a moment. There was a little smile forming around the corners of Dunbar's mouth, as if he couldn't help showing how pleased he was with himself for having thought of this bright idea.

"You've got to be kidding," Trumbull said after a while.

"I'm entirely serious."

"Which side are you working for?"

"Come again?" the FBI man asked.

"Let's assume that we've got a handful of saboteurs, which seems to me the likeliest bet. It probably isn't an invasion or we'd have had more action in the hours since they're supposed to have landed. So we've got something from one or two up to a couple of dozen men. No huge threat, maybe, but a potential nuisance value. They could disrupt things for us, give us some kind of scare . . . That's my first guess," Major Trumbull said. "But I can't imagine any kind of disruption they could manage to bring off that would come near cutting Long Island off from the rest of the country. All those commuters? You'd have either panic or a riot, or maybe both. And you don't have any idea who or what you're looking for anyway, do you?"

"You've got a better idea?"

The major thought for a moment. Better than trying to seal

99

off Long Island, they could do nothing, just sit on their hands. "I might cleck the immediate vicinity. Houses within a five-mile radius. The train stations, here in Amagansett and in the Hamptons."

"I've got men on the way," Dunbar said, implying that he'd already started on both those lines of investigation.

"Fine," Trumbull said. "Anything you need in the way of personnel, you just let me know."

"It's all under control," Dunbar said.

He'd used that word before. Trumbull wondered why it was annoying. Because it was so patently untrue? "Those men on the way," he said, "are coming from New York. Is that how you're doing it?"

"That's right," Dunbar said. "Any objections?"

"Yes, as a matter of fact. I think someone ought to check the railroad stations now. There weren't any trains during the night, but they start pretty early. After the trains have been through, there isn't a whole lot of point to it."

Dunbar glared at him. Trumbull glared right back. Where did Hoover find these people? The white shirts and the clean fingernails and the dry palms—the Director was rumored to hate candidates with sweaty palms—and the really short crew cuts. And all of them morons.

"All right," Dunbar said. "You take the Amagansett station. I'll check Westhampton and Southampton. You find anything, you call the New York office of the Bureau. You understand?"

"Anyone in particular?" the major asked. Of course he understood his own plan. He also understood that his agreement to call the Bureau was the condition upon which Dunbar was willing to cooperate even this far.

"Special Agent Kelly. John Kelly."

Trumbull nodded and went back to his car, trying to keep it all in perspective. Dunbar was merely an asshole; these others were Nazis, which was worse.

When Karl came back from reconnoitering the hulking shape of the building, it was with good news. "It's a small farm. There's a farmhouse, a barn, and another building for machines and tractors. There may be dogs, but I was quiet and there wasn't any barking."

They discussed their possible options. The noise of the engines on Montauk Highway had not been reassuring. They agreed that the safest thing was to assume that the trucks had been full of men who would spread out, searching from house to house. In the dark, it was too risky to try to move. The barn and the shed seemed the best of the choices. They made their way, painstakingly silent, reaching the shed and taking a full minute to open the door, a fraction of an inch at a time, avoiding any squeak of an unoiled hinge and alert to the possible barking of some watchdog or the crow of some silly rooster.

They crept inside and found places in which to arrange themselves, sitting on the floor and leaning against the walls, waiting out the couple of hours that remained until dawn. At one point, Johann fell asleep. His breathing turned into a snore. Karl nudged him. "Sorry," Johann said. But within minutes it was happening again.

The darkness seemed to be stuck like gum to the walls, the windows, the sky itself. They were supposed to be free now. But instead they were stuck here in some farmer's shed, with soldiers roaming around outside who were almost certain to mistake them for dangerous enemies of the United States. It was unendurable. And there was no alternative but to sit there and to endure. Elfreda envied the equanimity, the wonderful peace of mind that could allow someone like Johann to doze off so that the time passed with the painlessness of a surgical procedure.

Finally, it began to get light. There was some hesitation about whether they should move immediately or wait until it was lighter still. They discussed in brief phrases the relative dangers of darkness and light.

"The whole idea was to wait for it to get light."

"It'll be light soon."

"But it isn't yet, really."

"We could be ten miles from here in the time we're wasting on this talk."

"What difference does it make?"

"We're going for the car, aren't we? Why not now?" Peter asked.

Karl said, "Not the car. The house. They'd hear the car. They'd hear the motor start. They'd see us drive off. They'd call. We can't let them do that."

"Cut the phone wire?" Johann suggested.

"We could," Elfreda agreed.

"Do you know which one is the phone wire and which one is the power line?" Karl asked. "You have tools? You have a ladder? You want to risk getting electrocuted?"

He was probably right, Elfreda thought. It wouldn't be so terrible to go in there and tie people up so they'd be unable to sound an alarm. What difference would it make to them, in the long run? And to the four of them in the shed, it could be critical, that extra hour or so.

There were no further objections. They opened the door and looked out. They could see the barn. They could see the house. There was a small garden with vegetables and herbs laid out in rows. There was a stretch of lawn over which a big willow tree presided. There was a wrought-iron bench underneath the tree. At the side of the house, there was an elderly Dodge with a black leather roof. In front, there was a more recent and better-kept-up black Ford.

"Were there two cars last night?" Johann asked.

"I don't remember. I couldn't see," Peter said.

"We couldn't have seen that one," Peter said, pointing at the Ford.

"Let's go back to the shed and watch for a little while. Let's give the thing ten minutes. They could have two cars. Or a visitor."

"At this hour?" Peter asked.

"For the weekend, maybe," Elfreda said.

"Or it could be police. Let's give it some time," Karl said. It seemed a reasonable enough idea. Why not? There was no particular advantage to hurrying.

They retreated to the shed, not going back inside but using it as a barrier between themselves and the house. Karl lay on the ground, the way they had been taught at the lodge, and looked out around the corner. He could see the Ford at the side of the road, parked at the end of the front walk.

They waited, watching him watch.

Lucky or shrewd, he was right, it turned out. "Look," he said.

He crawled back and let Johann stick his head out past the corner of the shed. "Two men," Johann said. "They're getting into the car. They're driving off."

"You think there's another one inside?" Peter asked.

"No," Karl answered. "They don't have enough people to leave one off at every farmhouse. But let's go. Now. They'll think it's those men coming back."

It made sense. They hurried across that back lawn, around the side of the house, and across the front lawn. Karl rang the doorbell.

Shouldn't they have worked it out better? Elfreda thought that only one of them should be visible from the house, but there they all were together, like children at Halloween, the oldest or the boldest in front and the rest of them huddled together at the bottom of the front steps.

There was a wait of a few moments. That was worrisome. Had those been G-men? Had they instructed the residents of the farmhouse not to open their door to anyone? Had they left some secret knock that was a password? Would the car that had pulled away come racing back, warned by some radio dispatcher?

They stood there, helpless, waiting to be picked up, or so it seemed to Elfreda. The only reasonable thing was to run while there was still a chance. They could get away from the house, get back to the shed or to the field . . .

But the door opened. A white-headed man opened the door. He was wearing overalls, the kind with a bib and shoulder straps. Elfreda heard him say, "Yes?"

And then she heard the shot.

SEVEN

The door was open. A white-haired man had opened it. He was wearing overalls and a plaid flannel shirt. Peter could see the red and white of the shirt, much like the red and white of the man's head. Or what was left of it. The shot from Karl's automatic pistol had blown away most of the left side of the man's head.

The noise had disappeared almost at once, as if it had been a brief pain. But the smell of cordite hung in the air. Peter had no idea why Karl had shot the man. It seemed altogether irrational. But Karl stood there, perfectly reasonably. It was Elfreda who was acting like a crazy person. She was screaming. Or, no, she was shouting out a warning. "Get away. They're dangerous. They've come to kill you. Run! Get away. Get out of the house!" She broke and ran into the house.

It was as if she had accomplished in an instant what Peter had been hoping to do ever since the beginning of this business. She had simply walked through the door, leaving the German operation and going over to the American side. He could hear her, not screaming anymore, but calling out, "They have guns. They're dangerous. Get away. They shot the man who answered the door. Get away. Run!" Her voice grew fainter and louder as she went from room to room, trying to warn whoever else was in the house.

Yes, of course, Peter thought, she was absolutely right. He

made for the doorway himself, starting toward the house to help her, to join her, but he felt a hand on his upper arm. He tried to pluck it off, but the hand—Karl's—was very strong.

"Wait," Karl said. "There's nothing you can do. She's taken the risk. You can't reduce it. And if she's in no danger, then it won't matter, will it?"

In answer to this question, there was a loud blast of a gun from inside the house.

They hit the ground, the three of them. Peter looked in. He could see across the living room. Lying on the wide floorboards at the edge of the rag rug, at the bottom of the staircase, Elfreda lay. Or what was left of her. She had received a buckshot blast at very close range and it had torn her to pieces.

"We've got to get away from here," Johann said.

"We can't," Karl said. "Whoever is left in there will telephone. Or is calling now."

"We could run for it," Johann said.

They were both looking at Peter. He realized that he had to say something. He agreed with both of them.

"Come on, come with me," Karl told him. Karl got up and pulled Peter along. "You stay there," he told Johann. "We'll go around."

Peter followed him around the house. Was Elfreda dead? That man who had answered the door was dead.

"The shot came from upstairs," Karl said, whispering. "He knows there are more of us. So he'll be in the upstairs hall, looking down, expecting us from that direction. I've got to go in high and come at him from behind."

"Go in high," Peter repeated. "Right."

"We need a ladder. Or a place where I can climb up."

"The shed?" Peter suggested.

"No, we don't need the ladder. Look." Karl pointed to the back porch. There was a wooden railing. There was a low gable that came out over the projecting porch. An upstairs window looked out over the gable. Karl swung himself up onto the porch rail, then up again and hooked a leg over the edge of the roof. In a low crouch, he clambered up the roof and reached the window. He hesitated, looked inside, then tried the window. Peter was not surprised to see Karl raise the window without any trouble and disappear inside the house on the second floor.

Peter wondered whether he ought to wait where he was or go back to where Johann was waiting. If Johann was still there.

There were three shots.

Had Karl killed the person who had killed Elfreda? Was Karl dead too? Peter wasn't even sure what to hope.

"It's okay. You can come in now. Tell Johann," Karl was calling down from the window he'd entered through. He was waving, like a little boy on a merry-go-round.

Peter went around to the front door. There was no sign of Johann. Run off? Peter supposed so. He went inside to see if Elfreda might be alive. Maybe she'd been lucky. Maybe . . .

She hadn't been lucky at all. She had been stopped by a shotgun blast. She lay in a heap at the bottom of the staircase. She'd been blown back down the stairs. There were flecks of gore on the wall. Peter closed his eyes. He was beyond grief or even disgust. He felt exhausted. Why had they shot her? She'd been trying to warn them, for God's sake. She had risked everything to warn them about Karl and his gun. What reason could they have had for killing her?

Johann came out of the kitchen. He had a tablecloth. He covered her with it. "A shame," he said.

"I don't understand," Peter said.

"I do. I found out what happened," Karl said. He was at the head of the stairs, where the shotgun blast had come from. "He was a deaf-mute. He had these little cards in his pocket. He couldn't hear her when she called out to warn him."

"Oh, my God!" Peter said. Poor Elfreda! But the poor bastard, too . . .

"If he was a deaf-mute, how did he hear the shot?" Johann asked. "You shot the man who opened the door. And then he went for a gun. What sense is there in that?"

"He didn't hear it. He felt it," Karl explained.

"You think maybe we can get out of here now?" Peter asked. He was eager to get away, to get this behind him. And at the same time, he felt a helplessness, a hopelessness. Elfreda was out of it, had freed herself at last. It wouldn't be any easier for the rest of them. Their involvement was like the smell of gunpowder that still hung in the air. It would cling to them, wherever they went. He'd never be able to get free . . .

"We better put the bodies down into the cellar," Karl said, "out of sight. What if the police came back?"

It made sense. Just as, in a crazy way, there was a kind of sense in Karl's having shot that man who came to the door. They didn't want anyone who could recognize them, who could connect them with the landing on the beach.

But then why had they come to the door? Why had Karl rung the bell? Why not just steal the car and drive off? Or hide in the shed? It all fell apart.

He thought ruefully of his fantasies of walking ashore, strolling away, and leaving all this spy nonsense behind him. How in hell was he going to explain—or prove—that he hadn't had anything to do with this carnage? Who would believe him?

They carried Elfreda's body down first and put it in the pantry where the men in the farmhouse had been storing canned goods and sugar and flour in long rows on neatly arranged shelves. Then they went back up for the men, the white-haired one near the door and the deaf-mute from upstairs.

Then they washed the blood off their hands.

At half-past five in the morning, when Warren Wells opened the little Amagansett station, there were four men waiting to buy tickets on the first train to New York.

"No problem," he assured them. "I'll just get the wood stove going to take the chill off the room."

"When is the first train?" one of them asked.

"Comes in at five-fifty-eight. Gets to Penn Station at eight o'clock."

He got the fire started, went around into the ticket office, opened the window, and sold them four tickets to Penn Station. They looked as though they'd been out fishing, but he didn't ask and they didn't volunteer. There was nothing remarkable about their appearance, really. Weekend fishermen often came through on these early Monday morning trains.

The train came in and they got on it, the only passengers from Amagansett that early. And then, maybe twenty minutes later, the army major came in to ask about the morning train.

Wells thought it was a damnfool question. He wasn't required

107

to remember every single passenger who took the train to New York.

The major was patient and rather friendly. He said, "No, of course you're not required to remember. But you might remember. There were probably several of them. And they'd have looked a little scruffy. Maybe a little damp—like they'd been out on the water."

"Oh, sure, sure, sure. The fishermen."

"Tell me," the major insisted.

"Nothing to tell. They were here when I showed up at five-thirty, which is when I get here every day but Sunday."

"How many?"

"Four."

"You're sure?"

"I'm sure. Four. And one of them bought the tickets—four of them—for Penn Station in New York."

"And the train gets in?"

"Eight oh-one, according to the schedule."

"And what did they look like?" the major pressed.

"Four guys. Ordinary-looking guys. Middle height, most of them. The one that bought the tickets was taller. One of them had red hair. One of them was a little fat, maybe. Nothing remarkable."

"You've been a great help," the major said, and he charged back outside and piled into the jeep that was waiting for him. They roared away from the curb as if they meant to race the damned train to New York and meet it.

There was a gas station where Trumbull ordered his driver to turn in, where he phoned New York, collect person-to-person, for Special Agent Kelly.

Special Agent Kelly wasn't on duty. Nobody else would accept the call. The major dug in his pockets for change and clanked quarters and double-chiming dimes into the pay phone. He explained who he was. He mentioned Special Agent Dunbar's name. He described the four men who would be getting off at Penn Station, one fat, one tall, one redheaded, and all of them looking rumpled as if they'd been in the water. Meet the train. Hold the men for questioning.

Special Agent Barnes didn't seem all that happy about it, but he didn't have the nerve to refuse.

When Trumbull hung up, he felt better than he'd expected—more hopeful, certainly. He was able to look around and admire the cute little resort town. A nice peaceful place, he thought, and it ought to stay that way. He got into the jeep, ordered the driver to take him back to the Mobile Infantry Unit—there'd be coffee there and maybe some eggs—and relaxed a little.

Horst thought they'd made it. Willi agreed with him. Rudi was not so sure. Kurt was worried. "We look like bums," he said. "We look like escaped convicts."

"So? So, we'll buy new clothes. There's plenty of money for that kind of thing," Willi suggested.

"We don't even look good enough to go into a store," Kurt said.

It was a remark that was supposed to have been wry and witty, but Willi realized that it was true. The more he thought about it, the more he believed it.

"Huh? Go into a store to buy clothes so we can go into another store to buy other clothes? That's crazy," Horst said, and he produced a disagreeable kind of horselaugh.

Willi resisted any reference to a Horst-laugh. There were more important things to discuss. "If we went into Brooks Brothers, or even into Macy's, looking like this, and we bought new suits, all of us, they'd remember us, wouldn't they? It'd be unusual. So we want to avoid that. We should go into one of those fringe stores, those desperate places with cheap clothing, where people like us—who look like us—would go."

"What's the difference?" Rudi wanted to know. "Once we get to New York . . ."

"But that's it," Willi said, absolutely convinced now. "We shouldn't go to New York. We should get off this train before New York, and do our shopping, and then catch another train."

Horst thought that was wasteful. They'd bought tickets to New York. Why not use them?

Willi tried to explain it to them. Fortunately, there was nobody else in the car or all of this could have been awkward. But they were alone, with only occasional visits from the conductor who popped his head in after each stop to see whether anyone else had boarded. One wondered how the Long Island Railroad managed to stay in business.

"We were seen on the beach, right?" Willi began. "And whoever it was, he may have gone to report what he saw. We have to assume that. And we have to assume some kind of search. They might reasonably look in the railroad station. That's one of the first places I'd look. And the ticket agent might remember us. Four tickets, one way, to New York."

"So?" Rudi asked.

"So, New York could be dangerous. We should get out before. And either take another train or take a subway into Manhattan."

Horst was unimpressed and eager to get to New York City. Jamaica wasn't anywhere. There was nothing to do in Jamaica.

"There won't be anything to do in New York, either, if they arrest you when you get off the train," Willi reminded him.

Kurt agreed. He thought they should get off at Jamaica.

Horst accused Kurt of liking the idea because he'd thought of it first. "As far as I'm concerned, that's enough reason to reject it."

"Who are you to reject anything? I'm in charge of this team. And I say we get off at Jamaica. Understand?" Willi glared at Horst and Rudi.

"Well, fuck you!" Horst said after a while, as if it had taken him a little thought to come up with just the right reply.

Willi looked out of the window. He had gone too far and he knew it. The only question now was how to retrieve the situation, not so much to save the mission but to save face. He hated being made to look ridiculous. "Kurt and I are getting off at Jamaica," he said, very calmly. "I've already given you the reasons for that decision. I think we'll attract less attention if we get cleaned up a little before we get to Manhattan. And I'm worried about the police or the FBI meeting this train or having people at Penn Station. You two can do as you please."

End of discussion. Then it was a matter of letting them think it over in the uncomfortable silence as the train moved through the flat farm country of Long Island.

It was up to Rudi, then. Did Rudi realize that? Did he understand that there were risks involved in going on to New York? Was Rudi the kind of man who would destroy the mission at the first opportunity? Willi had no way of knowing. He tried to tell himself that he didn't care, that it was out of his hands. They slowed down. The conductor announced Jamaica. Willi got up. Kurt rose. Willi promised himself he wouldn't look around, but he did, had to, as if his head had been operated by someone else. And what he saw was Rudi getting to his feet and following.

What Horst did wouldn't matter so much, then.

But Horst, too, got to his feet. He glared at Willi, making it clear that he resented Willi's leadership. But he followed.

Willi led. He was surprised at how easy it was. He found a modest cafeteria where they could all have breakfast, dawdle over their coffee, read the newspapers, and use the bathrooms, without arousing any special notice. They were a little younger but not otherwise distinguishable from the clientele of sad sacks and near-derelicts scattered about the huge room.

Shortly after nine, they left the cafeteria and looked for the right kind of cheap haberdashery place where they could get underwear, precuffed trousers, sport shirts, and jackets and not have the salesman ask too many questions. The salesman might think of the questions, but he wasn't going to risk losing a cash sale by asking them. There was a dressing room in the back where they could try on the pants and change into the new underwear and shirts. The salesman wrapped their old stuff up in bundles. These they discarded later, in various trash baskets on the boulevard.

They went into a shoe store to get shoes. The ones they'd landed in had been soaked and looked awful, covered with striations of salt.

Finally, they went into a coffee shop across the street from the subway station. Willi said they had to make plans. What he was concerned about was that the temporary hold he'd managed to exert over them would prove to be short-lived. If Horst wanted to walk away, just cross the street and keep on going, what was to stop him? How could Willi order him to do anything? There had to be a way of finding out what authority he did or didn't have.

They ordered coffee. Willi reminded the others that the rendezvous was set for the next day at the Thirty-fourth Street Automat.

"So?" Rudi asked. "We know that."

"I'm just reminding you."

"How many more times are you going to do that?" Horst asked.

"I'm not," Willi answered. "That's the point. I think it would be safer if we split up into two groups. It's less unusual for two men to check into a hotel together. Four is already a large crowd."

He waited. There wasn't any objection. But then, he hadn't really thought there would be.

"Kurt and I will go off together," Willi announced. "And the two of you should wait for another ten minutes or so. Then you go to Manhattan and find hotel rooms."

They nodded.

"Maybe I'll go to the movies tonight. A movie and a show at the Roxy or the Capitol," Kurt said.

"What I want," Rudi said, "is a hot bath and a good warm bed with clean sheets and soft linen."

"For me," Willi said, relieved that the moment had passed and that he'd succeeded, "a thick juicy steak and a piece of hot apple pie."

"A chick," Horst said. "Maybe two of them." And he laughed that ridiculous horselaugh.

The waitress refilled their cups. Willi asked for the check. He paid it, drank his coffee, and said "See you tomorrow" to Rudi and Horst, with a heartiness that did not betray his very serious doubts.

Once Willi and Kurt had left, Rudi suggested to Horst, "You want a piece of pie, maybe?"

"That's Willi's dream, not mine."

"We're supposed to wait here, though, remember?"

"Oh, for Christ's sake. So? So what if we don't? Who's going to know? What's going to happen?"

"I don't know," Rudi said. "What?"

"I'll tell you what. Nothing. Exactly nothing."

There were six special agents who met the train from Amagansett at Penn Station, two of them down on the platform, two of them flanking the stairs, and two more at the gate. They were all wearing sidearms in shoulder holsters, dark-gray suits, white shirts, and dark-gray fedoras.

They gave the once-over to every passenger who got off the train, looking for men in groups of two or four, looking for men in rumpled clothing, looking for anyone unusual or suspicious.

Special Agent Cassidy waited until the last of the passengers had got out of the train. His lips were blanched white by pressure. His eyes flicked from one face to the next. He stopped one of two middle-aged men, not redheaded or fat, maybe, but rumpled. "I beg your pardon, sir, but could I ask you for some identification?"

"Who, me?" Sam Feibish asked, a little surprised.

"Yes, sir."

"You want my identification?"

"That's right, sir."

"You don't have any?"

"FBI," Special Agent Cassidy said, and he snapped his wallet open and then shut.

"Not so fast. Let me see it again. Closer," Sam Feibish said. "You closed it up so quick, I couldn't tell if it was forged. Or if it was from the five-and-dime."

"Could I see your identification?" Cassidy asked, not bothering with "sir" any longer.

"For a tenth of a second, like yours? Or you really want to see it?"

"Aw, Sam, don't give him a hard time," Sam Feibish's companion said. "He's just doing his job."

"That's what worries me," Feibish said. "He's doing his job. As if this were already Nazi Germany. As if they'd won and we all had to go around with papers and identification."

"Easy. Nice and slow!" Special Agent Cassidy said.

Sam Feibish produced his wallet. He opened it up. There was his identification in the glassine window, showing that he was Samuel J. Feibish, Deputy United States Attorney.

"I'm sorry, sir. Just following orders," Special Agent Cassidy said, coming as close to an apology as he was likely to get.

"That's what they always say, isn't it?" Feibish said to his companion and neighbor, Marty Bryant. "As if that took the curse off it."

Feibish walked past the FBI men, leaving them alone on the platform. They'd come up empty.

"It is ironic, isn't it?" Karl observed. "Because he was a deaf-mute, he was immune to lies."

"What?" Peter asked. "What lies? What are you talking about?"

113

"Elfreda was not speaking for us," Karl pointed out. "Those warnings of hers . . . he never heard them. But even if he had, I'd have had to kill him."

"Why?" Johann asked, not in outrage but in order to follow the argument. "Why would you have had to kill him?"

"Because I'd killed the other one, the one who opened the door."

"But why did you have to kill him?" Peter asked.

"He could have identified us . . ."

But Peter had already figured that out. "No, no. It isn't that," he said. "The real question is why we came to the house at all. Why didn't we just steal the car and drive away?"

"It would have been dangerous. They'd have telephoned."

"I know, I know . . ."

"But you are not satisfied. Why else did I come to the door? Why else did I kill? What good has been accomplished?"

"None that I can see," Peter said.

"Only harm," Johann said.

"Not quite," Karl said. "You are implicated now. It is not so easy a matter for you to . . ." He broke off and extended his hand palm up as if there were a variety of possibilities available to choose from. "Walk away? Betray the expedition? Save your own skin at the expense of the others? I make no accusations. These are simply logical possibilities. Otherwise, nothing has changed."

"For them, it's changed," Johann said, gesturing toward the cellar door.

"But we're at war, no?"

"Elfreda, too," Peter said.

"She violated discipline. She endangered herself. There was no way we could have protected her."

It was nearly eleven in the morning. They had not yet taken the old Dodge. They'd talked about it, but Karl had said, "In a way, we're safest right here, where they've already checked."

"But what if they return?" Johann had asked.

"If the same man returns—and *if* he remembers who was here this morning—there could be a problem. My guess is that if there is a second check, it will be by a second man. And we will tell him what they must have told the other one—that we have heard nothing, have seen nothing, have not been disturbed."

"He's right," Johann had decided, grudgingly. "We'd do just as well staying here."

Peter, however, had had the growing certainty that Karl was actually enjoying the time they were spending in the company of the three corpses. As if he were proud of them.

"What we must do, though," Karl was saying, "is to look more like farmers. Both for the possible visitor and for our trip. We must get out of these clothes."

They rummaged around the farmhouse, looking into closets and chiffoniers, into dressers and chests. There were more of those bib overalls, and some decent flannel shirts that made perfectly convincing farmer suits. There were also the little printed cards announcing "I am a deaf-mute." Karl put several of them into his overall pocket, either to use or as souvenirs.

There were eggs in the kitchen. And bacon and coffee. And English muffins! Karl was delighted to find English muffins and marmalade.

They were making breakfast, putting plates out on the table's cherry red oilcloth, rummaging in drawers for flatware and for napkins, behaving in ways that were almost domestic, when Johann picked up the gun that Karl had left on the countertop next to the bread box. He didn't do anything with it for a moment, but just stood there holding it.

It crossed Peter's mind that he'd never even asked himself how it was that Karl had had a gun. It seemed altogether natural that Karl should be armed. But why? Why he and not the others?

That thought took only an instant to flash in Peter's mind. Johann had also been thinking quickly. "You're not so smart as you think you are, my friend," he announced. "What you've said would work if Peter and I didn't do anything. But we're not helpless. I'm not, anyway. I'm going to turn you in. I didn't kill anybody. He didn't kill anybody. Only you. And you'll answer for it, not us."

"You're crazy," Karl said. "You just came ashore from a German U-boat! You think they're going to overlook that?" He was standing next to the stove. He had an egg in his hand. There was a black iron skillet on the fire. The butter was melting. The butter will burn, Peter thought.

"You turn me in, and you sign your own death warrant. You understand that? We're all involved together. All of us."

"I'll take my chances," Johann said. His eyes were wide with nervous energy. Or terror.

"You're a traitor, you know. To both sides. There's nowhere for you to turn," Karl said. It was as if Karl had the gun instead of Johann.

Peter realized that he'd missed yet another opportunity. Not now, but before. Back when they'd been approaching the house and Karl had killed the man at the front door. All that had kept Peter from running off was his ignorance of what Johann would do. And Johann had stayed for the same reason, not knowing what Peter was going to do. Every one of them distrusted everyone else.

It was just nuts. And there was no way for Peter to let Johann know that he agreed with him. As long as Johann had the gun in his hand, he'd never believe anything anybody could say to him. He couldn't afford to.

The refrigerator started to hum, switching itself on as if it were an ordinary morning in a Long Island kitchen. Karl seemed to think so. He stood there at the stove, melting butter into a frying pan as if Johann and the gun in his hand were figments of an overactive imagination.

EIGHT

The man in the Grand Central phone booth was very nervous. He missed when he dropped the nickel into the coin slot. It fell out and rolled around on the floor. He left it there, fished another from his pocket, and tried again. He got it right this time and dialed the number he read off the piece of scratch paper, one digit at a time—and got it wrong, which was typical for Horst.

Instead of getting the switchboard of the New York office, he got a direct line higher up on the rotation, and was connected through to the car-theft unit in another office two blocks away. The car-theft unit of the FBI took up a lot of room. There were rows upon rows of files of serial numbers and engine numbers of automobiles that had to be cross-checked all the time when vehicles were recovered that had been used in the commission of a crime. A stolen car, transported across state lines, allowed the Bureau to enter what would otherwise be a purely local case—if it wanted to involve itself.

Jerry Hawkins answered the phone when it rang. "Special Agent Hawkins," he said, reaching for a pencil in case there should be anything to write down.

"Is this the FBI?" a voice asked. It was accented and low, resonant, either coming from a phone booth, or sounding like that—as one could if one put a wastebasket over one's head.

"That's correct. Federal Bureau of Investigation," Hawkins

said, taking no chances. "Special Agent Hawkins speaking. Who is calling, please?"

"I'd like to speak to Mr. Hoover."

"Surely," Hawkins said, grinning. He toyed with the idea of lowering his voice and saying that he was Hoover, but that seemed risky, even as a joke. "Could I ask what you want to speak to Director Hoover about?"

"I am a German spy," the voice at the other end of the line said.

Hawkins covered the speaker of his telephone set and called Fred Jerome, his office mate. "You want to pick up on this? You'll love it!"

". . . landed from a submarine last night on the beach in Long Island."

"I see," Hawkins said, "and where are you calling from?"

"A phone booth in a hotel lobby. I don't know what the name of the hotel is. But there were eight of us."

"You want to turn yourselves in, is that it?" Hawkins asked.

Jerome, who was listening on the extension, made a circular motion with his index finger next to his temple.

"You are not understanding me. The others do not know I am making this telephone call. I wished to come home, nothing more. But you should know that Macy's is in danger. And Gimbels. And Saks. Those department stores Hitler hates must be guarded. I must speak to Mr. Hoover and explain this."

"Well, you've got the New York office. The director is in Washington, you know. And you'd have to come in to talk with somebody . . ."

Jerome was having trouble restraining his laughter. It was for Jerome's sake that Hawkins continued to play it straight, which was by far the funniest way to play it.

"The director is a very busy man, you understand," Hawkins reminded the caller.

"Then you must get the message to him. Those stores should be protected. The crowds of people . . . It would be very bad."

And then there was a click. The man had hung up.

"Wonderful," Jerome said.

"Can you believe it?" Hawkins asked.

"Of course not."

"No, I mean . . . can you believe that somebody'd spend his

time thinking up a wild story like that? At this hour of the morning?"

"And expect us to fall for it?" Jerome asked. He was still smiling. "Unless . . ."

"Unless?"

"Unless it's some kind of security check. We're supposed to put through a report, maybe?"

"That somebody called us here in the hot-cars office?"

"It happened, didn't it? So we report it. What's to lose?" Jerome asked.

"Just a regular memorandum to the special agent in charge?"

Jerome nodded.

Hawkins pulled the dust cover off the Underwood and put in a couple of pieces of paper with a carbon between them. "I feel like a real asshole, you know?"

"Why? You're just doing your job. They called you, remember. I heard it, too."

"I guess I could use the walk," Hawkins said.

"And on your way back, you can pick up a couple of Danish and some coffee."

"Yeah, yeah," Hawkins said. "What other stores? Gimbel's, Macy's, and who else?"

"Saks, I think."

"Saks Fifth Avenue, or Sachs Thirty-fourth Street?"

"Oh, for Christ's sake! What difference does it make? I don't think he said which one anyway."

"If I'm going to do it, I might as well do it right, hunh?"

There was no answer to that one.

It had been easier to get rid of Horst than Rudi could possibly have hoped. The two men had taken the subway in from Jamaica, and the plan was to find a hotel room. From the hotel they could begin looking for more economical long-term living quarters, a roominghouse on the upper West Side perhaps, or even a small apartment on a month-to-month sublease. Rudi had expected that Horst would cling to him like a barnacle, but as they emerged from the Forty-second Street stop of the Lexington Avenue subway, Horst announced somewhat shamefacedly that he had to go to the bathroom. They went into the Commodore Vanderbilt Hotel. Horst went downstairs to the men's room, leaving Rudi alone, in the hotel lobby. All Rudi had to do was walk through the passageway and into Grand Central Terminal. He did so, looking back over his shoulder every few seconds. No sign of Horst. He bought a coach seat to Chicago, then ducked into the newsreel theater on the upper level to wait for the train and watch pictures of Rommel's advance in North Africa, the President's appeal for rubber and tinfoil, and the announcement of a new bond drive. He sat through the whole show twice, looking behind him every few minutes, waiting for someone to burst through the doorway.

He knew that there was no chance of Horst's finding him, that he was safe. But he kept looking back.

"You're a hypocrite," Karl was saying. "You don't care a damn about them. They were garbage. A couple of homosexuals. And one of them was a defective. But when it's your own skin you're worried about, then you become a great humanitarian. It makes me sick."

"I'm not going to argue with you," Johann said. "This speaks for me," he said, nodding to his right, toward his gun hand.

Peter just stood there. Karl was a killer and Johann was a fool. It was as though he'd woken up suddenly in a cage where a couple of gorillas were fighting each other but could at any moment turn on him.

"Guns don't talk," Karl said. "You want to spend your life in jail? It's what you'll get if you make that call."

"I didn't shoot anybody."

"We're all involved," Karl said, wearily.

Peter was exhausted. He'd been up all night. All three of them, he realized, were stretched to the utmost, faced with impossible questions and forced to answer them under the worst possible circumstances. Taking a long view, Peter could feel sorry for all of them—himself, first of all, but Johann, too, with that sorry smile and the gun in his hand, and over near the stove, Karl, who had been putting more and more butter into the pan, mechanically, as if his behavior had got itself stuck in that mode like a needle in an old, worn phonograph record.

It would be ridiculous to have a skillet full of eggs be the instrument of their downfall. *Their?* Peter noticed his own pronoun and realized that he had no expectation whatever that any of them could emerge alive from this charnel house. Three corpses already were down in the cellar. Three more to go. And all because Karl had put down the pistol so that he could make the eggs.

"What if we leave the farmhouse? What if we all go somewhere else to turn ourselves in?" Peter asked. "It could be a way out of this. We would just walk away from all these dead bodies. We'd just agree not to mention we were here . . ."

"No," Johann said. "That requires that we trust each other. And we don't. We can't. Besides, they'd connect us up sooner or later. There must be fingerprints all over the house. Right here in this kitchen . . ."

As if to wipe off his fingerprints, Karl reached for a potholder. It wasn't enough, Peter realized. But there was no point in trying to get through to him and make him understand that. He'd been watching as Karl put in more and more butter during the weird conversation, so that there was now a half pound or so in the skillet. But Peter had missed the point. He saw that at once as the pan blew through the room, trailing its bright festoon of melted butter. It looked a little like a comet.

Karl had been planning this. Karl had been melting all that butter deliberately.

Johann had no idea what to do. One can't shoot a frying pan. One can't shoot melted butter as it comes at him. But one can't just ignore them, either. He ducked. He dove . . .

The gun dropped. Or maybe he'd thrown it. It skittered across the floor.

There was a scream as the burn of the hot fat registered somewhere in Johann's busy brain.

Karl was on the floor too. Karl and Johann were grappling, playing like children, it appeared. And the prize was the pistol.

"Kick it. Kick it away!" Karl shouted.

Peter realized he was the one Karl was calling to. He kicked the pistol and sent it spinning across the linoleum floor, making an irregular spiral because of the weight of the butt with its full clip.

They tumbled over the floor, wrenching, grasping, looking almost as though they were enjoying themselves. And then, suddenly, a hand came up. Karl's? Peter couldn't be certain. He saw the hand and the flash of the light on the blade of the kitchen knife. And heard the grunt. He didn't connect it with the knife. It sounded more like the kind of grunt a man makes when somebody has kicked him or punched him and knocked the wind out of him. Peter realized he'd never before heard anyone get stabbed.

That it was a stabbing was clear, because there was blood on the floor, not in huge quantities yet but enough to make it quite clear that somebody was bleeding. They were still grappling, fighting for the knife now rather than for the gun, which lay in the corner like a discarded toy.

It occurred to Peter that he could go get it, pick it up, and shoot whichever of them got up from this struggle. Or both. Or just keep it, for his own protection . . .

Peter supposed that the only sensible thing to do was to get out of there while there was still a chance, with or without the gun. But he stood there, watching the two men on the floor, fascinated and helpless, a rabbit caught in the headlights of an oncoming car . . .

There was another grunt, this time followed by a groan, and suddenly much more blood.

Karl picked himself up.

Johann lay there, gasping. He couldn't breathe. He was moving his mouth, trying to talk. He managed to get words out, partly voiced, partly gurgled through the blood. "Crazy. Fucking. Bastard."

And then he died, moving his head a little and then not moving.

"Do you suppose he was talking about me? Or about Hitler?" Karl asked. He was standing at the sink. He was, quite sensibly, washing his hands.

"Hitler?"

"Or whoever thought up this enterprise."

"Maybe both?" Peter suggested. He was looking at the gun, still on the floor in that corner. Go for it? Or was he intimidated now by Karl's recent success?

Karl filled a glass with water from the tap, drank it, and had another glassful.

"Thank you for kicking that gun away," Karl said. "I was worried there for a moment."

Peter didn't know how to answer that. *You're welcome* seemed wrong, somehow—too little or too much. "What now?" he asked, instead.

"I think the time has come for us to leave this rustic spot. Unless you force me to make it three in a row?"

"No, no."

"I'm very glad to hear that. I like you," he said. "We can take the car to New York. Or maybe Babylon and get a train from there, can't we?"

"I think so," Peter agreed. "And then?"

"And then we shake hands and say goodbye to one another. If that's agreeable to you. You have your stores to blow up. I have other tasks."

"Yes," Peter said.

"I mention it only so that you'll be able to deliver the message to the other team. It will have to be the five of you, I'm afraid. You can send my regrets. The key is behind you."

"The key?"

"The key to the car. On that little hook."

There it was. He took it. "What about the gun?" he asked.

"Leave it. We don't want it now. They can match the bullets to those in the bodies downstairs. It'd take too long and be too messy to cut the bullets out of the bodies. Easier to get another gun," Karl said. He watched as Karl washed off the kitchen knife. For the prints, he supposed.

"These knives stain if they aren't wiped dry. Good carbon steel will do that," Karl said. He put the knife back in the rack. "I'll go and get a clean pair of overalls," he said. "Be right back."

Peter was alone in the room. With the gun on the floor. And the keys to the car. Grab the gun and run? It had to be a test. His impulse was to pick up the gun, but he remembered that Johann had had the gun in his hand and it hadn't done him a lot of good. For all Peter knew, Karl might be upstairs, looking out of the window, staring down the barrel of some larger weapon . . .

It was unlikely, but everything was unlikely. There was no reasonable way to project into the future. He was immobilized. He stood there, the key on one side and the gun on the other, feeling like the stupid donkey who starved to death between two piles of hay that were exactly the same distance on each side of him.

He could tell himself he was a jerk. A moron. But he couldn't budge.

Karl reappeared. He was wearing a different pair of pants,

dungarees this time without the straps or the bib. They were just a little large.

"Let's go," Karl said.

Willi Morath liked New York and his own role in it as a man-about-town. Not quite a playboy, which was a little too rich for his blood and station, but what Europeans would more modestly call a boulevardier. He'd been a young man when he'd gone to sea for the Hamburg-American line, working as an oiler on one of the transatlantic liners. Unfortunately, he had caught the eye of the second engineer, a sadist and pederast. Willi had jumped ship in New York, found a job in a restaurant as a busboy, worked up to waiter, and then had been fired when a customer had flung a hand backward in conversation and knocked over his tray of drinks. Willi had gone to the employment agency that had placed him as a waiter, and there, in the waiting room, he'd met Inge, a narrow, rather severe-looking woman, four or five years older than he. She had suggested to him that they pretend to be a couple, so they'd be eligible for the better jobs in big country houses.

He'd been more than half convinced she was teasing, that it was a joke of some kind. But he'd agreed to play along, not imagining that there'd be any result. After all, for such jobs—for such *positions*, as they were called—there had to be references. But Inge was ready for that question. She produced a letter of reference from her bag.

"And we can telephone Mrs. Cannon?"

"Oh, no. She passed away two months ago."

"I understand," the woman behind the desk in the severe navy suit said. "You have other references though?"

Inge claimed that the two of them had worked for Mrs. Cannon in Pound Ridge for four years. Nearly five.

Willi thought it was all crazy, but the woman in the navy suit either believed it or took it as evidence that the couple was bright and eager enough to be given a chance. There was, in fact, a position available . . .

So they went up to Ardsley to be a couple, she a cook-housekeeper and he a gardener-chauffeur. There was an apartment over the garage that they were to share. The rules—as Inge set them down—were that he was to sleep on the rollaway in the living room and she would have the bedroom. He was not to bring women to the apartment. She would do her own socializing elsewhere. It was simple and clear-cut, and the threat was that if he in any way even thought of presuming upon their charade marriage, she'd quit and he'd be out of a job.

Good enough, he thought. And he counted himself lucky to have found so comfortable a spot, not much work to do, a beautiful garden to look after, a Packard and a Cadillac to wash and polish and, once in a while, even to drive. Good food. What more could a man want? He wasn't even particularly attracted to Inge. Or not at first. He saw her parade around the apartment in her dressing gown that now and then fell open to reveal not much in the way of bosom but a very dark and luxuriant pubic thatch he kept thinking about, despite himself. And in the bathroom, there was her diaphragm kit, and her douche bag, both of which she packed up and put in her little tote bag every time she went to New York for her day off—not that she was flaunting any of this but he still knew about it and felt challenged by it. Not threatened, because they weren't married. But challenged, because they were living together in this oddly sexy sexless way. And whether she meant to be provocative or not, she dropped hints all the time about her exploits in town, which he felt obliged to try to match.

So he was more or less obliged to go to New York on his days off, to pick up girls when he could, or to pay for them when that was necessary. The pursuit of women became obsessive, so that when he got back he would tell her what he'd done and enjoy her angry smirk of acknowledgment.

She must have realized what she was doing. She flaunted herself and extorted from him a kind of slavish admiration he did not understand but could not withhold.

And it was only a matter of time before his idea turned from possibility to plausibility and then took on the dimensions of hard fact. He approached her one night. She hit him in the side of the head with a bookend from the little shelf beside her bed and knocked him cold. When he awoke, he was in the St. Agnes Hospital in White Plains with a man in a uniform at the foot of the bed. She'd turned him into the Immigration Service, having gone through his papers and found out that he was an illegal alien . . .

As soon as he was well enough to move, the Immigration people drove him to New York and put him back on the Hamburg-American Line, as a tourist-class passenger this time.

So? A weird encounter, the kind of thing to think about in a bar maybe, twenty years later. But nothing to take seriously. Willi Morath got a job at Krupp. He was home. It had been a mixed kind of trip, but it could have been worse. He'd been lucky to come away as little hurt by it as he had. Inge, after all, could have killed him with that bookend.

He found himself thinking of her. He found himself unable not to think of her, as if the relationship were contagious and he had contracted the ailment from her. In his blind way, he had been happy with Inge. And he realized he wanted to return to her. But that was more expensive than he could manage. And then it became politically impossible, war having been declared between the two countries. Then, suddenly, he'd been presented with this unlikely opportunity.

He accepted, of course, not so much to serve the Führer as to serve Inge and whatever master and mistress she elected for them. To return to some servants' quarters and put up with whatever she demanded of him. That would be going home.

What the others wanted or intended never much impressed Willi. The Abwehr officers, the instructors at the lodge, the rest of the expeditionary team seemed to Willi no more real than the girls he'd screwed in order to have something to tell Inge. Alone, he was nothing, and the others were less than nothing. He'd worked hard during the training period, eager to be included in the mission. But he never took it seriously—until the end, when they were so pleased about his simple idea of climbing back into the truck. Willi had thought it was just a good idea any lazy man might have had. But the Abwehr people thought it was inventive and displayed leadership abilities. They had made him a team leader and had given him almost twenty thousand dollars to use for emergencies and equipment for the rest of the team.

His immediate thought, as he'd considered it in his narrow bunk in the U-boat, had been just to run off with the money. He'd be a rich man, he thought, with all that money in his pocket. But then, he'd had an even better idea, a thought so attractive that it was hard to keep from smiling. In order to show off to Inge and let her know how lucky he'd been, he'd have to find her. And that could take time. But if he had the help of the FBI . . .

They'd be perfectly willing to trade him the information he wanted for the information he had. He could even get a medal for his outstanding service to the country. No more citizenship problems! And Inge would have to acknowledge that he'd done well, admiring him and forgiving him at the same time.

So from the time he'd waded ashore with the others, he'd been intent on going to the G-men. It wouldn't be difficult. He was giving the orders, after all. But he'd had second thoughts on the subway ride from Jamaica into Manhattan. He didn't mind selling out the others. None of them had been particularly friendly or even individualized in Willi's mind. But Kurt was almost a buddy. He trailed around like a big faithful dog. He didn't want to do anything that would hurt Kurt, not unless he had to.

And as they emerged into the daylight, coming up out of the subway stairs into the glare of Times Square, he saw how to manage it. He could use Kurt. They could back each other up. They could go together. There'd be enough glory to share between the two of them.

Unless Kurt really wanted to go and blow up Abraham and Straus!

They bought a couple of suitcases, stuffed them with magazines to give them heft, and checked into the Astor Hotel. Willi's plan was to break the idea to Kurt as soon as possible. Not in a hotel room, though. Somewhere out in the open, in a public place. Like a restaurant.

"You hungry?" he asked.

"Oh, yeah. I'm hungry."

"You want to go for Chinese?"

"Yeah, sure," Kurt said.

They followed the bellman down the long carpeted corridor and inspected their rooms. They took their keys. Willi tipped the bellman for both of them. And they followed him back to the elevator. Willi was feeling very shrewd about the idea of a Chinese restaurant. He remembered that the Chinese didn't put knives on the table.

NINE

Even if Dunbar hadn't been a little prick, the nature of the organizations would have made the cooperation between G-2 and the Feds a matter of grudging ritual exchanges of information. That was just how it was. If a soldier finds something, what is he going to do with it? Run to a phone booth and call the FBI? Of course not. He's going to tell his lieutenant, who is going to report it to headquarters. Just as one of Hoover's people who turns up anything is going to call it in to his boss in New York or Washington.

And that, Trumbull supposed, was assuming gentlemanliness and decency on both sides. Assume something less admirable and there'd be two suspicious men, each of them looking to cover his ass, hoping for glory and credit but even more worried about looking like a jerk and having to deal with another man whom he had no reason to trust and some to fear. Their styles were different. Trumbull was Yale and Dunbar was Fordham.

Those were Trumbull's thoughts at lunch, at the improvised headquarters at the mobile infantry station. It was a meal he never finished—and was just as glad he hadn't. The message came almost immediately after he'd sat down that they'd found something and he'd better come right away.

"Found something?" he asked. "You know what it is?"

Jenkins, his driver, had no idea. "All I know is that they said it was a disaster."

There was the blood, first of all. There was blood in the

kitchen, where the dead man lay on the floor. But there was blood in the living room, and more blood up at the top of the stairs. The bodies of two more men and one woman had been found down in the cellar in a pantry.

What the hell had happened?

There was no reason to reject absolutely the possibility that it was a coincidence, that on the same night as German spies had come wading ashore on the Long Island beach, there might not also be in a farmhouse three miles away some berserk burglary that had resulted in this carnage. From the point of view of pure logic, it was certainly possible.

But it was unlikely. Particularly if one of the weapons lying on the kitchen floor was an Italian automatic pistol.

So Trumbull called Dunbar and was astonished to hear that Special Agent Dunbar was occupied and could not come to the phone.

"Tell him it's an emergency. Tell him that he's got four corpses to deal with, unless he wants me to call in the local police department. You got that?"

"I'll tell him that, sir," the belligerently smarmy voice replied.

Trumbull waited, wondering why Dunbar was playing games. Refusing to come to the phone. What could be so important? What was Dunbar sitting on?

"It's pretty much over," Dunbar told him. "We've got it cracked wide open."

"We do?" Trumbull asked, looking around. He was calling from the kitchen of the farmhouse. The body was still on the floor, and the blood had turned black and tarry.

"*We* do," Dunbar corrected him.

"What is it that you've got?" Trumbull asked, giving Dunbar the pronoun but putting it into a direct question.

"We've apprehended two of them."

"At Penn Station?"

"Nothing like that. That was a waste of time," Dunbar said, as if it were Trumbull's fault that the idea hadn't paid off.

Trumbull wasn't going to argue with him, or not about that anyway. "And do I get to talk to these two?"

"Not at this time. The authorization would have to come from higher up in the Bureau," Dunbar said.

Trumbull heard the language, the official jargon. *Appre-*

hended. At this time. The man had a gift for sounding like one of the Bureau's reports.

"Fine with me. But you let them know, higher up in the Bureau, that we've got at least one of them. Maybe more than that. And unless you get it cleared for me to talk to your suspects, I'm going to treat this as an ordinary homicide. Three men and one woman are dead out here. And one of the men was apparently a deaf-mute. You like it? You'll have it all over the *World-Telegram* and the *Sun* and the *Journal-American* by this afternoon. You hear me?"

There was silence. Dunbar was thinking. Trumbull could all but hear the machinery clanking in Dunbar's head. Trumbull figured he'd help the poor bastard along a little. "Do you have authorization for *not* cooperating with the United States Armed Forces?"

"Well of course not."

"I'd want that, if I were you. And I'd want it in writing."

"All right," Dunbar said, after a beat.

"All right, what?"

"All right, you can talk to them."

"I was hoping you'd see it that way. Where are they?"

There was a series of holding cells and interrogation rooms in the basement of the United States Attorney's office in Manhattan. Dunbar gave Trumbull the address, as if it were a speakeasy or a whorehouse, wonderful, valuable information he was not supposed to write down anywhere, even though it was in the phone book under United States Government, Department of Justice.

In return, he gave Dunbar his assurances about not bothering the local police with these corpses. Dunbar promised that a couple of special agents would be out there in half an hour and the crime lab people soon thereafter. If Trumbull hadn't been smart enough to remember that these corpses had turned into bargaining chips and that Dunbar was collecting them for the access to the spies, he'd have supposed Dunbar was offering to do him a great favor by sending out the men that quickly. It was the intonation as much as anything.

Trumbull managed to restrain himself from the instinctive response of thanks. "Whatever you like," he said. "I'll see you very soon."

"I'm sure," Dunbar told him.

A ridiculous story. Or stories. The careers of Kurt Engermann and Willi Morath were both so inconsequential, so haphazard, as to leave Trumbull puzzled. He was perfectly willing to believe them. That wasn't the difficulty. But there were still questions. Were they telling the whole truth? Did they know the whole truth? And if this was all there was to it—as Dunbar was so eager to believe, because that would make it a quick, easy administrative triumph for him—then what did that mean about the German espionage system? Could they be an entire collection of madmen, picking on losers for missions that made no goddamn sense at all?

Eight of them. Seven men and one woman. Less these two, left six. Less the man on the floor in the kitchen and the woman down in the cellar, left four.

He had promised Dunbar that he wouldn't let either of them know anything about the killings on Long Island, which was reasonable enough as Dunbar's requests went. But it made no sense. As long as he assumed that Morath and Engermann were telling the truth, then there was no reasonable way to account for the carnage. Of the two farmers, sure, but of the two spies?

Trumbull splashed water on his face, groped in the direction of the towel dispenser, saw that it was empty, looked at the old roller towel that looked to be on its third trip around, and settled for blotting himself with his handkerchief. No wonder Hoover liked people who didn't sweat. They didn't have to wash and use up valuable space on the roller towels.

Back upstairs, he had another session with Kurt Engermann, who didn't seem to be holding back anything. All he wanted to know was the size of their reward, when it would be paid, and whether he'd get a medal with it or just the money.

"It's early yet to say. And I'm not the one who decides these things," Trumbull said, both of which statements were true, he supposed, although misleading.

"But you could guess," Engermann insisted.

"I never like to guess about these things," Trumbull said, as gently as he could. "One more time, though, let's go over it one more time."

"The whole thing?" Engermann asked. He wasn't impatient really but bored. Tired of it. He had been promised a treat and the treat wasn't forthcoming, and he was getting just a little bit

131

fatigued. His round face, almost a moon face, looked darker for the one wrinkle that crossed his forehead.

"Mostly the beginning. The way you were recruited for it."

"I told you. I was a translator at Seehaus . . ."

"The Abwehr listening station."

"Yes, that is right. I had been six years in Winnipeg, when my father was there working on a construction job and then on a farm. I could speak English like an American. Or Canadian. I could listen to the broadcasts and I could write down what I heard."

Trumbull pushed him a little. How had he got that job? How had he come to apply?

"I could speak English. I could understand it. So I was qualified. And it was a good job. You could do that job and not have to serve in the army. You could stay in Berlin. It was safe and comfortable."

"So why did you leave?"

A shrug. A sheepish look. "I made mistakes. My reports weren't what they wanted. I'd leave out things. Or I'd leave out the wrong things, because they wanted everything short. And I couldn't tell what to put in and what to leave out."

"So they fired you?"

Engermann nodded.

"And then?"

"Then?" Engermann asked. "Then, it looked like the army, after all. I'd had my notice. I was supposed to report. But I got this phone call to come for an interview. And there was this offer of going to the States."

Trumbull thought about that. It was all very casual and even serendipitous. "You have family in Germany?"

"Some cousins in Freiburg. No one close."

"Your father?"

"Dead. He died in Canada. I was sent to live with an aunt in Cologne, but she died two years ago."

"You never married?" Trumbull asked.

Engermann shook his head.

"So there was no pressure? No hold they had over you?"

Engermann didn't understand. Trumbull had to spell it out for him. "There was nobody they could put into prison or kill if you didn't take the assignment? Or if you turned yourself in, as you've done?"

"Oh, I see," he said, cheerful now that he understood. "No, nothing like that."

"Then how did they persuade you to do this rather than go into the army?"

"Some of the jobs in the army are not so pleasant, you know? They showed me. It isn't all parades and pretty girls in Paris. They also guard the prisons and the concentration camps. They showed me one of them. And they gave me the choice. I chose not to do that. So I had to do this. It seemed less . . . disagreeable."

"I see," Trumbull said. "I'll be talking to you again."

"I look forward to it," Engermann said.

It wasn't tight enough to be a cooked-up story. It didn't have enough inner logic, Trumbull thought. Which was a disturbing consideration. Trumbull was inclined to believe it, to accept everything that Engermann had told him. And Morath, too. The two of them were more pathetic than dangerous. The money, of course, was real, a serious sum for a serious purpose.

But those two? Nazi spies? He just wasn't happy about it.

It was possible, of course, that the Germans figured the FBI or the police or the army would make a big public demonstration about the spies, creating just the kind of spy scare the Nazis wanted to see. He remembered Dunbar's first plan of closing off Long Island. Without referring to that, he asked Dunbar whether the idea might be just to create some sort of home-front panic.

"No," Dunbar said. "Or if it was, then it won't work. There isn't a word that's going to get out about this until we've got every last one of them under lock and key. And then, it'll be the decision of the Bureau as to what gets out and when and how."

That was a little self-serving maybe, but it was reassuring. "Still, it's funny, isn't it?" Trumbull went on, taking a slightly different tack. "These two guys are landed on the beach on Sunday night, and by Monday afternoon, they've turned themselves in."

"What's funny about it?" Dunbar asked. He was sitting at the desk in an empty room in the United States Attorney's office. The light of the desk lamp cut across his face to make it look severe if not actually intelligent.

"You don't think it's odd that the Abwehr didn't keep some kind of hold on these people? That they just picked a couple of amateurs and pointed them at our country and waved good-bye—doesn't that seem fishy?"

"Maybe they're not very smart," Dunbar said. "I don't think they're all that smart."

The implication was clearly that if Trumbull wanted to give the Germans credit for any more shrewdness than they seemed to be displaying, that he was practically a Nazi sympathizer.

"Meanwhile," Trumbull said, "there are four more of them out there."

"Looks like," Dunbar said.

"And you've got the lid on, until they're all caught?"

"Caught or killed," Dunbar said.

"What about *their* lids?"

"What are you talking about?"

"What if they call up the *Daily News* or the *Post* or the *Mirror*, tell a convincing story, get it on the front page . . . what do you do then?"

"I don't think that'll happen. I don't think anything will happen until tomorrow."

"Why not?" Trumbull asked.

"Because they're supposed to meet tomorrow afternoon at the Automat on Thirty-fourth Street. We've got it covered."

Trumbull didn't say anything. He didn't have to. Dunbar sat and stewed for thirty seconds. "You're welcome to come along to observe," he finally said. "But just you. Nobody else. Understood?"

"I'm looking forward to it," Trumbull said. "An epidemic of snap-brim hats. It ought to be something to see."

"You're quite the funny man, aren't you?" Dunbar asked. He gave Trumbull a look of real hatred, which Trumbull enjoyed.

About twenty minutes after Major Trumbull left the office, Dave Carnahan came in with a couple of pieces of paper in his hand. He unfolded one of them and put it down on the desk in front of Dunbar.

"What's this?" Dunbar asked.

"Read. You won't believe it. I didn't believe it either. But I figured you ought to know about it."

Dunbar looked at the paper. It was a report, dated that day from J. Hawkins in hot cars. Who in hell was Hawkins? He read on. A man had called on the direct line to stolen cars division at 9:22 A.M. claiming to be a German spy who had landed on the shore of Long Island the night before. The purpose of the mission, according to the informant, was the sabotaging of prominent New York City department stores, mention having been made of Gimbel Bros., R. & H. Macy & Co., and "Saks (Fifth Avenue) or possibly Sachs (Thirty-fourth Street)."

How did this get to hot cars?

"Maybe he misdialed," Carnahan said, answering Dunbar's unasked question.

Dunbar explained that he didn't think anything was going to happen at least until the next day. He didn't think it would do any good to send bomb squads out to all the stores. And it could do a lot of harm, if word got out somehow.

"Still," Carnahan said, "you can't not respond to a thing like that, can you?"

"Right," Dunbar said. "I guess I'd better go see the special agent in charge."

"What'll I do with this?" Carnahan asked. "File it?"

"No, I'll take both copies," Dunbar said.

"Fine with me," Carnahan said.

"Appreciate it," Dunbar said.

If it turned out at the end that they needed a record of the call, it'd be where Dunbar could put his hands on it. If, on the other hand, they wanted to have a nice clear collar of a Nazi spy, they might not want these pieces of paper kicking around in the files to confuse the issue. One just never knew how one was going to play the hand until all the cards had been dealt.

Meanwhile, he had to arrange for the bomb squads. Not to protect the populace or the store owners, but for the record. To protect the Bureau.

Peter and Karl left the car at the Long Island Railroad's Babylon station. They bought tickets for Penn Station and sat down to wait for the train. Karl bought a newspaper, but after a quick glance at the front page, folded it under his arm. Peter shook his head. "There wouldn't be anything, yet. Not in the paper. On the radio, maybe. But go find a radio."

"In the hotel. There will be radios in the rooms."

"I suppose so," Peter said.

They discussed their need for new clothing. They couldn't check into decent hotels wearing these farmer suits, not without attracting attention.

"We could go to Macy's," Peter suggested. "That'd be funny, wouldn't it?"

"Why not?" Karl agreed, but he wasn't smiling.

They sat there, waiting. There were fewer trains in the middle of the day than at the rush hours in the morning and late afternoon. A couple of groups of women appeared, evidently on shopping trips. A professional man, a lawyer or an accountant, toting a large briefcase, set it down, and began to read from long typed pages. Karl sat there like a puppet whose puppeteer had abandoned him.

Peter was thinking that the only trouble with Johann's maneuver was that it hadn't worked. Johann had underestimated Karl. But so had Peter. He'd known that Karl was a killer, but he'd just thought of him as a predator, like a big cat, gracefully deadly but not very complicated. Karl wasn't a cat but a human being, and a clever one at that. It was intricate and nasty for Karl to have thought of killing the poor bastards in that farmhouse in order to implicate the other members of the team, bind them to him, or at least ensure against their betraying him.

There was no hope now of just walking away. Sooner or later, the police, the FBI, the army, or some combination of those forces would catch up with anyone who tried that. The only hope now was to use Karl as a bargaining chip, to find out what he was up to and present him on a plate to the appropriate authorities. But if this was clear to Peter, then it was also clear to Karl. That explained Karl's plan in which they were to split up and go their different ways in New York.

"The train is coming," Karl told him quietly. "Wipe your face. You've broken out into a sweat. It's suspicious-looking. And unattractive."

Peter had no handkerchief. He wiped his forehead on the smooth worn flannel of the plaid shirtsleeve. Together, the two men boarded the train. They sat together in a non-smoker, and Karl read the newspaper he'd bought. An observer in the car, seeing them side by side and dressed the same way, would have assumed that they knew—and hated—each other.

Neither of them had said anything when the train pulled into Penn Station or on the short walk to the store. It would happen on the way out of the store, Peter supposed. It would be then that he'd have to decide. Make some move or just stand there and watch Karl merge into the crowds of pedestrians on the sidewalks, disappearing forever.

That was all. What else could he do? He'd had his chance. When Johann had been struggling with Karl for the gun, it had come within Peter's grasp. He'd kicked it away but he could almost as easily have grabbed for it, picked it up, and used it—to kill either or both of them.

There would not be such a moment again. He was there, in the haberdashery department, and not there. He was half there and half outside, at the door of the store, watching Karl's back as it disappeared into the bobbing sea of other backs. He was in the men's clothing department, trying on slacks and a sport coat, watching Karl who was studying himself in a three-way mirror so that the slender figure and the hatchety face with those peculiar eyebrows were multiplied to make a whole gang of natty thugs, but at the same time Peter was downstairs on the street, watching the back disappear, boarding a bus or descending into a subway entrance.

A hotel. Almost certainly, Karl would be going to a hotel. If somehow Peter could manage to follow him and see where he checked in, then he might find some opportunity of proposing that they work together. He might figure out some way of earning Karl's trust—the key to everything. There had to be something with which Peter could counter Karl's clever use of those dead bodies. But what?

Something would present itself. It had to. The only alternative was letting go, which was tempting as it is to a shipwrecked man at the point of exhaustion. But if Peter let go of Karl, he was doomed. So, hold on, hold on . . .

The scene kept playing and then the two of them were going down the escalator together, their old clothes under their arms in Macy's boxes with big red stars on them. There was the door. The double vision of present and immediate future came into focus together. There were counters of cosmetics with sampler bottles of perfume and eau de cologne. There were shoppers coming into the store and leaving it. Karl went through the door first. He was waiting outside when Peter appeared.

"Good luck to you," Karl said.

"And to you," Peter answered.

They stood there, toe to toe, neither one offering a hand but neither one moving. It was funny, really. Karl grinned. Peter grinned.

Finally, Karl waved, turned, and crossed the street, darting from the curb to the island just ahead of the rush of traffic.

Peter watched him. He gave him the north side of Thirty-fourth Street and crossed south, but then, when the light changed, crossed to the east, perhaps thirty yards behind Karl.

He was convinced that at any moment, Karl might look back. Ought to look back. Given the odd situation, and given the training they'd both had back in Germany, it was inconceivable that Karl did not check his rear. But he crossed the second part of the double intersection, and then turned south, so that Peter had to turn away and pretend to dab at the corner of his eye with one of his new handkerchiefs.

Of course, he'd been seen. But it could still be a coincidence. He hadn't attempted an approach. He let Karl go further, giving him half a block. He saw him turn west on Thirty-third Street. He followed, keeping to the buildings so as to be able to duck into a doorway if necessary. But Karl plodded ahead like an automaton. Never a glance to right or left, let alone to his rear. It was stupid. And Karl wasn't stupid.

It was a setup, then?

He had no alternative. He had to take his chances. It was like the vision he'd had in Macy's, of the disappearing back. But there it was again, in the tan jacket. He watched as Karl turned south on Seventh Avenue. He hurried to the corner, slowed, and looked down Seventh. He was gone.

Peter stood there, not at all sure about his feelings. He'd been stupid and arrogant, had wildly overestimated his own abilities, and now, because of his incompetence, there was a dangerous man at large in New York. On the other hand, that sense of his own limitations spoke another way. He was relieved. It was out of his hands now. He'd only been kidding himself. What could he really have done?

Slowly, he started walking south on Seventh Avenue. He had no real sense of where he was going. There were a couple of hotels down the street. He could try one . . .

"Peter, my friend."

He turned. The man had come up behind him, had grabbed his arm just above the elbow and held on with a strong grip. It was Karl. "You're following me," he said. "Why would you want to do that?"

"I thought . . . we could have dinner together. To celebrate. I mean . . . we made it. We've come through it all. I'd been about to suggest it back there, but you crossed the street. I called to you."

He hadn't. But it sounded plausible. "I waved," he said. He remembered how Karl had avoided looking around. "I had just given it up."

Did he have another gun? A knife? Would he dare to kill in broad daylight out in the street? Could he be sure that Peter was lying?

A grudging smile spread across Karl's face. Peter was convinced that Karl saw the joke and enjoyed it.

"Why not?" Karl said. "Dinner? It'd be very pleasant."

"Where shall we meet?" Peter asked.

"How about the Berliner Bar, up on Eighty-sixth Street?" Karl offered. "You know the place?"

"No, but I'm sure I can find it."

"At seven, shall we say?"

Peter agreed. Karl released his upper arm. They shook hands this time.

Like fighters before the start of the fight.

TEN

In back of him, through the large window, the sun was just touching the hills across the river. It was one of those impressive panoramas that one sees in travelogues, a fitting backdrop, Rudi thought, to his homecoming. He'd been all around the world, after all, and he was satisfied with himself. He put a crisp fifty-dollar bill on the little black tray and called the waiter. "Another Canadian Club and soda," he said. That was what explorers drank.

"Is that the smallest you have, sir?" the waiter asked.

Rudi nodded. Actually, he had twenties in his wallet, but he enjoyed the idea that the smallest bill worth carrying around was a fifty. "I'm afraid so," he said, but he added, "I'll be drinking up a lot of it."

"That's a lot of drinking," the waiter said, flashing a grin.

"I'm celebrating," he explained. "I'm finishing a trip around the world."

"Congratulations," the man at the next table said, raising a glass. "That's quite an accomplishment."

"I'm proud of it," Rudi acknowledged.

"Especially in times like these," the man said. He was wearing a brown suit and tan shoes, and he had a fringe of hair that skirted the back of his head. "The Pacific. The Atlantic. How'd you manage that?"

"I'm not at liberty to talk about it," Rudi said, almost whispering. "But there are ways, believe me."

"I'm sure there are," the man said.

"Have a drink with me? Celebrate my homecoming?"

"I'd be honored," the man said.

Several drinks later, Rudi and his new friend, John, were still talking. John had suggested a game of cards to while away the time. Rudi wasn't interested. "I'm no good at cards," he said. "I have no head for cards."

That was not the worst news John could have heard. The only problem was how to get Rudi to start playing despite his admitted inadequacies—before he passed out from the Canadian Club he was swilling down. Rudi's agenda was quite different. He was interested in playing the sophisticated world traveler. "My worry now is the home front," he said. "America is vulnerable. It's only a matter of time before the enemy decides to take advantage of that. We're too complacent."

"Sure, sure," John said. "You're absolutely right, sir."

"Of course, I'm right. And you mark my words. The Germans will make their move, attempt to terrorize us, attack us at home."

"You think so?" John asked. He never argued with a mark.

"I'm sure of it. My guess is sabotage. The coasts are vulnerable. Do you realize how easy it would be for them to land saboteurs on our shores and send them to our department stores to blow them up . . . Macy's! Gimbels! Marshall-Field! The May Company!"

"Why in hell would they want to do that?"

"To terrorize the population. To do here what the blitz is doing in London," Rudi explained, his voice low. "Believe me, I know what I'm talking about."

"I'm sure you do," the man said.

Rudi finished his drink. He didn't feel all that good. He'd drunk more than was sensible. And he was talking too much. But what harm was there? They'd just think he was drinking too much.

That seemed a very clever stratagem, letting them think he was drunk. He called for the check, left a tip, and tottered through the club car, overcompensating against the swaying of the train.

It was supposed to have been different. His plan had been to go to the club car, pick up some blonde, buy her dinner, get her a little tipsy, and then bring her back to his roomette. But there hadn't been any women in the club car. And he'd forgotten to eat dinner and then, all of a sudden, the dining car was closed. And he was going to bed alone.

He shrugged it off, the way he'd done for most of his life.

Brigadier General Ralph Armistead III, arrived from Washington, got to HQ, had listened to Colonel Buck's recitation, and was ready to talk with Major Trumbull by ten after five.

Trumbull marched into the office the general had commandeered, snapped to attention, and waited for the superior officer's "At ease, major." The general stared at Trumbull for a few seconds. "In fact, why don't you sit down. Make yourself comfortable. Smoke?"

"No thank you, general."

"I believe I will." He went through the whole ritual with the silver cigar cutter and the wooden match. He was a man who took his pleasures seriously. He was plump, pink, and in a number of ways smooth. "Before we get into this, let me make one thing clear, major. Hoover is a maniac. We can agree on that, I think. And a lot of the people in the Bureau behave badly because he's got them scared crazy—which isn't all that hard to do if you work at it long enough and with enough authority. He's also a terrific publicity hound. If he were as good a cop as he is a press agent, I'd be a fan, almost. The question is what have you done, and what is he likely to do? And how the hell do we manage to play this without any more friction than we absolutely need?"

"I appreciate your frankness, general," Trumbull said. Armistead waved the cigar in a generous arc. He didn't say anything but waited, leaning back. Trumbull ran through the events of the previous twelve hours. He was as brief as he could be.

The general asked about the bodies in the farmhouse. "You found them?"

"No, sir. I didn't, but the MP unit that did reported them in to headquarters. They radioed me. So I was there pretty soon afterward."

"As far as you know, that was one of the houses the Bureau had covered earlier in the day?"

"They should have. It was within the perimeter of their search."

"So that evens out the business about the train," Armistead said, puffing on his cigar.

"The train? Is there a problem there?"

"There have been certain questions about your order that Penn Station should be covered. They came up empty."

"Yes, well, one of the Germans thought of getting off at Jamaica while they were riding in. Otherwise, they might have gone all the way. They'd bought tickets for Penn Station."

"Fine."

"They're upset about that?"

"They've asked certain questions. It's up to us to infer who is or isn't upset. The real question seems to be whether you threatened to call the local police into the case."

"I did make that threat, sir. It was the quickest way I could persuade Dunbar to let me talk to the two men who'd turned themselves in. I never intended to carry it out. But I think he was going to make me go through channels and I had no idea how long it would take before somebody in the Pentagon twisted the right arm over at Justice."

"When he refused to let you see these two men, was there a witness?"

"No, sir. Do I need witnesses?"

"It might not be a bad idea. Dunbar keeps his rear protected. I'd hate to see one of our people doing any less."

There didn't seem to be any reply that was necessary. Trumbull waited. The general puffed at the cigar, took it out of his mouth, examined the long even ash as if he were admiring his own handiwork, and said, "Keep on with it, but watch yourself. And keep in mind what the shape of it is likely to be at the end."

"Sir?"

"Assuming we get out of this without a lot of egg on our faces and without a lot more dead bodies, it's going to be a triumph for J. Edgar Hoover."

"I'm not sure I follow you, sir," Trumbull said.

"You'll follow me. His reputation, earned or not, justified or not, is a powerful weapon. Let the enemy think that he's as good as he thinks he is and they may not try another stunt like this for a while. For public confidence here and for the propaganda value abroad, it's going to be Hoover's triumph. You got that?"

"Yes, sir."

"With that understanding, I want you to tag along, observe, try to keep them from doing anything too flagrantly stupid. It's a tough assignment. You can't get any glory out of this. And you can very easily screw up. Within the service, though, you can rest assured that we have our eyes on you. We're counting on you."

"I appreciate that, general."

"Now, how about a drink?"

He checked into the Statler, went up to the room, and sat there for a couple of hours, listening to the radio, turning the knob from one station to another. Four dead bodies ought to make it into the news, he supposed. Or a report of a German submarine landing spies on Long Island's beaches?

Peter had to figure that they were keeping quiet about the submarine. And that they just hadn't found the bodies yet. The myth was that crime was dangerous, that there was risk to it. But apparently it took a whole lot of bad luck to get caught at anything. It was dismayingly easy to kill four people and just drive away . . .

The soap operas gave way to the kiddie programs. Jack Armstrong the All-American Boy, Captain Midnight, and Tom Mix seemed to be in collusion with the Germans, trying to keep the public from suspecting that they were in danger.

Take a tip from Tom,
Go and tell your mom,
Shredded Ralston cain't be beat . . .

What was the matter with these people? Didn't they understand that there was a war on, that their survival was at stake?

Annoyed, frustrated, angry at himself for the helplessness he felt, he went downstairs, crossed the street, bought a bottle of gin and a couple of small cans of grapefruit juice, stopped at a drugstore, and went back up to listen to the news again, think, drink a Sea Breeze or two, and rest. He lay on the bed, sipping his gin-and-grapefruit-juice concoction, hearing Uncle Don prattle on to all the boys and girls out there in Radioland, and trying not to blame himself. He'd felt so clever about making up the story about having dinner, and calling out and waving, that he hadn't kept his mind on the real issue. He still could have followed Karl, could have stuck with him. After that last conversation about dinner, Karl would have been less suspicious. It would have been easier to track him to whatever hotel he'd chosen.

Bullshit! He'd been lucky to get out of it alive. To admit that he was afraid of Karl was the beginning of wisdom. It didn't make the prospect of dinner any brighter, either. Karl was no fool. And if he began to suspect Peter, if there were the slightest hint of Peter's duplicity, then Karl's reaction would be obvious and immediate. Whatever Peter did, the dangers were clear. He was tempted to walk downstairs, cross the street, go into Penn Station, and buy a ticket to . . . where could he run? He'd be safe for a matter of weeks, maybe, but what kind of life would it be with people on his trail all the time?

Maybe Karl would fail to show up. Peter would be spared the encounter, but his long-term prospects would be bleak. He wasn't sure what he wanted. All he knew for sure was that it wasn't fair. He'd killed his German. If everybody in the United States did as much, the war would be over and won. He decided to drink to that, opened another little can of grapefruit juice, poured it into the bathroom tumbler, and laced it with another dollop of gin from his pint bottle. He drank it off, then stripped down and took a shower. He toweled himself dry, combed his hair with the pocket comb he'd picked up with the toothbrush and the razor in the drugstore down the block. What he needed was more clothing. Fresh underwear. It was dispiriting to get out of a shower and put on the same clothes one had worn before.

At last, there was news on the radio. From North Africa. From Washington. From New York. With beeps that were supposed to be Morse code at different pitches. But there was nothing about a house on Long Island full of corpses. Or about a submarine landing people on the Amagansett beach. They were keeping it quiet. It had to be that. The soldier on the beach couldn't have failed to report it, could he? Or maybe they didn't believe him. Maybe there was nothing to worry about at all.

He turned off the radio, locked his door, and went off to meet Karl at the Berliner Bar. Eighty-sixth Street looked strange, although Peter argued with himself that it was his own nervousness rather than anything unusual about the street. Still, its lights seemed to him too garish and sharp, its shop windows too cutely staged. In a bakery window, there was an elaborate wedding cake, or cakelike construction, that had been decorated a long time ago and was starting to discolor now around the edges. Next door, there was a display of hospital supplies, trusses, and prosthetic devices, disposed in a rigidly geometrical pattern. Beyond that, there was the small shop of a clockmaker, his narrow window cluttered with timepieces of various sizes. *Gather ye rosebuds.*

The Berliner Bar was one of a number of establishments that had catered to Yorkville's large German population for years. There were half a dozen of these places, all within three or four blocks, and they were as little affected by the declaration of war as the spaghetti parlors down in Little Italy—or around the country in small cities and towns. Not even the German-American Bund, a pro-Nazi group active there before the war, had dulled Yorkville's attractiveness. People still came here to enjoy the schnitzels and wursts of the old country, to drink beer out of steins, and to sing the old songs. The waitresses were dressed in the style of their cousins back in Germany with their dirndls and their long blond braids.

Peter entered, looked for Karl. There was a woman in a booth who had the same angle of cheek and chin, the same way of carrying herself, as Elfreda. But the face, when she turned her head, was altogether different.

He tried to get hold of himself. Once more, he felt a queasy urge to flee.

"Peter! Am I late?"

"No, no," Peter said. "I just got here, myself."

"Good, good. Had a drink yet?"

"No."

"A beer, then? Or something stronger?" Karl inquired, leading the way past the bar to a table.

"Something stronger, I think," Peter said. He wasn't optimistic about mixing beer with the gins he'd drunk back at the hotel. He wouldn't necessarily have to finish this drink. But not to order anything might be to arouse Karl's suspicion—which was the last thing in the world Peter wanted.

A waitress came up to take their order. Karl asked for a schnapps. Peter ordered a gin and tonic. She went off to fetch the drinks.

"I wondered whether you'd come," Peter said, plunging in at once.

"Why not?" Karl asked.

"I had the impression this morning that you wanted to keep clear of me. Of all of us. And I can understand why. I mean, with a different project than the rest of us have, it could be perfectly reasonable . . ." He broke off. He wasn't sure where he was going. And Karl was looking at him as if he were about to fling a pan full of hot butter.

But quite abruptly Karl's expression changed. He smiled. "But I'm here, you see," he said. "I trust you."

"Well, what do I do now?"

"Eat dinner, I should think," Karl said.

"I mean, if I'm reading it right, and you're going to be otherwise occupied . . . You're the leader. You're in charge." Peter saw now how to do it. "You're the one I'm supposed to be taking orders from. What are the orders?"

"Go to the meeting tomorrow. Take orders from Willi. Our contingent has been sadly diminished, wouldn't you say?"

The waitress brought the drinks and set them down, putting them on little square cork coasters that bore the logo of Beck's beer.

"I guess it has," Peter agreed.

"You'll have better luck, perhaps, with the other fellows," Karl said. "To luck." He lifted his glass.

Peter lifted his. They drank. After a moment, Peter asked, "Do you think it's likely, though? Knowing who they are and what they're like?"

"What difference does it make what I think?"

"This difference. Suppose that I go to the meeting tomorrow. And suppose that Willi isn't there. He could have been picked up. Or could have disappeared. Or got into any of a thousand kinds of trouble. It's possible, isn't it?"

"Anything's possible," Karl agreed. "What's your point?"

"What do I do then?"

"I'm sure you'll think of something, old man."

"I might have, yesterday. But after what happened today . . . after the way you contrived to get us all committed to the project?" Peter assessed Karl's expression, or tried to. He'd make a good poker player, Peter thought. He took a sip of his drink. "What I'm getting at is that I'd like a transfer. From their project to yours, whatever it is."

"You don't know what you're talking about."

"No, not altogether," Peter admitted. At least Karl wasn't being overtly hostile. "But I know what they're supposed to be doing. And I have a sense of what the chances are. It just seems a waste. Of their lives. Of my life. Of all that involvement of time and effort. I don't see that anything's likely to come of it."

"You volunteered," Karl pointed out.

"I had no idea what the project was. And I was eager to get out of the internment camp. I had no idea it was going to be . . ." He groped. He wasn't sure how far to go. But what could he lose? ". . . both suicidal and silly."

"And you think that what I'm doing must be sensible and safe, is that it?"

"I don't know. I wouldn't have thought it was risk free. But there must be some point to it. Most of the others were clowns, more or less funny or sad, depending on where you were sitting. You're not a clown."

"No?"

"You know you're not," Peter went on. "And my guess is that they grafted you onto this because they wanted to get something useful accomplished. That you're a kind of ringer . . ."

"If I weren't, I'd say no. And if I were, I'd still say no, wouldn't I?" Karl asked. He signaled to the waitress for another round.

"The fact remains that you have a different objective. It can't be as foolish as what the rest of us are supposed to do."

"What would you say to sinking the Staten Island ferry?" Karl asked. He kept a perfectly straight face for about ten seconds, then broke into a broad grin and a single bark of laughter. "Hang on for a minute, will you? I'll be back before the drinks get here." He went back toward the men's room.

Peter finished his gin and tonic, needing both the liquid and the liquor. It had been nervous work and he had no idea whether he was doing very well or very badly. Or something in between. Maybe it would be reassuring if he left it open for Karl to get in touch with him, rather than asking for an address. He couldn't push too hard.

He sat there, jiggling the empty ice cubes in his glass and wondering where Karl was. He pushed the glass away from him and fiddled with the salt and pepper shakers. The man seemed to be taking a long time in the bathroom. Had he skipped out? Was that possible? Yes, of course, it was possible. Anything was possible. But Karl wouldn't leave loose ends like that.

Peter looked for the waitress. Karl had promised to return by the time the waitress had brought the new round of drinks. So, if the waitress came, that would mean Karl was coming wouldn't it? Peter realized he was being stupid.

He slid the pepper shaker along the table and caught it with his other hand. That was stupid too.

"Peter King?"

He looked up. There were two men in dark suits and striped ties.

"Yes?" he asked, looking up, holding their eyes with his own, or trying to.

"Come with us, would you? We don't want any trouble. We're with the Federal Bureau of Investigation."

ELEVEN

It never occurred to him to doubt them. He wondered how Karl had managed to set him up, how Karl had been able to accomplish what he had tried to work out and couldn't. But Peter filed that question away. He had other, more immediate problems to solve. What could he use as a weapon?

Unscrewing the top of the pepper shaker wasn't hard, really. It just took an act of concentration to keep their eyes fixed on his, as he stared at them like a trapped animal. Then he felt the metal top come loose. He threw the pepper at them, using the instant of their surprised, sneezy immobilization to bound up from the table and make his break.

It almost worked. The closer one, who was a little shorter than the other, got enough of the pepper in his face so that he doubled over, his eyes closed and streaming, his sneezes repetitive and explosive. The other one managed to duck or close his eyes. And he was able to lunge after Peter, charging toward the door past the startled customers and the annoyed waitresses. Peter made it to the door, made it out to the sidewalk, assumed that there would be more FBI agents waiting there, was relieved that there weren't, and he turned to make his getaway dash. He didn't see the woman.

He didn't knock her down. He didn't even bump her very hard. But he did graze her, and he didn't stop to apologize either to her or her escort. The escort, a middle-aged man, bald, and dressed in evening clothes, was Old World in his bearing and his standards. He took the inadvertent jostle of the woman on his arm as a personal affront, reached out, grabbed at Peter, caught him by the wrist in a surprisingly strong grip, and barked, "Ruffian!"

"I'm sorry. I didn't see her."

"Apologize to the lady," the bald man insisted.

"I'm sorry. I said I was sorry."

But the delay was enough for the men from whom he'd been fleeing to catch up. The taller one grabbed him. The other one was still sneezing but he'd recovered himself well enough to be able to keep up.

"One more stunt like that, and you're a dead man, you hear?" the taller man said, grabbing at Peter's arm almost as tightly as the offended bald gentleman.

Peter's spirits sank. It wasn't just a phrase. He could feel something physical, down around his stomach and diaphragm, falling away. Another couple of inches and he'd have got by that woman, and the man with her, and he'd have got away from these FBI people . . .

But they weren't! He looked around for the car, the backup team, the local police who might be cooperating. There was nobody but these two thugs—who hadn't shown any identification. That was how Karl had done it. He had been the bird dog, but not for any FBI agents. These were German agents.

Which might not be so bad, he thought. Not if he played it right.

"Where are we going?" he asked.

"You'll see," the taller one said. The other one was still sniffling.

"You've got identification?" Peter asked.

"You got a fondness for pain?" his captor asked. He had Peter's arm twisted behind his back. All he had to do was raise the arm a little and he could produce a sharp, searing pain. A little too much, and the arm would break.

Still, it wasn't hopeless. They were out on a public street, walking south on Second Avenue. They'd gone a couple of blocks. These people—if Peter was right about them—didn't want to attract attention. There had to be some way of using their vulnerability against them. A cop? Some passersby?

151

But the block was almost deserted. There had been pedestrians back up on Eighty-sixth. They were near Eighty-second, and nobody was around but a teenager walking a dog, and an old woman across the street, carrying bundles. They turned east at the corner of Eighty-second and stopped at the steps of an old graystone, once a private house but now broken up into apartments. There was a series of mailboxes and a panel of buttons and nameplates inside the front door. The shorter man had a key, which he produced from one of his pockets. He hunted for the right key, sneezed, found the key, and opened the door.

"Inside," the taller one said, twisting the arm.

"This is a mistake," Peter said.

"We'll talk about it inside."

Peter walked through the doorway. The hall was dimly lit, which was a mercy. The old wallpaper was coming off in strips. There were odd stains and bulges up on the ceiling. The linoleum on the floor was worn through to the backing. There was a smell of old garbage—one hoped it was garbage rather than cooking. The banister was shaky and the treads sagged, but the staircase held. The second-floor hallway was slightly less dim than the entrance below. There were four doors, all of them scarred and crusted with layer upon layer of peeling paint in a murky chocolate. They stopped at one of them and the shorter man used three more keys to open the locks. Peter went on into the apartment. Or room, actually. It was a single room with a pullman kitchen—gas stove, refrigerator, and sink against one wall, with a curtain in front of it. It looked to be a shower curtain and even had mildew at the bottom. There may have been a bathroom. There were two windows overlooking a courtyard. There was a fire escape, Peter noticed, wondering whether it might even be of some use. He could imagine the feeling in his calves, a kind of muscular hallucination of clambering down the metal rungs of that fire-escape ladder.

There was a wooden folding chair near the far window and an upended orange crate. There was an iron cot along the wall opposite the windows. There was a foot locker in front of the cot—a coffee table to the cot's sofa.

The shorter man closed the door and locked the locks. For a room in which there was nothing at all of value, the security was impressive. There was even a New York Police lock with its iron bar and metal plate in the floor.

The taller man let Peter go. Peter glanced at the window. There was no way. The man smiled, having noticed Peter's glance. Producing a long knife with a triangular blade from a sheath that was attached to his belt, he said, "Go on, try it."

"You want to explain what's going on?" Peter asked.

"What's not clear?"

"You're not from the FBI. That's for sure."

"So? If you know that, then what's to explain?"

"What your connection is with Karl. We're on the same side. You and Karl, and Karl and I. So you and I, we're together."

"Turn out your pockets," the man said.

"You want to call Karl? You want to do that?" Peter asked.

"What I want to do is get this over with, you dumb fucker. That bit back there with the pepper? You think that was cute? I ought to cut your goddamn liver out for you. Just do what I tell you, okay? Empty out your pockets."

Peter emptied his pockets. He had a hundred and fifty dollars with him in cash. A handkerchief. His hotel key. That was annoying. He had to assume that they'd go and search his room. They'd find the rest of the money. If they were going to kill him, he hated to tip his assassins. But they couldn't just kill him.

"It doesn't make any sense for Germany to have invested all that time and money training me and sending me over here, and then have a couple of German agents kill me before I've done the job I'm supposed to do. You've got to check this out, I tell you," Peter said.

The man picked up the money and the hotel key, put them into his pocket, and said, "Lie down on the bed."

"What are you going to do to me?" Peter asked.

"Just lie down, will you? You want to find that rope?" The latter question was addressed to the shorter man who had been standing near the sink, dabbing at his eyes and nose with a handkerchief that was none too clean. But it answered Peter's question, at least in part. They were going to tie him up. What for? He believed his own argument, could not imagine that they wouldn't see its logic, and therefore he hoped that they were going to keep him tied up while they sent back for more instructions. If things turned out well, Peter supposed he'd have more to trade, more names and faces with which to bargain.

Even so, he wasn't enthusiastic about being tied up on that

cot. The shorter of the men had begun cutting a length of clothesline into shorter pieces. There was a dish towel on the chipped enamel drainboard of the sink. The taller man threw it to the other one, who held it up in front of Peter's face.

"Open your mouth."

"I'm not going to scream," Peter said, his teeth clenched, his lips barely moving.

The shorter man punched Peter in the midriff, hitting his solar plexus and knocking his breath out of him. He gasped. The man stuck the sour dishcloth into Peter's mouth and pushed him backward. He collapsed onto the cot. There was no point in struggling.

The short man started to tie him up. He wasn't having an easy time of it because he was still sniffling. And every now and then, he had to wipe his eyes. Peter figured it was something to exploit. If he tensed his muscles and flexed them, he could keep a little play in the rope. He had no idea how long he'd be tied up. The looser the better. It was the only thing he could think of.

They tied his feet together and then tied them to the bottom of the cot. His hands they tied down separately. He lay on his stomach embracing the musty mattress with his wrists tied to the metal bars that ran the length of the cot on either side. He could turn his head toward the wall or toward the room. He was facing toward the room, watching as the two men emptied the closet. There were pieces of radio equipment, fairly large, that fitted into suitcases. A transmitter, almost certainly, and a receiver too. There was a hot plate. There was a photographic enlarger. There was a percolator. And there were some odd items of clothing, including the most garish jacket Peter could remember having seen in his life. It looked like a stage costume. Orange and black stripes, it was cut like a blazer and had brass buttons . . .

And a straw boater? It was too silly.

Altogether, it was as much stuff as the two of them could manage to carry. They piled it into the foot locker and put it next to the door. Then the shorter one, sniffling one last time, went to the stove and blew out the pilot light. He turned on all the burners. And the oven.

"We will be back tomorrow to cut the ropes off you. And to telephone the police about the suicide."

154

"The door!" the other one urged. The gas was hissing into the room. Understandably, he wanted to get the hell out of there.

So did Peter.

The shorter man opened the door. They moved their baggage out into the hall. The door closed again, and one after another the various bolts slid closed. Peter could hear the footsteps on the staircase, descending in an exquisite diminuendo.

Horst had been puzzled at first when he'd come back to the lobby of the Commodore Vanderbilt Hotel to find that his companion had vanished. He'd gone down to the men's room to look for Rudi, in case Rudi had gone down there to look for him—that was where Horst had said he was going when he'd gone to make the call to the FBI.

But no Rudi. It crossed Horst's mind that Rudi might have gone to another telephone booth to make exactly the same call, but that seemed too much of a coincidence. It was enough to suppose that Rudi had simply gone home—to wherever he had lived before the war. That was what Horst thought he'd probably do, himself. He had money now, more money than he'd ever had in his whole life. He planned to buy a boat with it and make a decent living, chartering it out a week or two at a time. Gas was not so easy to get, maybe, but the war wouldn't last forever. And some of these rich people who chartered yachts had connections and could get the gasoline.

A German citizen, Horst Lempe had come to America in the early thirties to find work, even though he was a believer in Nazism. He found its professions of racial superiority entirely plausible and he liked its moral toughness. He hated the leftists and the Jews whom he saw as Germany's enemies and his own, sapping the strength of hard-working and upright men everywhere. He had lived for several years in the States, working on pleasure craft mostly. In '35, he'd gone back to Germany to participate in the new program of the Fatherland his own father had fought and died for in the Great War.

He'd gone to Bremen and found a job in the shipyards. He'd been around boats and ships all his life, was willing to work, and was good at what he did. And there were sailors in Bremen, so the odds were good that he'd meet people like himself, strong, hearty companions. He wasn't interested in limp-wristed pansies. He wasn't like that. It was just that he was uncomfortable around women and liked his own kind better. But the Party put homosexuals in the same category as Jews, Gypsies, Communists, and mental defectives, persecuting them as if they were in some way a threat to the ideals of Nazism in which Horst still believed.

But that belief became more and more difficult to cling to. More and more, he had to pay attention to the business of survival. A man never knew whether the good-looking fellow down along the bar was out for a good time or looking for someone to turn in to the police—either to save his own skin or to bargain for that of a dear friend.

Horst found the ground slipping out from under him. His own country had turned him into a kind of foreigner. It was even worse than life in the States had been. Less and less idly, he thought about giving up his apartment, going through France to Spain to South America, and then crossing from Mexico into California or Texas. It was always there as a possibility, something to do if the situation got just a little worse. But then the war was declared. The police began following him around like dogs that can smell the fear and are enraged by it. They knew and were toying with him. He stopped going to bars, stopped talking to people.

And then they offered him this passage on a submarine to America. He thought of Port Washington or places across the sound in Connecticut where he could get himself a berth on a graceful old cruiser with a beautifully kept teak deck . . .

He couldn't believe his luck. Of course, he accepted, having a pretty good idea what would happen to him if he didn't leap at this chance. He went through the training. He landed in Amagansett and came to New York, where he called the FBI to warn them and square himself with his adopted country.

He asked for a room at the Commodore's registration desk, signed in, and told them his bags were still in Grand Central. They asked him for a deposit, which he gave them. He went up to look at the room, approved, and tipped the bellman a half a dollar. He ate lunch in the Oyster Bar in Grand Central and then went back up to the room to take a nap.

He left a call for eight o'clock so he could wake up, shower, and go out early enough in the evening to enjoy himself. He had no question at all in his mind about what he wanted to do. He was free now. Without the terrible risk of somebody denouncing him to the police, he could go down to one of the bars in Greenwich Village and pick up someone, or get picked up by someone, and celebrate. A little good, hearty masculine fun.

He was dead.

That was the assumption to work on, at any rate. The fact that Peter was able to move his hands back and forth a little bit, and that he could just manage to get the clothesline in contact with the outer edge of the bedspring on one side, was merely tantalizing, a part of the torture. He had no idea whether to exert himself and fight to slice through the bonds or not. If he did try, then the exertion would increase his need for oxygen and he'd take in more and more of the gas from the hissing stove. On the other hand, if he didn't try to escape, then he would be, in a real way, collaborating with them in his own execution.

All he needed was one hand. With that, he'd be able to get his other hand and then the rest would be easy. The trouble was that it took so much effort to pull on the clothesline and get the wrist in contact with the sharp edge of the spring. But because the guy had been sneezing and his eyes had been watering, there was just enough give to allow Peter to do that. And the plan was simple enough—to saw through the line on that bedspring edge. But he was breathing hard and that scared him. He could smell the gas, or not the gas but whatever the gas company put into it so that people would know that the stove was on and gas was leaking. He *was* grateful to the gas company. He *was* alerted. He was fully cognizant of the fact that the stove was leaking and the gas was pouring forth from all four burners and the oven unit below.

He had to keep the pressure on that now aching arm, to keep the line as hard on the steel edge of the bedspring as he could, to believe that it was possible, that each stroke was weakening a strand of the line. It wasn't very good rope. Just clothesline. Not intended for hard wear, after all. It couldn't be much longer. And the room's size and high ceilings were an advantage. The building once had been a more or less gracious dwelling for some prosperous member of the middle class. No mansion, maybe, but a comfortable house. The ceilings had to be twelve feet up. And the gas? Did it rise or fall? He couldn't remember.

It felt a little different. Or he thought it did. There seemed to be a little more play than there had been before. Of course, that could be a sign that he'd tugged the knot tighter. It was impossible to see around to where he was working. It was all by feel. And he had scraped his wrist several times. There was blood, although he had no idea how much. He was also feeling the beginnings of a dull headache, which could be the result of the gas or of the effort and the tension.

But there *was* play in that hand. Peter tugged. He yanked hard. It hurt but he yanked again. He felt the line begin to give. He pushed again and scraped more. He tried to keep calm and to breathe normally, not to let the prospect of success excite him too much. Peter scraped and tore and yanked and then felt it almost give and then really all but yield, and then, yes, his right hand was free.

It was messy. He'd torn the skin pretty badly. He flopped over and could almost reach the other arm. He flopped again, harder. And a third time. He could reach it but not comfortably. It was arduous work, trying to pick the knot open without being able to see what he was doing. And his right arm and wrist hurt a lot now, sore and abraded as they were. It was infuriating to have to work blind. But after a number of unsuccessful attempts, he found one strand of the knot and that led to another, and he pulled the line until he found an end. After that, it was a matter of feeling the end, working up the line, coming to the knot, and pulling whatever crossed his free end, over and over again.

Peter had no idea how long he had been working. He felt his headache as much more severe. He was beginning to be giddy, too. But he kept on with what was now agonizingly close and possible. He didn't want those two bastards to come back and see him with one arm free, the other all but untied, and yet still there, on the cot, dead as a carp. He yanked the left arm and it came loose. It was free. He flopped further around, lowered himself into a fetal crouch, and was able to swing around and over the bed. He couldn't reach the knots that held his feet, but he could tip the bed over. He crawled along the floor and got to the stove. He reached up and turned off the gas. He pulled out the broiler pan and threw it through the window, breaking the glass and allowing some fresh air to come into the room. He pulled out that drawer from the cabinet under the sink. He was in luck. He found a small paring knife they'd left behind. He reached around to the clothesline on the top side of the bed and cut through it. Then he stood up, grabbed the dishrag they'd used as a gag, tied it around his bloody wrist, and went for the door.

One of the three locks was the kind that needed a key, even from the inside. But there was the fire escape. Peter unlatched the window, opened it, climbed out onto the fire escape, and, just as in the vision, saw himself, felt himself descending, the calf muscles at last doing what they were supposed to do.

TWELVE

There was a telephone booth on a street corner, but he didn't have a nickel to make a phone call. He had to panhandle, approaching passersby as he walked down Second Avenue. "Excuse me, sir. I've been robbed. I need a nickel for the phone . . ."

Some disbelieved him and walked on, uncomfortable with the declaration of need. Others found his story plausible enough but unacceptable, distasteful. A youngish man in a dirty cream-colored raincoat gave him a dime. He didn't have any nickels.

But the dime would work. Peter called information, and it came clinking down into the coin-return slot. Information gave him the number he wanted—of the Federal Bureau of Investigation. Peter redeposited the dime and called that number.

He asked for the man in charge of the investigation of the Long Island beach incident.

"I'm sorry? What Long Island beach incident is that, sir?" the voice at the other end of the line asked.

It was a male voice, crisp and efficient in its rhythms, but still that of a switchboard operator. Bureaucracy being what it was, the man at the switchboard was not the first person to be informed of the important business of the Bureau. "Eight German agents were landed on the beach last night at Amagansett," Peter told the switchboard man. "I'm sure that the FBI knows about it and that they're investigating. I want to talk to someone who is connected with that investigation. I have some information that's important. I want to give it to the right people."

"One moment, sir. I'll connect you with someone who can help you."

He waited. He began to get impatient. "Hello? Hello? Anybody there?" But he'd been put on hold. He supposed they were recording the call. Or trying to trace it. He wondered how long he ought to risk it, before they sent their agents out to pick him up. And then he realized that his position was different now. He'd been attacked. Damned near killed!

But the bastards who'd tried to kill him had done him a favor!

It was exciting and frightening, the kind of feeling he remembered from playing chess, when he'd glimpsed a possible combination. Only he didn't have time to think it all the way through, looking at all the possible countermoves. It came down to a matter of basic trust. These FBI people were our guys, after all. That had to count for something.

There were several clicks, and he was at last put through to a man who identified himself as "Special Agent Harrison. Can I help you?"

"Are you connected with the investigation of the landing of eight German agents on the beach at Amagansett last night?"

"No, but I know about it."

"I'm one of them. I'm at a phone booth at the corner of Seventy-eighth Street and Second Avenue. There's just been an attempt on my life. Could you send somebody to pick me up?"

"We'll be there in fifteen minutes," the man promised.

"Faster, if you can manage," Peter urged. "They'll kill me if they see me. I'm out here on the street corner in a phone booth."

"We'll do what we can."

He hung up. He stood there in the phone booth. The door was open. He'd left it open so that the light wouldn't go on. He tried to think ahead. There was proof—on his hands and up in that room he'd just escaped from—that people had tried to kill him. Nobody else knew he was here in New York except the Germans. So the FBI would have to believe that it was a couple of Nazis who'd just tried to murder him. Which meant that the Nazis thought he was an enemy. So the FBI had to see him as a friend, didn't they?

He couldn't see any holes in it.

Those two clowns had issued him credentials. In a little while, it'd be over. He'd tell what he knew, and get his hands bandaged, and that'd be the end of it.

They went over it and over it. Coffee was sent in. A doctor showed up to examine the wrist, paint it with antiseptic, and bandage it. Dunbar sat there, doodling on a yellow evidence pad, listening, while two other men took down every word that was said.

"So, when you made it to the beach, there was a soldier?"

"That's right," Peter said.

"So, why didn't you speak up then? Why didn't you tell the soldier that you and the others had just come off a U-boat?"

"To tell you the truth, I had no idea it was going to go the way it did. I wanted to get ashore and just walk away from it. I wasn't planning to blow up anything."

"But the others were, weren't they?"

"Some of them might have been. Some of them might have come along for the ride. I had no idea which were which."

"And it never occurred to you to let us figure out who was dangerous and who wasn't?"

"I didn't see how I could do that without turning myself in."

"Aha!" Dunbar exclaimed.

"Or without turning in the woman. I wanted to protect her. And some of the others might have been . . . perfectly innocent."

"You'd all sworn an oath to Adolf Hitler and the Nazi government, hadn't you?"

Peter nodded.

"So why should I believe you now?"

"I called you, didn't I? I didn't have to do that."

"Didn't you? They'd tried to kill you. You were afraid they'd try again and that they'd be more efficient the second time. That's one possibility. Or maybe they just staged this. It's a dumb way to try to kill somebody, if you ask me."

"Why would they have staged it? Why would I have called you if I hadn't been afraid?"

"You tell me," Dunbar said. "Somebody want to get some hot coffee? This is cold."

One of the stenotypists came in with a fresh roll of paper for his machine. The other one waited for him to set up, then took a break.

Peter tried one more time. He didn't have any particular hope that this time he'd be more convincing than before. But he couldn't think what else to do. He was telling the truth. Sooner or later, somebody was going to have to believe it. At least check it out. He told how he'd intended to find out more before making his move. He wanted to be able to give them as much information as he could, to make the best possible deal for himself. He hadn't killed anybody there on Long Island, but he'd been there. And he was afraid that unless he was able to produce some really important information, his presence at that farmhouse would be enough to get him locked up.

"Oh, yeah. I can see that," Dunbar agreed. "But if they hadn't tried to kill you and you didn't need protection, maybe you wouldn't have called. Is that possible?"

"I might not have called right then. I wanted to find out what Karl was supposed to be doing. His mission was different from ours."

"So you say."

"So he said."

"But you can't prove that. And you don't know what it is."

"That's right," Peter said. "I think the reason they tried to kill me was that they were suspicious because I'd been pushing too hard."

"Maybe. Let's go back to Germany one more time. From the beginning."

The man brought the coffee. It came in a cardboard container with little cardboard ears for handles. Dunbar actually used the handles. He hadn't offered Peter any coffee.

"Twelve guys, to start with," Dunbar recapitulated. "And nobody uses last names. That right?"

"Eleven guys. One woman."

And so on. For hours.

Peter was exhausted. He felt gritty all over. His eyes were itchy. The light in the room was much too bright. It wasn't that lamp-in-the-face of the third degree, but a kind of sickly glare from the overhead fixtures. There was an electric clock on the wall which seemed to be Peter's adversary as much as Dunbar was. All Peter had to do, he told himself, was wait out the time. Sooner or later, Dunbar would get tired and give up. Someone else would come in to take Dunbar's place. But at least Peter would have won the first round, would have endured through the first shift.

The next interrogator would probably be more congenial anyway. Peter wasn't just thinking of the odds and of Dunbar's lack of charm, but of the methods of interrogation. There was the bad guy to set you up and the good guy came in to finish you off. You'd talk to him. They were just doing their job. The hands of the clock were doing theirs, sweeping around to bring in the dawn. Peter was the only one who had the freedom to do what he wanted. The rest were his creatures, his puppets. He worked the strings. If he hadn't made that phone call, these people would all be at home in their beds.

And eventually Dunbar got up, smiled, adjusted his tie, and announced, "You can sit here as long as you like, and just keep on smiling for whatever it will get you. But remember, we're going to fry your ass. You hear? You're going to fry and I'm going to be there to watch you."

The next fellow was a uniformed army officer, which surprised Peter a little. He'd expected that the new guy would be less formal rather than more. But he started out pretty much the way Peter had assumed he would, asking whether Peter had eaten.

"No, I was supposed to have dinner with Karl—but I never got that far. I had one drink a thousand years ago."

"I'm not sure I can get you another drink, but I can work a sandwich and coffee. Can you stand any more coffee?"

"As the dormouse said, I can have more but not less. I haven't had any."

"Jesus! I'm John Trumbull, by the way. G-2. That's Military Intelligence. We've got to go over some of this, I'm afraid. I've read the first part of the transcript. But there are a few questions I've got. And then we can see where we are. Any objections?"

"No, no objections."

Peter and Trumbull went through it once in short form and then with the explanations. Why didn't they use last names? Peter explained that the Abwehr didn't want any of them to be vulnerable. If one of the team got caught or turned coat, he wouldn't be able to name all the others.

"You think they expected some of you to turn yourselves in?"

"I'm not sure. I never could decide. They were certainly allowing for it. But I don't think they were planning on it. I mean, what would it get them? Where are they better off, now that I've blown the whistle."

"And you're not the first one."

"I'm not? Who else?"

"Willi and Kurt turned themselves in late in the afternoon," he said. "So that leaves out there only Horst and Rudi and Karl."

"It's two different operations. Horst and Rudi never seemed to me to be serious threats to anything. But Karl is different."

"Of course, that's what Willi thought about you, for that matter. You and Karl," Trumbull said.

"Just flattery. I mean, you can't imagine the low level of what they called training. It was a joke, mostly. Karl was the only one of us, as far as I know, who had contacts here in America. He told me, straight out, that he had a different assignment . . ."

"But he never told you what it was?"

Peter shook his head. "That's what I was hoping to find out. When I had that, then I was planning to come in. I'd have something to trade. Now . . ." He shrugged.

A man came in with coffee and sandwiches. There were ham and Swiss, roast beef, and turkey sandwiches. Peter picked the ham and Swiss. The major took a half of the roast beef. Between bites, he asked, "What was he like in training, this Karl person. Terrific? Better than the rest of you?"

"No, not especially. He was good. But not so good as to make the rest of us wonder. It wasn't on the training, really, but on the exercise that I understood that he was different." Peter explained about the training exercise and how Karl had killed the Gestapo man. It was both the manner of the killing and Karl's need to escape that were impressive.

"And you? How did you do on the exercise?"

Peter told how he and Elfreda had managed. It wasn't just an exercise anymore, because of Karl. They'd been in that orchard. Peter had taken the dead man's knife. He told about how he and Elfreda had killed the driver.

When Peter had finished, Trumbull leaned back on the two hind legs of the chair. "As you say, it's not just what people say. It's what they do . . ."

"Yes?" Peter asked, not quite seeing where the major was going.

"Take a break, boys, would you?" The major rocked back down to all four points of the chair, rubbed the side of his nose with his finger, and said, "It's nothing we need to take down. I'm going to be talking. He'll be listening."

The stenotype team got up and went out into the corridor. When the door closed behind them—it worked with one of those air-compressor devices—the major said to Peter, "I can't make any promises, mind you. I have no idea whether I can get approval for this, or what it will amount to if I do. But it seems to me that you were on the right track, really. You were trying to get something to bargain with. Would you still be interested?"

"In what?" Peter said.

"Let's say we put you out there again. Or that you escaped. You'd be right back where you were, before you called us. Not much future on your own. But with Karl's head on a plate, in not such bad shape. Right?"

Peter nodded.

"You think you could find him again?" the major asked.

"I don't know," Peter said. "I could try."

"Of course, there's the other side of it. You'd be looking for him. But he might be looking for you. As you've discovered, it's not without its risks."

"On the other hand," Peter said, "the prospects aren't all that rosy if I stay where I am, are they?"

"They're not terrific," the major said. "You think about it. I'll see what I can do. And until we have another chance to talk, you don't say anything about this to anybody. The Bureau wouldn't be very happy about it."

"I understand."

"You have no idea at all what his mission is?" Trumbull asked.

"My guess is that he's not a saboteur. He's a killer. But I haven't the vaguest idea who it is he's supposed to kill."

"No?"

"In fact, in a funny way, I have the idea that that's what the Gestapo was trying to find out, too. This was an Abwehr operation. The two services didn't get along."

"They didn't get along? I can't understand that," the major said. He got up and went to the door to call a couple of guards.

"This man needs some sleep," the major said. And to Peter, "I'll talk to you tomorrow. Maybe something will come back to you when you're not so exhausted."

"Thanks," Peter said.

"I'll get back to you," Trumbull said.

It was still dark. Far off, two or three blocks away, there was the thin, almost wiry sound of a siren—ambulance or police car—that ululated briefly and then died, underscoring the quiet. A truck engine sputtered, roared, and diminished. The two men walked along the pavement with the sounds of their leather heels clicking on the pavement improbably amplified by the stillness of the city at just a little before half-past five in the morning. The taller one tried to walk more quietly by keeping on the balls of his feet. The other one didn't care. He just walked.

They climbed the steps of the old graystone and let themselves in through the locked double doors. Upstairs, the shorter man opened three locks and then pushed the door open. He had taken a deep breath and was hurrying into the room to turn off the gas and open the window, but he never reached the stove. Out of the corner of his eye, he saw that the cot was empty. Turned over. That Peter King was gone . . .

"What?"

"What's the matter?" the other one asked.

"Look. He's gone. The gas is off. The window's open . . ."

"I never liked it. It was too . . ." He made a rolling motion with his hand that could have meant complicated, or drawn out, or both.

There was no way to answer. The emptiness of the room, the open window, the cot on its side were irrefutable. The taller man shook his head. "We better call in," he said.

"I guess."

The shorter man locked the door as they left, even though it made no particular sense to do so. On the other hand, just to walk away and leave the door open would have been admitting more than he was ready to admit. The taller man waited patiently. They descended the stairs, went back out to the street, and walked to a telephone booth on the corner.

"You want me to do it?" the taller man asked.

The other one nodded.

"You got a nickel?"

The shorter one fished in his pockets and produced a nickel. He held it out. The other one held out his palm like a little boy. He took the nickel and dropped it into the slot. He dialed and waited.

"*Ja?*"

"Kieffer there?" he asked.

"*Ja.* Who's this?"

"Hubschmann."

"Hang on."

He waited. Then Kieffer came on the line. "Yes?"

Hubschmann told him what had happened. That the man was gone. The room was empty. The gas was off. The window was open. "It was Otto's plan," he said, not so much to blame his partner as to exculpate himself.

"We'd better meet."

"Your place?" Hubschmann asked.

"Yours. Half an hour." The line went dead.

"Well?" the shorter man asked.

"I don't think he was very happy."

"That's not surprising. What else?"

"He wants to meet us."

"Now?"

The taller one nodded. "Back at my place."

They went to Hubschmann's apartment, a one-room studio with a little kitchen, not unlike the flat in the graystone. But Kieffer never showed up. Instead, Karl came, the man they'd met earlier that day, and the one who had pointed out their target in the Berliner Bar. He had a key. He also had a gun. He wanted to know what had happened.

They told him. Then explained about the pepper Peter had thrown in their faces and how he'd almost got away then. But they'd caught up with him and brought him to the apartment . . .

"I know that. Kieffer told me that part of it. Then what happened?"

Hubschmann explained about the gas stove and the clothesline. It was something he'd read in a mystery story a few months before, where the killer had wanted to make the death look like suicide. And it was slow and unpleasant. And he'd been angry about the pepper.

"Did the killer get away with it? In the novel?" Karl asked.

"No, there was some other clue . . ."

"Didn't that tell you something?" Karl asked.

"It won't happen next time," Hubschmann said, not quite wheedling but worried.

Karl shot the shorter man from across the room. Then he approached Hubschmann and put the gun directly to his head. "No, it won't," he said. And he squeezed the trigger.

He pressed the gun into Hubschmann's hand. It would look like a lover's quarrel. The one man would appear to have shot the other and then to have turned the gun on himself. As in a mystery story.

THIRTEEN

Horst had a terrible headache. His hangover was particularly savage because of the capriciousness of his selection of drinks the night before—beer at the Café au Lay then rum in some funkier bar down the block, then brandy in another bar, and finally, in the small hours of the morning, mescal in the apartment of a fellow who had brought back several bottles from Mexico, a big Swede with a dumb beefy face and mean eyes but a nice hard body, all muscular angles. Horst had roused himself, looked for his wallet, had been somewhat surprised to find it with the money still in it, and had crept out into the dazzling sunlight of West Fourth Street to find a cab and go back to the hotel. There, he had bathed, drunk several pots of coffee and three iced tomato juices, and swallowed a couple of aspirins. But the solution turned into the problem as the headache got better and the stomach got worse. Now, severely nauseated, he lay on the bed taking deep breaths and trying to imagine grassy fields.

By two, he was still pretty fragile but well enough to move if he had to. And he had an appointment he was resolved to keep. He had to let them know that the mission was no good, had to be called off because the FBI had been warned . . . That was the only fair thing to do. He had to stop the others from trying something crazy. Horst felt that it was the least he ought to do to keep the others from walking into some trap. He assumed there would now be special security at all of those stores. He had to let the other members of the team know this—and his plan was to blame Rudi. For one thing, Horst was a little annoyed about the way Rudi had just disappeared. That was not the decent or gentlemanly thing to do. For another, he had to suppose that Rudi wouldn't keep the appointment at the Automat. It would be easy then to blame Rudi as the man who'd squealed. Horst wanted to divert their attention from himself, after all.

He took a taxi to the Thirty-fourth Street Automat, but he had to get out at the corner of Sixth Avenue. The traffic was tied up on Thirty-fourth with a Con Ed crew working down in a manhole over which they had erected a gaily striped tent. There was a Brink's truck parked next to the tent, so that two lanes of traffic were effectively blocked. Across the street, a van was unloading office furniture. Horns sounded. Pedestrians swarmed into the spaces between the cars and trucks. Policemen looked on with a kind of dejected fatalism. The cabbie was unhappy that he'd committed himself to this impossible block, especially when Horst decided that he could make faster progress on foot.

It was a few minutes after three. Horst didn't want to be the first to arrive. Or the last, either. It was better to be somewhere in the middle. His intention was to sit quietly, let the others talk, and keep his own counsel until the very end. Then, if it looked as though he might get away with it, and if Rudi didn't show up, he'd tell them that the authorities had been warned. At the very least, that would cause a delay of a week or two. And by then, Horst would be away, on the foredeck of some yacht, leaning over a brightly polished railing and looking into clean blue water.

Strange, but he didn't see any of them. The place was not crowded. Indeed, a part of the large eating area was roped off and men were mopping the crushed stone floor with great wheeled buckets and large gray string mops. Here and there, at the section in which there were customers, a man lounged over coffee and a piece of pie or read a newspaper that was folded and propped against the lazy Susan in the center of the table. He looked, but he could not see Karl or Peter, Johann, Elfreda, or Kurt, or Willi . . . Not a single one?

He didn't have to worry after all.

None of them was even going to do so much as light a match in any of those stores. He hadn't needed to call the FBI. Or come to this depressing Automat with its smell of disinfectant, too strong for his still delicate stomach. It was all a joke!

He turned to leave, or at least to go outside to wait there, in the less offensive air, in case any of the others might still show up. He heard someone say, "Hold it right there. Hands up."

He looked around. He saw a man with a submachine gun. A holdup? He looked behind him. There were others. The men mopping the floor. The man with the coffee. They had pistols, revolvers, submachine guns. And they were holding up the Automat? It didn't make sense.

Then it made sense. They were after him.

They were from the FBI. He put his hands over his head. Several of them converged, holding out handcuffs, ankle shackles, billy clubs. He was afraid they were going to hit him. But all they wanted to do was look in his mouth for the cyanide pill they were sure he had hidden in there and frisk him for weapons. It was during this procedure that he saw Willi led from the Con Ed truck into a waiting car. Willi had been the Judas.

And he'd come here to keep them from getting caught.

It was a joke, but not the one he'd been so ready to laugh at.

It was, Trumbull thought, a hell of a show. In an idle hour, he imagined, he might figure out the cost of that operation, multiplying the number of men by an hourly rate and throwing in the cost of the equipment . . . They really did like to come on like Gangbusters.

Compared to that circus, the taproom of the Yale Club seemed sensible and sane. People like himself appeared to be killing time between their afternoon squash game and their evening's amusements. It wasn't the case, of course, but the affectation was of idleness and freedom. Trumbull thought it civilized and, in its way, admirable. Harry Davenport, sitting at a corner table, looked altogether relaxed in his tweeds and his glossy loafers. Trumbull felt a little out of place in uniform, even though Harry was a Deputy Secretary of the Army for Research and Development. He was also a Yale Senior Society brother of Trumbull's and an old friend. Davenport looked tired, a little sallow, and his cheeks and nose showed road maps of blood vessels tracking the pallor. He had a Scotch and water in front of him. Trumbull waved and went to the bar to get himself a mug of stout.

He sat down at the table and said, "It was good of you to see me on such short notice."

"Good of me? No, no, old buddy. I was curious. You are into some very treacherous bureaucratic waters here, you know? If there's anything I can do . . ."

"That's not it, Harry. I mean, the one thing I want from you is your opinion about whether it's worth it for me to go down the drain on this. If that's what it takes, okay. But if I'm just deluding myself, if I've got some kind of martyr complex going, you can talk me out of it. What I'm not after is any kind of rescue from you. If I'm going down, then there's no reason to involve you too."

"I understand."

"It's friendship, of course," Trumbull said. "But it's more than that. You're a hell of a useful man. It'd be a shame for them to lose both of us."

"All right. Enough preface. Now what is it?"

Trumbull told him, in more detail than he'd been able to do on the phone, about the landing of the eight saboteurs, only three of whom were still at large. He told him about Peter King, whom he believed.

"You do?"

Trumbull nodded. "I'd bet on him."

"Against Dunbar, you mean?"

Trumbull nodded.

"How much?" Davenport asked. "How much will you bet? Your whole career? The national security?"

"Well, I'd cover myself as much as I could, but . . . yeah! I think he's telling the truth."

He went on to tell Harry Davenport about Karl, whose threat was of a different magnitude entirely. The operation, without Karl, was small potatoes. But if Peter King was telling the truth, Karl could be really dangerous. "Which is one of the reasons I'm going along with him. What Peter King is saying is the worst possible case, which is what we should be worrying about."

Harry took a sip and thought for a moment. "So?" he asked.

Trumbull took a breath and dived in. "What I thought I'd do is let King go. He wants to find Karl as much as we do. He needs Karl—to bargain with."

"You think he can find him?"

"He might. Or Karl might find King."

"You're throwing him out like chum?"

"Not exactly. He's got a chance. And as far as I can see, it's his best chance. But the Bureau doesn't think so. And that Dunbar is a standard-issue FBI type. He does arithmetic. He thinks we've got it five-eighths closed out. I don't think the other seven together are as dangerous as that one man."

"But the question is whether to let King go or not," Harry prompted.

"No, not really. I've pretty much decided that. The question is how to do it. Do I try to get the Bureau's cooperation—which could take weeks if I ever get it at all? Or do I just go ahead and move on my own?"

"You don't seem to have much use for these people."

Trumbull described the great Horn and Hardart Automat raid with sixty men and ten vehicles to grab one unarmed and startled fellow.

"It sounds funny," Davenport said.

"It was pathetic. The jerks against the losers."

There was a bowl of peanuts on the table. Davenport grabbed a handful, nibbled at them, and nodded. "I think it's worth doing. Cover yourself where you can, though. Don't take more heat than you have to. And if there's anything I can do, call me, you hear?" Draining the last of his drink, Davenport grabbed a last handful of peanuts and said, "Got to run. I'll be seeing you. Good luck, now."

It seemed perfectly normal, but that was because of the room, the building, the middle-class protection that all of them assumed they had. Trumbull sat there in the comfortable room, thinking about the Automat raid and how dumb that had been. The rivalry between bureaucrats and the fear up and down the lines of command were depressing. That poor bastard they'd picked up had seemed to Trumbull less a menace than a victim. Of the same kind of interbureaucratic bullshit. Say the Abwehr and the Gestapo . . .

He caught at that. His mug froze in midair, on the way to his lips. That's what had to have happened. That's why the thing was so screwed up! It was some fancy double-dealing between the two rival outfits. It wasn't that the Germans were stupid. They were just busy as hell trying to cover their asses.

He finished the last of the drink. He felt satisfied by his insight, although it brought him no closer to finding Karl. But he knew what he had to do, himself, with King.

Rudi didn't go straight to his parents' apartment. He didn't want to shock them, ringing the bell and having his mother open the door, see who it was, and drop dead of a heart attack from sheer joy.

Call her, then? But she might have just as strong a reaction to the sound of his voice. His aunt and uncle, then? They would be less excited by his return. And one of them could tell his mother, judging just how gently to break it to her.

So, from the railroad station, he first went to the apartment of his Uncle Wilhelm and Aunt Anna, who were not only unexcited but unimpressed. "So, like a bad penny, he pops up!" Uncle Wilhelm remarked. But then Uncle Wilhelm had always been a sarcastic man, the classic wise guy.

Rudi explained why he had come. Uncle Wilhelm thought he was giving himself airs. "I hate to break it to you, kid, but I think you don't have a lot to worry about. They're not going to fall down. They're not even going to blink."

Aunt Anna thought it was considerate. She made the call to Rudi's mother and said that she had heard from Rudi. She covered the mouthpiece of the phone. "She's very happy," she whispered. "She's coming over."

"She'll open the door. She'll see me!" Rudi protested. It was just what he'd wanted to avoid, only the positions would be reversed. His mother would be out in the apartment hallway and he'd be inside in the living room.

"No, no. You'll hide in the bedroom. We'll tell her. She'll be sitting down. When I tell you, you'll come out."

"Oh, I see," he said. He had a quick feeling of humiliation. Why hadn't he thought of that?

Still, when Uncle Wilhelm asked him if he was broke or if the police were after him, he was able to reach into his coat pocket and pull out a roll of bills—only a small portion of the money he'd been carrying in his money belt—and display it. There was a thousand dollars or so in the fan of bills he displayed.

"You robbed a bank!" his uncle said.

"No, no. It's nothing like that."

"You earned that money?"

"Yes," he said. In a way, it was true.

He went and hid in the bedroom. His mother came. They sat her down on the sofa and told her that they'd heard from Rudi, and she asked to see the letter. It wasn't a letter, they told her.

"A telephone call? From where?" his mother asked. There was apprehension in her voice. She, too, assumed that he was in trouble.

"Not a phone call," Aunt Anna said.

He came out of the bedroom. "Mama!"

"Ruuuuuu-di!" She didn't faint. But she was excited. She held out her arms and he ran to her and hugged her. And Aunt Anna made coffee. And Uncle Wilhelm even endorsed Rudi's return, telling his sister-in-law, "He's done okay. He's earned money. He's going to be insufferable for a while, all full of himself. But he did okay."

"Now, tell us," his mother ordered. "Where have you been and what did you do?"

He told them. Not everything. Not all at once. But he told them how he'd been in Mexico and Japan and then had gone to Germany.

Uncle Wilhelm didn't believe any of it. He thought it was not very funny to be joking about such matters. Aunt Anna was troubled too, but she didn't say anything. Rudi told them how he had gone to Augsburg and had visited his great-aunt, his mother's and Aunt Anna's Aunt Sophie, and he described her and the house she lived in. They believed him after that.

He told them how he had been unable to work without a permit even in Germany, and how he had been offered a secret mission to the United States.

"What mission?" Uncle Wilhelm wanted to know.

"It was nonsense. I just took the ride on the submarine, you know? And I got to New York and took a train here. It's okay."

They sat there, all four of them, considering that question.

"What can happen? How will they find me? Nobody knew my last name. Even the people on the submarine. Nobody knew where I live, not even in what city! How will they connect me to that business? I'm here. I live here. It's . . . it's all over."

"I hope so," his mother said. She finished her coffee and she took him home. She wanted to have him in the apartment when his father came home from work.

It was a good surprise when his father came home. And it was pleasant to tell his father about his adventure. But the best of all came that night, when he went down to see if Gerda still was in the same apartment. She was. She had had a miscarriage.

So the whole trip, the whole circumnavigation, had been unnecessary. If only he'd waited another month . . .

"Ah, well," he said. "Who could have known?"

"So? Where have you been?" she asked.

He told her, too. To boast a little. And to apologize, to let her know what had happened to him. But mostly because he liked telling it.

"You came back, at any rate," she said, when he finished his story.

"You glad to see me?" he asked her.

"I suppose you'll do," she said. She got up and went toward the bedroom. He followed her.

It was as if he'd never left.

Back at the Federal Building that evening, Trumbull found that Peter King had been transferred. King and the two others had been moved "for security reasons."

The Justice Department robot who told him this might even have believed it. It wasn't worth arguing about with him, Trumbull thought. He asked for Special Agent Dunbar, but Dunbar was off duty.

"Fine. Then let me see the special agent in charge."

The Justice Department functionary, as officious as any junior high school principal could ever hope to be, could not be encouraging. That was the way he put it. And he was so tickled not to be encouraging that Trumbull was snottier than he usually let himself get. "I don't need encouragement from you. This is official business. I'm doing a job, just like you. This has been set up in Washington with liaison people from the Pentagon and Justice, and you can call and confirm that if you want. But after you've put me in touch with the special agent in charge or have found out where the prisoners have been moved to. Otherwise, it's going to be your ass, you hear me? Now, what's your name? My name is Major

John Trumbull, G-2." He flashed his ID and the light glanced off the glassine as if it were a saber blade.

"I'm John McClatchey, Assistant United States Attorney."

"Great, Mr. McClatchey. Now, are you going to get on that telephone? Or am I?"

McClatchey went to the phone and called someone at FBI dispatch in another office in New York. He made three more calls, writing down names and telephone numbers. After ten minutes of effort, McClatchey was able to look Trumbull in the face and tell him, "They're in an observation ward in the Kings County Hospital. There are two agents out there who have been alerted to the fact that you're coming. There's a Dr. Lefcourt in charge of the hospital. If you need Washington juice, that's the man you want to aim it at."

"I appreciate your effort."

"Look, I'm just doing my job. I just follow orders."

"Right," Trumbull said.

Trumbull's driver made the best time he could, but traffic was snarled at the approach to the Brooklyn Bridge. It was the tag end of the rush hour. Trumbull had plenty of time to listen to horns honk and to reflect and plan. The fact that Dunbar and his people were playing games this way wasn't an absolute surprise. In a way, it made things easier for Trumbull. The Bureau's gesture of bad faith was an excuse for what Trumbull was about to do. Or to try to do. All he could do was propose it. The decision would be Peter King's to make.

He had to expect Dunbar would be there. Or would show up pretty soon, after having been alerted by McClatchey. But at the most, Dunbar would come out with one or two other agents. Like any bully, he wouldn't expect to be challenged. Trumbull got on the radio and asked for backup, to meet him at the front entrance . . . or, better, just inside the front door of Kings County Hospital.

There was a satisfied smile on his face. He caught himself. He had to remember that the point wasn't to get Dunbar or to show him up. The point was to respond to a foreign threat in the most reasonable and prudent way. And not to screw up the bureaucratic we any more than he had to. He and Dunbar were on the same side, after all.

If Dunbar was reasonable, there wouldn't have to be any muscle. It could all be decent and civilized.

The odds were against it, though.

The driver did well. They got to the front entrance of the hospital in a little less than forty-five minutes. The major burst out of his car as it stopped and charged in through the revolving door, his wallet already open to flash his credentials to functionaries and guards. A woman with hennaed hair and silver fingernails was knitting behind a semicircular desk. Trumbull held out his ID, but she didn't look up from the large liver-colored pile of knitting. Trumbull said that there were three FBI detainees in some observation ward somewhere and he wanted access to them. "Dr. Lefcourt knows all about it," he said, dropping the name he'd been told to drop.

She couldn't have been less impressed. "Down the hallway, take the elevator to the eighth floor," she said in a harsh nasal voice. "There's a guard up there. You can talk to him."

The guard, a barrel-chested man in a white uniform and what looked like a monk's tonsure, was expecting the major. He showed Trumbull into a conference room and within minutes brought Peter in.

"They treating you all right?" Trumbull asked

"Not bad. I can't complain."

Trumbull looked at him, his eyebrows raised.

"Really, it's okay."

Trumbull looked around the room for microphones. Up at the light fixture. Around the baseboards. If they were listening, they weren't being clumsy about it.

"You've had some time to think?" Trumbull asked.

Peter nodded.

"And?"

"It's a hell of a choice, isn't it?" Peter asked.

"It's not easy," Trumbull agreed. "It wasn't easy back in Germany. And it isn't easy here. I'll give you that."

"Thanks," Peter said.

"So?"

"No matter which way I go," King said, shaking his head, "it's a lousy deal."

"You think so?" Trumbull asked. "Look, I believe you. It could be worse if I didn't. Let's say I thought you had something and were holding back, just on the chance that I'd come up with an offer like this. You could be one of them, you know. You could even be the ringer, for that matter. But I'm with you. I believe what you're saying, and as far as I'm concerned, you can take your shot. But you've got to decide. Tonight. Now."

King looked shocked. "That's not true. I mean, I guess you could think that, but you'd be wrong. If I were the ringer, I'd know who the target was. And I don't have a clue."

"Then I guess you'd better get out there and find one. Otherwise, you're at J. Edgar Hoover's mercy, and he'll have a lot of fun deciding whether to hang you as a traitor or a spy."

"All right."

"All right, what?"

"All right, I'm willing to do what I can. Look for Karl. Or let him look for me."

"You realize that I'm sticking my neck out on this," Trumbull said.

"I realize that. But it's not for my sake. You want to stop Karl. So do I."

"All right, then. Let's go."

"Now?"

"Why not now?"

Trumbull called the guard, who came and unlocked the door.

"I'll be taking him with me," Trumbull announced, matter-of-factly.

"Hey, I don't know anything about that," the guard said.

"You don't have to. This is all you need to know," Trumbull said. He flashed his ID.

"But that's not what they told me," the guard said.

"Then maybe you ought to take that up with them," Peter suggested, pushing the call button for the elevator.

The guard picked up the phone. That was about what Trumbull had expected and he was glad—for the guard's sake.

The elevator door slid open. Peter King and Major Trumbull entered the cab. The door closed. "We may have some problems in the lobby," Trumbull said. "Don't let them worry you."

"I'll try not to."

"Just keep it calm and slow."

King nodded.

The elevator door opened, revealing a tableau in which Dunbar and another agent, in the classic crouch with sidearms pointed and braced, were posed for some poster announcing the Bureau's vigilance and spirit. "Where in hell do you think you're going?" Dunbar asked. "Hold it right there."

"I'm going back to New York," Trumbull said. "With the prisoner. I'm taking him back where he belongs."

"No, you're not."

"You don't think so? Look around."

"You've got to be kidding," Dunbar said.

"Why? There are two of you. You can take your eyes off us for just a moment. Go ahead. I promise you, we'll just stand here. We don't have to do anything dumb."

Dunbar looked around to see the six men from G-2, all of them in uniform, and each of them carrying an M-1 rifle that was pointed at the FBI men.

"You're out of your mind," Dunbar said.

"Am I?" Trumbull asked. "Why?"

"You can't kidnap an FBI prisoner."

"I said I was bringing him back to Manhattan. You're the ones who look like the kidnappers."

"I'm a special agent of the FBI!"

"And I'm a member of the United States Army. You showed the guns first."

Slowly, Dunbar lowered his gun. "We can talk about this," he offered.

"Send me a memo," Trumbull said. "Come on," he told Peter King.

"You can't go! You can't do that!" Dunbar said, but his voice was higher-pitched than before. He was a desperate man, trying to unsay what was happening.

"Try me," Trumbull said. "Or, more to the point, try them. See if they're willing to blow your head off or not." He led the way through the lobby and out through the revolving door.

The car was directly in front. The door was open. Peter dived into the back seat. Trumbull followed, slamming the door behind him. They were off in a squawl of rubber and a whine of engine strain.

"That was fun," King said. "But it complicates life a little, doesn't it?"

"I'm afraid so," Trumbull said.

"They'll be looking for me. Pictures plastered up in every post office."

"I don't know about the post offices," Trumbull said, "but there'll be pictures in police stations. All the agents will have them. Bus terminals. Railroad stations. Airports. Life will be—what was your word?—complicated. Yes, indeed."

"What do I do if I find him? How do I get in touch with you?"

"That's the next order of business."

They spent most of the rest of the trip attending to these details. Trumbull would be available every afternoon at four o'clock at Schrafft's on Madison Avenue and Fifty-fourth. And there was a telephone number for Peter to call, ringing twice, hanging up, and ringing twice. That would set a meeting in the extreme right section facing the screen of the Capitol Theatre, two hours after the signal. Only in emergencies was he to keep ringing after that second ring, in which case the major would answer the phone. "But I have no idea how secure the phone will be."

"I see. About money?"

"You don't have any?"

King explained about the money he had left at the hotel. Presumably, the men who had nearly killed him had gone for the money. They'd had the room key. Or the FBI had found it, going over the room. It would be dangerous going back there.

"I guess," Trumbull said. He pulled a couple of hundred dollars from a black lizardskin wallet and handed them over. "That ought to do you for a few days. If you need more, I can get it for you."

"All right."

"Now, let me make one last thing clear," Trumbull said. "I want to hear from you. Tomorrow afternoon, if you can make it. If not, the next day. You miss two meetings, and I assume you've taken off. In which case, Karl and the FBI will be minor headaches compared to what you'll get from me. You understand?"

"I understand."

"All right. Then good luck to you," Trumbull said. He held out his hand. Peter shook it.

"There's a subway entrance," Trumbull said.

"You got a nickel? Any change? I've just got these bills."

Trumbull flipped him a nickel. Peter caught it on the fly, touched a finger to his temple in an informal salute, and disappeared down the subway steps.

"Keep on going," Trumbull told his driver. "Back to Manhattan."

The woman with the hennaed hair and the liver-colored knitting was still at it. Her needles clicked in a syncopation that was particularly noticeable because of the silence of the rest of the lobby. The six G-2 men stood posed with their automatic rifles aimed at the two FBI men.

One of the FBI men looked at the other, raising his eyebrows in an unspoken question. The other, Dunbar, shook his head a fraction of an inch from side to side, deferring conversation. The G-2 men just stood there.

Quieter than the knitting needles, the men's wristwatches ticked. The leader of the G-2 outfit waited until his sweep-second hand had completed its fifth rotation on the dial. Then he nodded and began to back toward the door. He stood next to the revolving door and waited as the other five went through and out. Then, when he was left alone, he said, "Thank you for your cooperation, gentlemen," and ducked out, himself.

"Crazy," Carmody said, shaking his head.

"No, no," Dunbar said, "It was very good. It really was. He's got nerve, that fellow."

"But to come in with armed men," Carmody said.

"Why not? It worked."

Dunbar went to the front door and looked out through the glass panels. The G-2 cars were gone, of course.

"But what was the point?" Carmody asked.

"He's going to let him loose. They'll never get to New York—or not together."

"That's nuts."

"No, risky. But it's a way to go," Dunbar said. He went to the semicircular reception desk and asked the hennaed lady if she had a telephone he could use. She nodded toward the instrument. "Dial nine for an outside line," she said.

Dunbar called the Bureau to report what had happened. He wanted pictures of Peter King distributed to all law-enforcement officers and posted at railroad stations, bus terminals, airports, and the usual places. And he wanted a round-the-clock surveillance of Major John Trumbull, United States Army.

Carmody didn't ask the question. But his face did.

Dunbar explained it to him. "If he comes up with something, we'll know. And if he comes up dry, we'll have Trumbull. We win or he loses. That isn't too bad, is it?"

FOURTEEN

It was one of those decorated apartments, all pastels and curves, with a long wall of glass that gave onto a balcony with an impressive nightscape of Central Park and twinkling lights across the park and on Fifty-ninth Street to the south. It was a gentle spring night, but the glass doors were all closed, to keep the cream-colored rug and the white plush of the modern sectional sofa free of the city's grit.

A fat man in a dinner jacket sat in a small loveseat near the fireplace, almost filling it all by himself. He had a brandy snifter in his right hand. With the left, he traced the patterns of the crewelwork on the arm of the loveseat with a pudgy index finger. Opposite him, and separated by a stark glass coffee table Karl Roeder sat, not quite lounging but very much at his ease, leaning an elbow on his armrest and his chin in his upturned palm. He refused to be impressed by this man's status or weight.

If anything, the opulent if not vulgar surroundings spoke against this man in Roeder's mind. He had refused the offer of brandy or anything else. He had declined the small talk. It was a business matter they were supposed to be discussing.

"There have been mistakes," the fat man admitted. "But it is useless to haggle about who should bear the blame." He paused and took a sip from his snifter. "We must go on from where we are."

"I'm not interested in blame, either," Roeder said. "But to go on is to make certain assumptions. What's been bungled? Who knows what? How wide does the knowledge go?"

"They couldn't have given anything away, because they never knew anything. You must believe me about that. We've learned the habit of caution. It's no advantage to tell anyone more than he needs to know, and it's risky. So we don't. They had no idea who or where or when . . ."

"You know," Roeder said. "Who else knows."

"Four men back in Berlin. Maybe five. Nobody on this side of the Atlantic but you and me."

Roeder looked at the fat man. Kieffer held his gaze.

"We could change it, if you like. We could move it ahead. The advantages are that nobody but you and I would know, and I wouldn't know, myself, what date you'd picked. Or we can leave it as it was, for the reunion weekend, because there will be all those strangers and all the confusion . . . It'll be easier to blend into the crowd."

"Nobody ever said Einstein? Or Princeton?"

"Nobody," the fat man assured him.

"All right. We'll leave it as it stands. That's a week from Friday, then?"

"Any time that weekend. They start arriving on Thursday night and keep going to about Sunday noon. Friday or Saturday would seem to be the most advantageous."

"A week from Friday," Roeder said.

"You sure you won't have a brandy?" Kieffer offered.

"No thanks," Roeder said.

The fat man put his snifter down and heaved himself upright. He went to a cabinet at the far end of the room and reached inside it for the parcel wrapped in brown paper and tied with several turns of twine. "A Smith and Wesson .38 with ammunition," he said. "That ought to do you."

"In good condition?"

"Brand new. Factory fresh."

"That'll do," Roeder said.

The fat man showed Roeder to the door. Then, when he was alone, he stood looking out through the glass at the familiar panorama, not really seeing it, but thinking about the blazer. He hadn't mentioned it to Roeder because he hadn't wanted to spook him.

And he'd been perfectly right not doing so. Who was going to connect a silly thing like that garment with the death of Einstein?

"You're a bastard, you know that?"

"You missed me," he said as if that were what she'd meant.

"Of course, I missed you. And this. You missed it too," she said.

"Oh, yes," he said, but in the tone of a man of the world. He kept asking himself what a man of the world would say.

"I missed you, Rudi. I missed you a lot. At first, I was going to kill myself. And then, after it happened, after the miscarriage, I thought again I might kill myself. And then, I decided that, to spite you, I'd struggle on. I'd find a way to live. Even to be happy again. I'd make a life for myself and not let you be so important."

"Good for you," he said.

"And then the months passed and it didn't so much matter anymore. I forgot, you see, how good it is with us. How you make me into an animal. You turn into an animal and then you make me into an animal too."

He lay there, listening to her. He allowed himself the pleasure of hearing her words, letting them caress him. He played with the limp tendrils of her hair, wet against the nape of her neck.

"I even decided that you had run away from the child rather than from me. You were very bad to do that, but I think I understand. I forgive you, as you see. It isn't just the bed, you understand. It is everything, the life we can have together. You wanted a time of just the two of us. And you got scared and ran away. But it's all right now. And you're back."

"Yes, I'm back," he said.

"To stay," Gerda said.

"To stay? What do you mean?" He didn't want to commit himself.

"What do you think I mean?" she asked. "We're back together. We'll stay together now, no?"

"I don't know. I just got back. I have to get my bearings, you know? I have to see how it goes."

She sat up. The room was dark, but from the hallway, enough light came into the bedroom so that he could see her clearly enough at least in outline.

"You don't love me," she said. It wasn't a question.

"I don't know. I honestly don't know. It feels like it sometimes, but how the hell do I know? I don't even know if I've been in love ever. I'm not even sure what love is."

"It's this, idiot. This and being able to stand each other."

"Maybe."

"So?" she asked.

"So?"

"So maybe we should think about getting married."

"I don't know." He got up and started groping around on the floor for his underwear. "I'll let you know as soon as I know, okay?"

"No, that's not okay. Decide now. We get married or not?"

"Not," he said.

"Then get out," she told him.

"I'm going," he said.

It took him a couple of minutes to get dressed, or dressed enough to be able to pick up the rest of his things and leave her apartment.

He wondered what a man of the world would do—shrug it off? Smile? Figure that she'd come around in a day or two—a week at the outside—and welcome him back? She'd said, hadn't she, that they'd been wonderful together, that he turned her into an animal? It looked good, he thought. Just a little patience and she'd come around. She'd forgiven him before; she'd do it again. He knelt down on the coarse hall carpet to tie his shoes, realizing that he looked a ridiculous figure out there in the hallway, and rather enjoying it.

Inside the apartment, Gerda was enjoying it less. She sat there on the edge of the bed, still in the darkness, not having moved in all that time. She thought about what a fool she'd been. And about what a bastard Rudi was.

It was bad enough having to produce Karl's head on a platter as the evidence of his own good faith and loyalty. He had no idea where Karl was, how to find him, what Karl's target was, or what Karl's operating schedule might be. And while Karl was connected, apparently, with some kind of organization, some network of in-place agents, Peter was absolutely on his own. That was all bad enough, without the FBI hot on his trail, as they'd be now.

Time and time again, he ran it through in his mind, the impossible odds against his success, the dangers both from Karl and his people and from the FBI and their agents. He was between the devil and the deep blue sea, hanging helplessly. The shrewd thing would be to run. To take the money the major had given him and light out. Out of New York, as far away as he could get. Somewhere in South America, maybe, in some sleepy river town in Uruguay.

But the temptation was so obvious, there had to be a catch. There had to be some way Trumbull was going to keep tabs on him. Otherwise, Peter figured, he'd have a head start of almost forty-eight hours. He'd be a fool not to take advantage of that.

On the other hand, he was well aware of the fact that Trumbull had taken a chance on him. Trumbull would look bad if Peter tried to flee. And the FBI—Dunbar, in particular—would look good. That was the catch. Loyalty—not just to country but to actual human beings one liked. He was probably being a fool, but sometimes there are worse things to be.

But as the pendulum swung the other way and he felt the impulse to stay and try, he also felt his confidence ebb. How to go about the search? Where to begin? He had no idea where Karl was, still in New York or by now in Chicago or Washington or Los Angeles. It was impossible. And there would be G-men swarming all the hell over.

He was on the subway. He had been riding around, more or less aimlessly, changing trains every now and then, reversing directions. Manhattan was probably the place to begin. He asked himself why and couldn't frame an answer at first. But as he held onto the question it yielded a little. The Berliner Bar? Some waiter or waitress or bartender there? Or that house on Eighty-first Street. The apartment had to have been rented to somebody. Maybe there was a forwarding address? A thread of some kind that could lead to a line that might connect to a heavy hawser. It wasn't really such a promising idea but it was better than nothing.

Twenty minutes later, he was on that block and in front of that house. By now he was convinced that it was such a likely place for him to begin that the FBI would very probably have the place staked out. Not only that, they'd have gone over it, themselves, with a fine-tooth comb. What did he expect to find that they hadn't? What was the point? Still, he'd come up out of the subway and hadn't seen anyone loitering in a suspicious way. As long as he was here, he'd give it a try.

The bottom bell was marked *Super* and he pushed it. He waited. He pushed the bell again.

"Yeah, yeah. Coming. Coming," he heard. And then he saw the super, a huge fellow, at least six foot six inches, in carpet slippers and a three-year-old T-shirt with a faded representation of the World's Fair trylon and perisphere on it. The T-shirt wasn't quite long enough and it showed a crescent of hairy belly above the tops of the dungarees the man wore. "Yeah?"

"You're the super?"

"Yeah."

"I'm looking for the people who were in the apartment on the second floor in the back. The one that's empty."

"We got no empty apartment."

"The one that was empty the day before yesterday."

"No empty apartment," the huge super said. He had a gravelly voice and an odd way of holding his head to one side, looking past Peter.

"It was empty. I was in it."

"Then it wasn't empty was it?" the super said. He considered that, decided it was funny, and emitted a sharp "Ha!"

"I'm trying to find the people who rented that apartment," Peter said. "It's very important."

"No idea," the man said. He turned away.

"Wait," Peter called. "I'll make it worth your while."

The man stopped and turned back. He glowered. Or Peter thought he was glowering. With that face—the features were just as huge as the rest of him—it wasn't easy to tell. "I don't know nothing. I just keep the furnace going and take out the trash. The management company, they do all the renting. They're downtown. They can tell you something, maybe. But I doubt it."

"Who are they? Where do I find them?"

"Stelle Management. They're in the book."

"Stelle?"

"S-T-E-L-L-E," the man said, spelling it for him. He turned away again. This time Peter let him go.

It was a lead. More encouraging, it was the kind of hint the FBI types might have overlooked. If they'd bothered to ask, that is. It would have taken at least a rudimentary knowledge of German to know that a *Stelle* was a command post, a station, a center. In the Abwehr they went from an *Abteilung* to a *Hauptgruppe,* to a *Gruppe,* to a *Referat*—or desk. And out in the field, reporting to a *Referat,* there was the *Stelle.*

A coincidence? Maybe. But it was also in character. Peter remembered how Karl had reported that his target had been, in some way, a kind of joke. They liked jokes. Or somebody did—Canaris or one of his lieutenants.

He'd try Stelle Management in the morning. Meanwhile, he could use a meal and a bed. And a drink or two.

The doorbell? At . . . What time was it? Mrs. Muller looked at the dial of her Big Ben alarm clock but couldn't make out the time. She groped for her eyeglasses on the nightstand and put them on. She still couldn't see. It was dark. The doorbell again. She switched on the light next to the bed. Twenty past five.

Mr. Muller grunted.

"The doorbell," she said. "A fire, do you think? Some emergency . . ."

But the only emergency she could think of was one involving Rudi. For a fire, there would be the clanging bell. So it was something else. Gerda?

Not even that hussy would dare, at this hour of the night, to come ringing the bell and wake people up.

She dragged herself out of the bed. She looked at her husband. Wake him? Or not? She could always come back to wake him, she decided. She put on her robe and went to the front door. The bell sounded a third time as she approached.

"Yes, yes? Who is it? At this time of night . . ." She looked through the peephole in the heavy metal door. There were three men in suits and ties and hats. "Yes?"

"Open up, please. FBI."

"You must have the wrong apartment," she said, still whispering. But she was afraid now. It was Rudi. It had to be.

"Mrs. Muller?" the one in the middle asked. "You're Mrs. Muller? And Rudi Muller lives here?"

"I'll go call my husband," she said, and she closed the metal disk over the peephole. She turned around.

Rudi was standing there, in his pajamas. "The FBI," she told him. "What shall we do?"

"Tell them I'm not here," he said.

"They won't believe me! They'll want to come in."

"Fire escape," he said, and he disappeared back into his room. The fire escape included one window of his room and one window of Mr. and Mrs. Muller's bedroom. "No," she whispered. She didn't know what to do.

The doorbell sounded again. She went back to the door. She opened the peephole. "He's not here. He's not in his room," she said.

"Would you open the door, please?" the man said. "We've got a warrant."

"I tell you, Rudi isn't here!" she said. She was on the verge of crying, unable to protect her son and afraid not to.

"Open the door, Mrs. Muller, or we'll knock it down. We'll shoot the lock out."

"No, no. I'll open the door. But let me call my husband!"

"Now, Mrs. Muller. You've got five seconds."

She went toward the door and was actually reaching for the upper lock, the brass knob that controlled the deadbolt, when she heard the burst of gunfire. She recoiled. She was sure they were shooting at the door. But no, it sounded as if it came from behind her, from outside . . .

She forgot about the door and ran to Rudi's room. She saw the window open and the curtain billowing. She went to the window. She looked down. She saw the men, half a dozen of them, and the cars, and the searchlights. The little spot of blue in the middle of the circle of the men was Rudi. His pajamas. And she heard more gunfire, but this time from the front door. And the men came into the room.

"Help him," she said, staring down at the blue of his pajamas. "Help him."

"I'm afraid he's beyond help, ma'am. You should have opened the door."

They pulled her back into the hall. Two of them went to get her a robe. They found the husband asleep still, or pretending to be. They arrested him, too.

There was no office for Stelle Management. Instead, it was one of a number of enterprises that were run out of a dreary set of offices on a low floor of a seedy building in the East Thirties. There was an elevator, but Peter walked up the stairs to the third floor. Down the long, ill-lit corridor there were several doors, each of them with a panel of that beaded opaque glass. On each door, along with the names that were painted on the glass, there were additions—printed or typed cards stuck in the corners of the panes. Stelle Management Company was one of these small cards in the corner of a window. The central name on the window was Walter Geppert, Attorney at Law.

Peter opened the door. There was a swath of linoleum with three wooden chairs, then a low wooden rail, and beyond that a half-dozen desks, some of them surrounded with barricades of file cabinets. There was no receptionist. Peter asked a tall bald man at the desk closest to the door whether he was connected with Stelle Management. The man shook his head but didn't say anything.

"You know who is?"

The man shook his head.

"Stelle Management?" Peter called out.

There was only one other man in the room, at the desk by the window. The other desks were empty. The telephones—the two or three that Peter could see—all had locks on them. Nobody answered Peter.

He pushed his way through the gate in the low wooden railing and walked toward the end of the room where the other man sat at a battered oak desk, studiously ignoring him. He was reading a *Herald Tribune* and drinking coffee out of a cardboard container.

"Mr. Geppert?"

The man lowered the paper a fraction of an inch and peered over it. He was hollow-chested and sandy-colored—his hair, his suit, his tie, and the frames of his glasses. "Yes?"

"You have any idea who runs Stelle Management?" Peter asked.

"No, sorry."

"This is your office, isn't it?"

"This part of it," Geppert admitted. He took a sip of the coffee, as if to demonstrate that he wasn't concerned.

"No, no. The whole thing. You rent out space, right?"

"So?"

"So you know who you're renting to."

"Not always. They pay cash. I don't much care who they are. You look into these things too closely, you can scare off good tenants."

"They never come around?"

"That's my idea of a good tenant," he said, grinning and revealing a set of yellow—almost sandy—teeth.

It was perfectly possible that the man was telling the truth. On the other hand, maybe he was lying. And Peter was up against it. If this lead gave out, he had absolutely nothing left. "There must be a name," he suggested, affably enough.

"Nope."

Peter grabbed the man's letter opener, a long chrome blade with a scuffed leatherette handle, and put the point of it at the base of the man's right ear. "I don't believe you," he said. "There has to be a name."

"What are you, crazy?"

"No. But it's important to me. It's more important to me than you are. You understand what I'm saying?"

"You're crazy!" It was almost a whisper but it carried.

The other man, the one near the door, reached for his hat and ran out. To get help? Peter figured he had a few minutes anyway. He pressed a little with the point of the letter opener. "The name!"

"In the file. I don't remember," the man said. "I swear to God!"

"Put your hands behind you. In back of the chair," Peter ordered.

Geppert did so. Peter took the telephone off the hook and made a quick coil and knot around the man's wrists with the phone wire. Then he went into the filing cabinet. "Alphabetical or what?"

"Yeah, alphabetical," the man said.

Stelle Management was a Mr. Charles Kieffer of 1111 Fifth Avenue.

"You have the leases in here on the buildings Stelle manages?"

"Two drawers down."

Peter rummaged a while before he found them. The building on Eighty-first Street was one of them. It had a Manila folder to itself. Peter flipped through it. There was a note in block letters, either ordering or reminding: 2-R: LEAVE VACANT.

"That's better," Peter said. He untied Mr. Geppert. "Let's go," he said.

"Where? Where are we going?"

"Eleven-eleven Fifth Avenue."

"No."

"Oh, yes. Otherwise, you're likely to call Mr. Kieffer and tell him people have been asking for him. I wouldn't want anything to spoil the surprise."

"I'm not going anywhere," the man said.

Peter slapped him twice in the face, back and forth, not hurting him much but scaring the hell out of him. "Let's go."

There wasn't any argument anymore. But Peter took the letter opener, for its persuasive value.

The cab was crawling north on Fifth Avenue, behind a couple of double-decker buses that were playing a kind of leapfrog with each other. Geppert shrank to the farthest corner of the seat and cowered, like a girl on a date with a monster. Peter hardly noticed him. He was thinking ahead to Mr. Kieffer, about whose connection with Karl there could be no doubt at all. The notation that the room was to be left vacant. The radio equipment. The name of the management company. They all pointed toward some tie-in with Karl. But how much did Kieffer know?

"What are you going to do with me?" Geppert asked.

"Nothing," Peter told him.

"Nothing?"

"I'll send you back to your office," Peter said. He gave Geppert a five-dollar bill, which was more than enough to cover the round trip. "I just didn't want you to make a mistake in the heat of the moment and try to warn Mr. Kieffer. You do that, you see, and he'll know where I found him. You keep quiet, though, and I'll keep quiet about you."

Geppert was thinking about it.

"I could have knocked you out back there in the office. Or killed you. But I didn't. You look like a reasonable man. And I dislike excessive violence."

Geppert nodded. He disliked excessive violence too.

"You say anything about me to Kieffer and he won't be pleased. Neither will I, for that matter. Either way, it'd work out to be very bad for your health. You understand?"

Geppert nodded.

The cab pulled up to the apartment-house entrance. Peter instructed the driver to take the other passenger back downtown. He got out and gave his name to the doorman. "I'm Walter Geppert," he said. "To see Mr. Charles Kieffer."

"Is he expecting you?" the doorman asked.

"No," Peter said. "But he knows me. I'm a business associate of his."

"I'll call up," the doorman said. "It's sixteen C," he added.

"Thank you," Peter said. Clearly, Kieffer was at home. "Sixteen," he told the elevator operator. In the mirrored panels of the elevator, he saw his reflection and did what a Geppert might do, smoothed his hair and straightened his tie.

The next moment was tricky. This was where it could all collapse. Just as Peter expected, the elevator man held the door open, waiting for Mr. Kieffer to acknowledge and welcome his visitor. Kieffer would know immediately that Peter wasn't Geppert.

"Yes?" A fat man opened the door and peered out.

"Geppert sent me," Peter whispered. "It's about the Stelle . . ."

The fat man's mouth opened and then closed. The door opened wider. Peter entered the apartment. The door closed. The man had a small pistol in his pink pudgy paw.

"What is this about?" the man asked.

"Are you Charles Kieffer?" Peter asked.

"Yes, that's right."

"Where's Karl?"

"Karl who? I don't know any Karl."

"Karl from Germany. Karl from Munich. Karl from the Abwehr."

"I don't believe I caught your name," Kieffer said.

"I'm Peter King. I was on the U-boat. Everybody's been captured or killed except for Karl and me."

"I have no idea what you're talking about."

"Oh? Then call the police. Or do you plan to shoot me right here in your apartment? You'll mess your nice rug, and it'll be hard to explain. Shall I call the police?"

"No, I don't think so," Kieffer said, gesturing with his pistol.

"Shall we talk?" Peter suggested.

"Why not?"

They crossed yards of carpet and made their way toward the sofa that cut the living room in two. Like most men who haven't had much experience with guns, Kieffer made the fatal mistake Peter was hoping for, allowing him to come too close. He lunged, grabbed not at the gun but at the much easier right forearm, and hit it sharply. There was a very loud report for such a small weapon.

They grappled. Peter had the man's arm up, pointing the gun at the ceiling. He kicked Kieffer sharply in the shin, then punched him hard in the side of the neck. With his left hand, he brought Kieffer's right arm down suddenly, behind his back. The gun dropped. He kneed Kieffer in the groin. The man went gray and collapsed onto the carpet. Peter went for the gun, got it, and sat down on the edge of the sofa, waiting for the fat man to recover.

"I know about the building on Eighty-first Street. I know about Stelle Management. You're Stelle."

"Stelle . . . just means . . . place. Like a . . . a shelf. The shelf in . . . Geppert's office . . ."

"It is also an Abwehr outpost. And you know where Karl is."

"No, I don't. I swear . . ."

"And where he's going."

"No."

"It can't be a coincidence that those two thugs brought me to a building your manage. That Stelle manages. You want to tell me now? Or you want to suffer first. I am part of the team. I need to get in touch with Karl."

"Then I'll tell him . . . you're looking for him."

"No. Your goons tried to kill me. I don't trust you. You tell me where he is."

"I swear to you, I don't know."

There was a lot of flesh. The hard thing would have been to hit something vital. But there were all kinds of fatty areas around the thighs and the ass, great globs of the man, into which it was no great feat of marksmanship to place a bullet from five feet away. Peter placed one.

"Eeeeh!"

"Where is he?"

"I don't know."

He placed another. There was blood on the carpet. The man was crawling around the end of the couch. This was a relatively useless maneuver. Peter simply got up and followed him.

"Whom is he after? Whom is he trying to kill?"
"Don't shoot. For God's sake, don't . . ."
"Who?"
"I don't know."
"Then why did he come here?"
"He didn't."
"Yes, he did. Or he called. But you've talked with him. And you know. The next one will be in the gut."
"No!"
"Who?"
"Einstein."
"And how can you get in touch with Karl?"
"I can't," Kieffer said. "I have no need to. He can call me but I can't call him. I swear, that's the setup."

Peter believed him. And shot him in the head.

He took the gun with him, carrying it in his pocket in case he had any awkward questions from the elevator man. But no one challenged him. The doorman saluted and offered to get him a cab. Peter said it was a nice day and he'd just as soon walk. He turned the corner.

Einstein! It made a certain amount of sense. A distinguished figure like that, a great man—and a Jew. It would be as outrageous as anything else the Nazis had done. He believed Kieffer had been telling the truth.

And then he stopped, sure of it, remembering what Karl had said at Maxim's. Two birds with one stone. One of Canaris's jokes. Of course.

In German, it was *Zwei Vögel mit einem Stein.*

The girl gripped his buttocks and felt the shudder of release. The man's eyes were closed, but hers were open—focused on his expensive watch.

Twenty minutes was pretty good. She could be back out in the street by half past, calling in or maybe finding another john on her own.

The watch was tempting. The money for the sex would have to get passed on, but the watch might bring a hundred or more, and she'd get to keep it all.

She waited until he withdrew, rolled over, and lay back on the bed beside her. Then she offered him a cigarette.

"Thanks, but I don't smoke," he said.

"A shame. You want a shower? You want me to scrub your back? It's there and you've paid for it."

"You don't have to bother," he said. But he got up and went into the bathroom. In a moment, she heard the sound of the shower spray hitting the porcelain of the tub. She began to get dressed, delighted that it was working out so well. Underwear. Dress. Shoes. He'd already paid her and the money was in her bag. All that remained was to stick her head into the bathroom, say goodbye, grab the watch, and beat it. He'd be stark naked and dripping wet, and once she was out in the hall she'd be home free.

She nearly made it.

She had the door open, had got that close, when she felt the force of the blow as he slammed against her.

"The watch, please," the man said.

"What watch?"

"I'll give you five seconds to hand that watch over. Otherwise, I'm going to wait until my cock gets hard again, and I'm going to fuck you one last time. And I'm going to strangle you while we're fucking so that I can find out if a strangled woman's cunt contractions are as strong as I've heard. You won't be faking it this time, ducks. It'll make an honest woman of you. You want to try it? Or you want to give back the watch? One. Two. Three . . ."

She had been looking at his eyes. She believed him. Or at least she wasn't sure she didn't believe him. She reached into her bag and gave him his Patek-Philippe.

He took it. He stood aside. She opened the door and ran.

FIFTEEN

He was home free. All he had to do now was go to Schrafft's, meet Major Trumbull, have a cup of coffee, and deliver the information about Karl's target. There would be no problem in protecting Einstein until Karl was caught. Or moving Einstein to some safe place. And there shouldn't be any great problem in working out the details of the arrangement, so that Peter could be released without any charges being brought against him.

A quick visit to Cleveland to see his mother, and then . . . There wasn't anything he couldn't do. The world was his oyster. He could get some sort of job with a commodities brokerage house, perhaps in Chicago. It was wonderful to imagine himself leading an ordinary life, doing ordinary things. He realized how much he had given in to the hopelessness of his position. He'd been walking around like a man with a fatal disease, waiting for the pain to confirm the doctor's diagnosis. Suddenly, he had his life handed back to him.

He was walking down Madison Avenue at a brisk clip. He stopped every once in a while to look at a window display or tie his shoe, but he didn't see anyone pull up short or avert his eyes. Peter had no particular reason to suppose anyone was following him, but it was a possibility. All he needed now was for someone on either side to snatch his success away from him. So he was careful. He cut to the west side of the street, then back to the east side. He backtracked north for half a block in the Sixties. Nothing. Nobody.

He felt the growing conviction that he'd done it, that it was going to be all right. A large mantel clock on display in a jeweler's window showed the time as ten to four. He had seven blocks to walk in ten minutes and then it would be all over.

But when he got there he saw no sign of Major Trumbull. It wasn't anything worth worrying about, he told himself. The man was only human and could get caught in traffic like anyone else. There was a fountain to the right and a sit-down restaurant off to the left. Peter sat at the fountain and ordered coffee. He could see through the plate glass window out to the street where, at any moment, the major would appear. Of course. What sense would it make for him not to come?

The counterman brought Peter his coffee. He stirred in a little sugar and stared out at the sidewalk. What kind of intelligence officer was late this way for a meeting? It was annoying more than worrisome. Here he sat with the answer to the great question, with the key to the whole damned problem, and the major was tied up in traffic. Ten after four?

He told himself to be calm. He ordered an English muffin and accepted a refill on the coffee. Let it go to four-thirty before jumping to conclusions. It'd be all right. The worst was past.

He ate the English muffin and drank the second cup of coffee. Peter supposed that Trumbull could be in some trouble for having let him get away. That would soon sort itself out. A simple phone call would fix it. And he had a phone number. If another six minutes passed, he'd call it, ring twice, call back, and ring through.

He paid his check, went to the men's room, came back out into the restaurant, looked around for Trumbull, didn't see him, and went to the phone booth in the corner. He dialed the number. He got a busy signal.

That was odd. But he forced himself to retrieve the nickel from the slot, redeposit it, and then, slowly and carefully, to dial again, checking that each digit was correct. Again, he got a busy signal.

"You're sure?"

"No question," Trumbull said. "You want to see one of them?

He's out on the corner. Leaning against the traffic light. They're not trying to be subtle about it. They want me to know."

"But what for?" Davenport asked, looking down.

"I can't meet him without the Bureau tagging along. I can't talk to him on the phone . . ."

"They're bugging your phone?"

"I have to assume so," Trumbull said.

"So, send someone else. Have one of your people meet him."

"It won't work. He's out there, worrying about the FBI just as much as I am. More than I am. How does he know whether some stranger who comes up to him is from the Bureau or from G-2?"

"I don't know," Davenport agreed. "You're right. It's tricky."

"Harry, it's worse than that. It's deadly. He's out there with no connection anywhere except to me. Everybody else is a threat to him. If he's got anything, we want to know. And if he doesn't, then we want to know that, too. Otherwise, he's going to bolt sooner or later. And they'll kill him."

"Who will? Us or them?"

"Either way, Harry . . ."

They were in an empty conference room of a Yale classmate's law offices, way downtown. It was a way they had figured out to meet without anybody being able to follow them. Trumbull was walking back and forth past the rows of law books. "I only wish I'd been able to think of a better system. But it was all I could come up with on the spur of the moment."

"You can't reach him?"

"Only at the meeting place, at the appointed time. Or at the fallback. He can call me. But I can't call him. I don't know where he is. And I couldn't set up any surveillance on him because there wasn't time, and there wouldn't have been any way for him to tell us from the Bureau. You've got to call them off, Harry. Just for a couple of days. Then, if we haven't got anywhere, I'll have him come back in. Or I'll take him. Or let them take him."

"I'll do what I can, John."

"It's so sensible for them to put their dogs out after me. But I didn't think of it. I didn't think of it, and I couldn't imagine Dunbar coming up with something I hadn't thought of first. That's two mistakes, right there."

"No mistake is that terrible—as long as you don't keep on making it."

"I wish it were going to help Peter King, though."

"He's not your responsibility, John. You didn't recruit him. The Germans did. Remember that, will you?"

"I'll try."

"And I'll do what I can. I'll call you at home, tonight."

"They'll hear."

"It won't matter. Whatever it is I'm telling you, they'll know by then anyway, won't they?" Harry Davenport laughed. "Got to run."

Trumbull let him have a ten-minute head start, then walked out of the building and went down into the subway to take a train uptown. He counted three different teams of FBI men. Six men! What enormous wealth of resources and personnel they had. Or, turning it around, they had their counterespionage unit set up, and he was all they had to work on.

He and Peter.

Down at the end of the car, he spotted one of them. And near the doors in the middle there was another. Both of them had cold vice-cop eyes. They made John Trumbull nervous—and he wasn't a fugitive.

"And now a bulletin. The FBI has announced the landing of a German U-boat on the coast of Long Island. All members of the landing party have been apprehended with one exception. The one German spy still at large is described as follows. Name: Peter King. Height: six feet, one-half inch. Weight: one hundred seventy-three pounds. Dark-brown eyes. Light-brown hair. No scars or tattoos. This man may be armed and is considered dangerous. Do not attempt to apprehend or detain him, but telephone any information to your nearest FBI office.

"Repeating that bulletin, a party of German spies has been landed on the coast of Long Island and all have been apprehended except one Peter King. Further bulletins will be broadcast as we receive them."

Peter switched the radio off. His first thought was that Karl had been captured. Or "apprehended." Did that just mean *captured*, or did it include *killed?* At any rate, the implication for

Peter wasn't good. His bargaining chip was gone. And with it Major Trumbull's support. Not that the man probably had much choice about it, but the signs were pretty clear. He hadn't been at the meeting place. He hadn't been waiting at the phone. And now this announcement from the FBI, which seemed to drive the last nail into the coffin lid.

Peter was at the Plaza, having decided that a first-class hotel was safer than any other. He could stay in his room and order from room service. He had been lying on the bed, listening to the radio . . . He found himself making plans. He would get out of Manhattan, head south and west, get to Mexico, keep on going. He had no real hope of success, but he wasn't just going to lie here on a bed in the Plaza Hotel, waiting for them to apprehend him, while he ordered club sandwiches from room service and listened to the radio.

There was a small voice, dwindling but still perceptible, that urged him to have faith. He tried the number again. It was still busy. He had a list of three John Trumbulls he had found in the Manhattan telephone book. Call them? He had no reason to think that Trumbull lived in Manhattan. He could be a commuter from Westchester or Connecticut. Or he could come in from Long Island every day. Still, the number the major had given him was a Manhattan exchange, Filmore 8, which was the upper East Side.

He called the first of them. No answer. He tried the second, got an answer, and asked for Major John Trumbull. "I'm sorry," a deep woman's voice told him, "You have the wrong John Trumbull."

"I'm sorry to have bothered you," he said. He tried the third—the one he'd been saving for last because it, too, was a Filmore 8 number. And it, too, produced a busy signal.

He ought to have hung up at once, but he didn't. He couldn't. He lay there, his feet crossed, his right arm behind him and braced against the headboard, and his left hand holding the phone to his ear as he heard the repeating blat of the busy signal. It sounded like a prison alarm, only very faint and far away.

Trumbull was on the phone. Harry Davenport had called—sooner than Trumbull might have expected—with the bad news. "There's no way," he said. "I'm sorry."

"There's no way to do what?" Trumbull asked.

"To hold to the deal with Mr. King. It's all off. You heard the report on the radio?"

"I heard it."

"That's what the director got out of the secretary of the army. There's a lot of muscle involved in this."

"I don't understand one thing. What about the one who's still out there? Or was? What about Karl?"

"He's out there."

"He's the only one who counts," Trumbull said.

"That's not true. King counts. King counts more than all the others, because the prestige of the Bureau is involved."

"And who decided that?" Trumbull asked.

"The Bureau."

"Well, they're just wrong, that's all."

"They may be," Harry Davenport agreed. "But they've got the clout to carry their point of view in this particular dispute."

"Hoover is blackmailing the Secretary? Or Roosevelt?" Trumbull asked the question not because he expected—or wanted—an answer from Davenport but because he assumed there was a Bureau tap on the line. Let them realize that other people knew what kind of operators they were.

"There's no sense getting paranoid, John," Davenport said.

"Isn't there? What do you think this does for King's mental health?"

"He made his mistake some time ago," Davenport said. "More important is your mental health. And your prospects. I want you to cooperate with the Bureau in its search for King."

"Cooperate?"

"I want you to go to Dunbar and let him know you're working with him."

"And see if I can get to King first?"

"That's up to you, John. But whoever gets to him first, he's a dead man now."

"Jesus!"

"I'm sorry, John. I know you can't feel much enthusiasm for this . . ."

"That's one way of putting it, Harry. But thanks for trying." Trumbull hung up. He looked at the desk for a while, then opened the top right-hand drawer in which there was another phone, its receiver off the hook. He hung that up too.

On a tray table near the desk, there were several decanters with whiskeys and liqueurs in them. He grabbed the brandy decanter, poured himself a drink, not into a snifter but into a double shot glass, and drained it in two gulps.

Roeder was puzzled by the announcement on the ten o'clock news broadcast. He had washed his hands of Kieffer. The man was more of a liability than an asset, and the organization seemed useless at best. Obviously, if it had been of any worth, there would have been no need for the Abwehr to send over people in the first place. Neither assignment was all that demanding, after all.

But this announcement was puzzling. Obviously, it was untrue. Roeder was still free. But did they know that? How could they fail to know how many there had been in the team? It was tempting to suppose that Kieffer had found someone to get captured in Roeder's place . . . but that was unlikely. He thought, however, that the fat man might be able to shed some light on this anomalous news bulletin. He telephoned him.

There was no answer. Had Kieffer, then, been arrested? Or killed? Or had he fled, frightened by the realities of espionage after all those months—or years even—of playing and pretending?

There was, Roeder expected, a rough justice to it. Kieffer had got what he deserved, one way or another. The only thing Roeder cared about was how Kieffer could hurt him. The risk was that Kieffer had tried to bargain for his life, offering up whatever he knew. Roeder would learn soon enough. If he got to Princeton and found that Einstein had been spirited away, Kieffer would be the one to blame. But it would be too late to do anything more than blame him.

He couldn't just let it go that way. He left the residential hotel—he'd taken a room by the week in the Hotel Paris on the upper West Side—and went to a liquor store to get a couple of bottles of Scotch. He then took a cab across the park and got out a block above Kieffer's apartment house on Fifth Avenue. He went to the service entrance of the building and told the security man that he had a delivery for Mr. Charles Kieffer.

"You're a little late, buddy."

"I'm sorry? What do you mean?"

"Kieffer's dead. Shot."

"You're kidding."

The security man shook his head.

"Any idea who did it?"

"They haven't told me."

"I'd better take these back then," Karl said.

"He won't be needing them. That's for sure."

Karl waved cheerfully and got the hell out of there. He took the booze back to his hotel room and tried to puzzle it out. Who could have killed Kieffer? It wasn't the FBI's style, unless they thought they were dealing with some public enemy type like Dillinger. But if it hadn't been the G-men, then Kieffer hadn't talked, or not to them at least. Friends of the clowns Roeder had had to kill? It was a remote possibility, but no real threat.

The only real worry was Peter. And he wasn't likely. Why would Peter care enough to kill someone? He seemed to Karl too smart to get involved in this business. Still, he'd been curious, fishing around to try to find out what Karl's real target was. To have something to trade? Peter was smart, but was he that smart? And even if he was, would he have found Kieffer? Would Kieffer have talked? If Kieffer had talked, would Peter still have killed him?

His instincts were to assume the worst. In which case, it was too bad for Peter. A shame, if a fellow like that should make a nuisance of himself. Karl had rather liked him.

He opened one of the bottles of Scotch and poured himself a generous nightcap, neat.

At five in the morning, Peter left the Plaza. It was still dark. There was a sweet freshness of morning dew from the park.

He knew he had to get out of New York, and soon. And that the FBI and the local police would be watching every bridge and tunnel. He had spent much of the night tossing and turning in the large bed, working it out. Now it was a mechanical exercise, putting his body through the motions and waiting to see what happened. He took a subway downtown and changed for the Hudson Tubes—the least likely way he could think of to get across the river and into Jersey. From the tube station on the Jersey side, he set out on foot, walking generally west and south, looking for a main road on which there might be some through traffic. His plan was simply to hitchhike out of Newark and get as far as he could from the focus of police scrutiny. He was vulnerable—had no papers, no draft card, and only a little money. He could get stopped by a local cop anywhere and he'd have a hard time giving a plausible account of himself. It was like being back on the exercise again.

He was looking for a big wide road with a route number on it, maybe with a truck stop or at least a gas station, so that he could stand there and let the drivers see him when they were stopped. It wasn't so easy to find, though. He went from one inconsequential street to another. It was beginning to get light, and he'd hoped to be on the road by daybreak, putting miles between him and the search. He was beginning to think he was lost and was trying not to get worried by it, when a truck honked at him, not from the roadway but from the right. It was pulling out of a garage, a large panel truck. In the still tentative daylight Peter could just make out the hand-lettered sign on the cab door: NEZHDET BANUSHI—ONIONS. Underneath the lettering there was a picture of a large bulbous object, probably an onion, but twice life size.

"Hey! Watch where you go!" the driver called. He had a black cowboy hat on his head.

"Sorry," Peter called. And then, "You going south?"

"Yeah, south. You want a ride?"

"Thanks!"

Peter climbed up.

"Where you going?" Banushi asked.

"Ocean City," Peter said. He'd grown up there. It was a couple of hours down the road.

"I take you most of the way. You're lucky. I could have killed you, you know?"

Mr. Banushi let Peter off at a crossroads not far from Glassboro. There was a roar of the engine—Banushi's muffler wasn't working—and the truck pulled away. Peter looked around him. There was a Farm Fresh stand that wasn't yet open. On the opposite corner there was a Victorian house with a hand-painted wooden sign, POODLES BOARDED AND CLIPPED. On the other side of the roadway there was another old house, this one painted a bright yellow and sporting a more professionally done sign: THE OLD YELLOW HOUSE—ANTIQUES. On the fourth corner there was a diner—which looked to be the likely place to go. Peter's nerves had unknotted enough for him to feel hungry.

He went in, sat down at the end of the counter, and ordered the breakfast special. He was on his second refill of coffee when the woman came in. She was young, probably in her late twenties, and neatly if inexpensively dressed in a plain blue frock with white eyelet material around the neck. Peter noticed her but he didn't pay any particular attention until she went to the telephone booth behind him and called Triple A for someone to change a flat tire for her. He couldn't help hearing—the phone booth was only six feet from his counter stool and she had left the booth door open.

"That's the best you can do?" he heard her ask. And then, after a brief pause, "So I have to wait here for an hour?"

He got off the stool and approached the phone booth. "Excuse me. It's just a flat?"

She nodded.

"You have a spare?"

She nodded.

"Tell them you've found someone who can help you."

She hesitated. "How much?" she asked.

"My pleasure," he said. "Free."

She hesitated further. He watched, unable to urge her anymore. He heard her tell the dispatch operator of the automobile association not to bother, that she'd found someone after all.

He paid for his breakfast and followed her out to the road.

"I'm afraid it's about half a mile down there. Maybe a little more."

"I've got nothing else to do," he said. "I was hitchhiking down to the shore . . ."

"I'm going that way," she told him.

"Great," he said. "My name's Peter. Peter Crown."

"I'm Alicia," she said. She didn't give him a last name. But that was all right. They started walking.

Half an hour later, he had her tire off and the spare put in its place. It was a warm day, the first really hot day of the year. He was sweaty and probably smelled of onions. "You can change your mind, if you want to," he told her. "My last ride was in an onion truck. I'm pretty rank, I'm afraid."

"It's nothing a shower won't fix," she told him.

209

Was that an invitation? Probably not, he thought, and yet . . . It would be a good thing if he could find someone to keep him for a while. He had to assume that the FBI and the police were looking for him. An informal arrangement with a woman like Alicia would be more than satisfactory.

But it was unrealistic. She didn't look like the kind of woman who picks up strangers and takes them home to live with her. But then, what kind of woman does? He was interested to hear that she was coming back from Camden where she'd gone to get some electric motors repaired. She ran a miniature golf course and the dragon's tail and the windmill's arms wagged and turned only if their electric motors worked. There used to be a man in Atlantic City who could fix them, but he'd joined the navy. The man in Camden had a wooden leg, so he didn't look to be in much danger of getting drafted.

"Oh?" he asked.

What she really meant was that she felt free to do business with him. He wasn't a shirker or a draft dodger, hadn't tried to get himself declared "essential." There was a particular energy, almost a bitterness, to the way she said these things.

"Your father is in the service?" he asked. "Or your husband?" She wasn't wearing a wedding band.

"It was my husband," she said.

There was a long silence. She was deciding whether to tell him or not, whether he was worth the effort. Either for his sake or for the sake of the telling, she decided to go ahead. She explained how he—Harold—had been in the Merchant Marine and had gone down off Greenland, sunk by a German submarine. She had heard the news only a month ago.

"I'm sorry," he said.

"Sure," she said, as if that were obvious, as if everybody was sorry. And then, still belligerent, she asked, "And what about you?"

"Me? Oh, I've enlisted," he said. "I have to report in ten days. I just wanted to come down and look at the ocean a little, you know? I was brought up around here. I thought I'd walk on the sand and watch the gulls."

"Yeah, I do that. It doesn't help," she said. "Maybe it will be better for you."

He asked about her miniature golf course. It had been Harold's father's, but he'd died, and Alicia and Harold had run it for a while. It was up for sale, but she thought she could get a better price if it was a going business, so she'd been working it, in season anyway, until she could find a buyer. It wasn't too bad. Six or seven months a year, and then she could head south. But it wasn't what she wanted to do, hand out golf balls and little pencils for the rest of her life, and take care of defective dragon's tails and windmill arms.

"Maybe I'll come over and play a round or two," he offered.

"Sure, why not?"

He thought again he might have heard a note of invitation. It was not impossible. A lonely woman, a recent widow, might be drawn to a young man about to go into the service. Should he claim to be going into the marines? The navy? And how could he explain his lack of money and a draft card?

"Are you good with mechanical things?" she asked.

"Sometimes," he said. "There are lots of people better than I am, but there are lots of people worse."

"Maybe you wouldn't mind trying to put these motors in for me and hook up the machines. It's a dirty job, but you need a shower anyway, right?"

"Be happy to try," he said.

Don't grin, he told himself. Don't, for God's sake, grin.

But it was okay. She was smiling, herself.

SIXTEEN

From Kieffer, Roeder had received a reunion schedule for Princeton University, a small orange folder printed in black, a Smith and Wesson .38-caliber automatic pistol with a box of ammunition, and that blazer. He supposed the folder was legitimate. But he wasn't ready to rely either on the blazer or the gun. The gun he tried one night in Riverside Park, shooting two rounds into the river. It didn't blow up in his hand. And as for accuracy, at the range he was expecting to shoot from that wasn't critical. But the jacket was harder to try out. He thought about it for a while and then telephoned the Alumni Affairs Office of Princeton University, identifying himself as James Dorsey of the class of '37. He wanted to know whether he could wear his cousin's striped blazer to his reunion instead of buying one.

"But I don't understand," the woman at Princeton said. "Your class doesn't wear blazers. Those are for the older alumni. The twenty-fifth-year men wear them."

"Oh, that's why they didn't offer them to us."

"All you need is in the reunion package that you get when your check has been received."

"I see. Well, thanks very much. I just thought all the people wore those jackets. But I understand. Thanks again." He hung up. He took the damned blazer, put it in a paper bag, and dropped the bag in a trash barrel on the corner of West End Avenue and Ninety-fourth Street.

The incompetent bastard. If he hadn't already been killed, it would have been something for Roeder to do while he waited. Not, of course, that he didn't already have plenty to do. It was necessary, after all his posturing back in the training school, that he accomplish the ridiculous task that had been set for the decoys. The police and the FBI had to be persuaded of the truth of their captives' stories. To keep them from wondering about his purpose, Karl had to fulfill their expectations, at least once, at least in a symbolic way. He had pretended to listen to all those tiresome lectures, and now he was the only one who had to put them to use. Fortunately, he had been bored enough to absorb them, having nothing else to turn his mind to. He was pretty sure he could do it. Not that it was all that complicated.

He went to a drugstore on upper Broadway and bought a number of small medicine bottles. At an art store, he picked up a bottle of sulfuric acid. At a hardware store, he purchased paraffin—to use, he said, for putting up jelly. And at a supermarket, he bought a small box of powdered sugar. The only difficult item on his shopping list was the calcium chlorate, but the difficulty was not at all insuperable. Downtown at a chemical supply house, he bought a pound of the stuff and was ready to tell them he was going to use it as a bleaching agent. Or his boss was. But nobody asked any questions. They just sold him what he wanted. Which was fine with Roeder.

He put the fuse together. He took a piece of writing paper, one of the medicine bottles half-filled with the sulfuric acid, and some of the paraffin, and he secured the paper over the mouth of the bottle, using the paraffin to hold the paper in place. Then he inverted the bottle, put it into the wastebasket, and watched it. According to what they had told him, the acid would take a few hours to eat through the paper. He checked his watch. He went out for a double feature in a theater just above Eighty-sixth Street and sat there, trying to concentrate on the films. He came back to the hotel and looked into the wastebasket. He went out for a light supper at a Chinese restaurant and came back. Nothing. He stared down, wondering what had gone wrong. How had he screwed it up? But as he watched, he saw it, the wonderful moment when the acid ate through the paper and spilled out into the metal wastebasket.

So, it worked. He poured himself some of Kieffer's Scotch to celebrate with, and then he set to work with the sugar and the calcium chlorate, trying the mixture in different proportions to see which burned best, either with a match to start it or with a drop of the sulfuric acid. When he had it right, he rigged his bomb, did another fuse with a medicine bottle, and put the bomb and the fuse on the dresser. He had a paper bag from the supermarket where he'd bought the sugar.

The beach was smooth and clean early in the morning. Peter stood on the hard-packed sand, below the high-water mark, and stared out at the glinting blue water, smelling the salt tang of the air and feeling, for the moment, good. Free. As if the expanse into which he looked were an expansiveness of spirit. Knowing that there were U-boats out there, that one of them had sunk Alicia's husband, and that another of them had dropped him on the beach on Long Island, didn't diminish the distances or the brilliance of the sunlit blue and foam-flecked white.

It had taken him a couple of days' rest and some long walks on this very beach to figure out how things stood, how they stood now and how they'd all been set up from the very beginning. He'd been badly used. They all had been. He thought of Elfreda. And Johann. And those two poor sons of bitches out on Long Island. And the Gestapo driver. And Kieffer. And that poor soul who'd been hanged in the detention cell.

He looked out at the water. He was tempted to walk out into it, not to a submarine this time but on foot. Swim out until he was exhausted and then take that one frightening, watery breath.

He had bought the newspapers and had read through them carefully, but the accounts of the captured German spies were very sketchy. No names. No photographs, aside from his own. What was the point of their holding back on the story now that it was all over? Peter would have supposed that they'd want to trumpet it as loudly as possible, showing how invincible they were and how efficient.

Did they have Karl or didn't they? He wouldn't believe it until there was some proof. Karl's picture. At least, his name and a description that fitted closely enough. If Karl was still out there operating, then Peter's choices were narrowed. He couldn't just run. He tried to imagine a phone call in which he told Professor Einstein—always assuming that he could get through to Einstein, that Einstein sat there by his telephone answering crackpot calls that came in—how there was a man out there the FBI hadn't caught, how a man named Karl was on his way to Princeton to try to kill him. Standing there on the beach, watching the people back on the Boardwalk strolling in the freshness of the morning, he could hardly believe it himself.

Meanwhile, he was safe for the moment, but only for the moment. Alicia didn't bother with the papers. She was a sweet, simple soul, the kind of woman who might not be all that smart but had a native shrewdness he admired because he thought he lacked it himself. He didn't suppose for a minute that she believed his story. But she had sensed in that moment in the diner that he was harmless, when she'd wrinkled her nose a little and given him the once-over. She was using him as a diversion, a stand-in for Harold, convenient and expendable—as the Abwehr had also used him as a convenient, expendable stand-in. The whole scheme of blowing up department stores had been nothing more than a diversionary tactic.

And he'd jumped at their offer as he'd jumped at hers, out of desperation.

He started to run back, keeping to the strip of smooth sand below the high-water line and forcing himself to go, to get the blood going and the rhythm established, as if it were the first fifty yards of a middle-distance race. He felt the thud of his feet on the beach and gave himself to it, imagining that they were cannons and that their shells were aimed at all the madmen who had conspired to put him in this terrible fix. And then, as the demands of the running drained more and more of his energy, he felt all of his anger and frustration fade away. There was only sand and water and sky and the rush of blood and the pleasant pangs of exertion.

Back at the house, he showered. He got into a pair of white duck pants and a polo shirt, both of which had been Harold's. Harold had been a big fellow, but if Peter rolled the legs of the pants up a little, the fit wasn't bad. Alicia was still in bed, although not asleep. Or not deeply asleep. She woke slowly, which could be very nice, Peter had found.

"You up?" she asked.

"I've been out running."

"Mmmhmmn," she acknowledged. "I heard the door close." She rolled over and looked up at him. "I thought you'd gone."

"You mean, for good?"

She nodded.

"Soon, I'm afraid."

He'd thought of just leaving. Or of leaving a note behind. But what was the point? She knew. She'd known all along. That was what she liked about him, that he was going away. It was crazy. Still, he felt better now that he'd told her.

"Close the curtains," she told him. "And then come back to bed."

"You don't like the light?"

"No. Not now."

In the dark, he could be whoever she wanted him to be. Harold, most likely. And she could be Elfreda. Or somebody else. He'd thought that maybe now that he was leaving, they could leave the curtains open or the lights on. But whom would they be fooling?

"Sure," he said. He closed the curtains and the heavy draperies that covered them. He took off his clothes—Harold's clothes—and got into Harold's bed, to have Harold's wife do to him whatever Harold had liked.

Peter thought of Elfreda, or tried to. She kept slipping out of focus. He tried to remember what Alicia looked like in the light. It didn't matter.

If one was good, two were twice as good. And he'd had enough material left for the second bomb. Or, not bomb, really, but incendiary device. He recalled the instructor's distinction, back in those lectures in Munich.

So Roeder went back to Macy's, browsed among the shirts and ties, looked at the displays of cameras and sporting goods, of kitchen gadgets and furniture. The furniture department looked like a good place to leave one of his packages.

"Excuse me, but have you a trash receptacle?" he asked. He did not want to sneak anything into their trash bin in a suspicious way.

"Certainly, sir."

"Thanks very much, indeed," he said, and he put one of the bombs into a large bin that had just been emptied. It didn't seem likely that it would fill again in the hour or so that remained until closing time.

It was pleasant to think of the fire as it spread to all that wonderful wood of the chairs and tables and étagères and bookshelves. He continued his browsing through the store and settled on a corner in the basement where another trash bin was parked near a fiberboard partition. There was no one to ask this time. Roeder simply put the other bag into the corner of the trash bin and covered it over with the tissue paper and excelsior that had been dumped in. That stuff would go up instantly and the fiberboard would catch.

Now that he was unencumbered, he bought himself a couple of polo shirts and a pair of casual shoes, so that he might fit in better at the Princeton reunion festivities. The *Schweinerei* with the jacket was merely amusing now.

But he was glad Kieffer was dead.

He walked out through the same door he'd used when he'd shopped there with Peter.

He felt bad about Peter. He wondered why the authorities were picking on Peter. Had they caught him and lost him? The publication of that mug shot certainly made it look that way. Roeder wished Peter well, but there was nothing he could do for him now.

Roeder treated himself to a good dinner and then an Ida Lupino movie at the theater near his hotel. Then he went back to listen to the news reports and pack for his trip. It was, he thought, an altogether satisfactory evening, intelligently planned and efficiently executed.

"What do you want?" Dunbar asked. But before there could be any answer, he let Trumbull know what he was thinking. "I must say, I think you have a hell of a nerve, calling here."

"The prisoner escaped," Trumbull said.

"Sure, sure. Tell me another one."

"Can you prove different?" Trumbull asked.

"If I could, you'd know it."

"All right, then. In that case, there's nothing to prevent my calling you, is there?"

"Go on. I'm waiting to be enlightened," Dunbar said.

"It's about those fires last night at Macy's. You're figuring arson. Or they are, so that you're figuring Peter King."

"And you're figuring differently?"

"Maybe. Karl is still out there."

"I thought you had him pegged for some different job," Dunbar said. "You just being contrary?"

"I did. I still do. But it could be that this is a signal to somebody. Or a way of covering for the stories we're getting from the people we've captured."

"We?" Dunbar asked.

"We're both on the same side, aren't we?"

"Well, I don't buy the signal idea. We tried to hush it up. We didn't want anything printed or broadcast about it. But those reporters have their connections right at the firehouse, when the alarm comes in. So it's a tough proposition."

"And the other idea? Covering for the stories you've been getting, so you'll believe them?"

"It's a logical possibility. But it's also a logical possibility that your Peter King isn't the lily-white boy you've pegged him as, isn't it?"

"It's possible. You'll keep me posted if you get a line on him?" Trumbull asked.

"I suppose that's an official request?"

"If you want it that way," Trumbull said.

"I want it that way," Dunbar said.

"You got it," Trumbull told him. He wanted to be there at the end of it. If Peter had been playing straight, then Trumbull thought it would be only fair to try to protect him against the Bureau's excessive zeal. On the other hand, if Peter had betrayed Trumbull's trust, then he wanted to take Peter out, himself.

On the boardwalk, Peter read the same small article in the *New York Times*, just a couple of sentences about two fires in Macy's that were believed to have been the result of arson. He tore out the page and carefully trimmed it. This was Karl's work. Had to be.

And if Karl was loose, Peter was back to square one. He had to do something. Call the FBI? That was the most reasonable course, but he didn't believe they'd listen to him. The fact that they'd lied about Karl, that they'd claimed to have captured all the members of the team except Peter, gave him little reason to trust them. Trumbull? But Trumbull had disappeared. Just vanished. And Peter more than half-believed the FBI had been the ones to take him away, angry at him for letting their prisoner escape. It was crazy, but there it was. Einstein then? He still couldn't imagine Einstein believing a caller who claimed a German assassin was out to get him. The fires at Macy's . . . To a paranoid, anything was evidence of anything else. So Einstein would dismiss it as the raving of a paranoid nutcake. Or a crank. Or a mischievous anti-Semite.

It was nevertheless becoming increasingly obvious that he had to leave for Alicia's sake. He didn't want to involve her in any of this. He didn't want to sully their time together. He looked down at the tiny news item in his hand, staring at it as if it were marching orders, or a warrant. He crumpled it up, then rolled the tiny wad into a ball.

He didn't run on the beach this morning. He just sat there on one of the benches, staring out at the slate-blue sea. Then, more weary than if he had run twice his usual distance, he returned to Alicia's. He had, the day before, painted the rails around the miniature golf course and the little white cabin in which Alicia sat to take the customers' money and hand out scorecards, pencil stubs, putters, and golf balls.

He approved of the job he'd done. The place looked pretty good. As good as it could. Maybe she'd get lucky. Maybe someone would come along to buy it. Or to take her away from all this and to change her life. He hoped so.

She was up, which was a little surprising. She had come down to the kitchen to make him breakfast. "That's really nice of you," he told her. "But you didn't have to."

"I know. That's the best part. That I don't have to."

"Yeah," he agreed. He tried to be cheerful and carefree and bright. He took the coffee she poured for him, and sat down in the little breakfast alcove.

She stood at the stove, scrambling eggs, and every now and then she looked over in his direction. "There's something wrong, isn't there?"

"No, no. It's fine. Great coffee."

"I didn't mean with the coffee. There's trouble, isn't there? With you."

"There's always trouble. Life is trouble."

"Yes, that's true. But that's not what I mean. There's something particular. Something bothering you."

He shrugged. He didn't know what to say. He didn't want to lie but he didn't want to lay any of it on her.

"Can I help? Is there anything I can do?"

"No," he said, and then he realized that he had more or less admitted the major premise—that there was trouble.

"You need money, maybe?"

"No," he said. He was touched by her willingness to do what she could for him. He was also bothered by it. He wanted to warn her to be careful, not to get involved with people like him.

"All right, be that way," she said.

"I'm not being that way. It . . . it doesn't involve you. And it shouldn't. You're better off out of it. That's the least I owe you."

"All right," she said.

"Now let's have that nice breakfast you've been making. We mustn't spoil it."

She looked at him for a moment. "You mean we mustn't spoil it because it's the last one?"

"I'm afraid so."

She didn't say anything. She didn't have to.

"I'm sorry too," he said.

She scooped the scrambled eggs out of the pan and onto the plates on the stove. She grabbed the strips of bacon from the paper towel they were draining on. She brought the plates over to the table and set one in front of him. She put the other one at her place and sat down but didn't eat. There were deep sighs coming from her as she struggled and didn't cry. She rubbed her eyes and kept the tears from coming. "Nothing's forever," she said. She forced a smile. "Maybe even your going away won't be forever. We can always get together again sometime, can't we? Like, say, in a year? Or five years? We can have a reunion. Five years from today. I'll go back to that diner near Glassboro and you'll be sitting there having breakfast. Why not?"

"Why not?"

"And we'll both wear just what we were wearing . . . Except that I already forgot what I was wearing. But it doesn't matter, does it. So just be there, May 28, 1947, at, say, ten in the morning? Okay?"

"Okay," he said. He picked up a piece of bacon and looked at it. There were tiger stripes of lean and fat running down the length of it. He remembered that blazer from the house on Eighty-first Street and realized it was a reunion blazer for Princeton.

He'd absolutely missed it. But with Einstein's name to connect it to, it made perfect sense. There'd be all those crowds of people at a reunion, all of them descending on the university and the little town of Princeton at once. A perfect opportunity!

"I say something?" she asked.

"Yes," he told her. "But it's okay. It's terrific."

"You'll be there? In five years?"

"If I can. If I'm walking around, I'll be there. Or I'll get to you before then."

She started to eat. Which was his cue for eating, too. He was hungry. And eager to get out of the house so he could make a phone call and get going. He gulped down his coffee.

"Look," he said, as he put the empty cup down on the saucer, "if I can, I'll be in touch with you within the month. If not, if you don't hear from me by then, just . . . just forget about me."

She nodded.

"You're terrific, you know?"

"Sure," she said.

"I mean it," he said. He bent over and kissed her on the forehead like a husband going off to work for the day.

From the Reading Railroad terminal, he called the Alumni Affairs Office at Princeton to find out what he hoped was true, that the reunion weekend was just beginning. Hoped and feared it was true. Because he knew where Karl was going and whom he was going for, and when he was going to make his move.

Once more, he tried the number in New York for Major Trumbull. This time, there was no busy signal. But there was no answer, either.

SEVENTEEN

In Philadelphia, at the Thirtieth Street Station of the Pennsylvania Railroad, Joe Gagliotta—he pronounced it in the Americanized way, Gag-lee-ot-tah—looked up as the next man in the long line came up to his window.

"New Brunswick, one way, coach."

"New Brunswick," he repeated. "One way."

Gagliotta stuck in the plate and punched the button so the machine would spit out a printed ticket to New Brunswick. It was all fast and efficient, a series of gestures he had performed hundreds of times that week. He didn't even look at the customer until he had the ticket in his hand and it was time to collect the fare.

"That's two-eighty," he announced, looking at the man on the other side of the grille.

The man was wearing a movie-gangster's hat with a big brim that he wore low over his eyes. Gagliotta saw the hat before he saw the face. But they were so close to each other, separated only by the little counter and the grille, that he saw the face too. Gagliotta's eyes flicked off to the right and then back to the customer's face. "Out of five," he said, keeping his voice just the way it had been before. He made the change. The man walked away with his ticket.

It was the man, all right. The man's picture was posted on the inside of every ticket window in Philadelphia, in every window of every station on the Pennsy, the New Haven, the New York Central, and the Delaware and Lackawana.

"One moment please," he said to the next customer. "I'll be right with you." Gagliotta went back to the assistant station master's desk and dialed the number from the poster. When he got an FBI agent on the line, he said, "This is Joe Gagliotta at Thirtieth Street Station. I'm a ticket seller. I'm calling to report that I just sold a ticket to New Brunswick to that Peter King you people are looking for. The next train is at eleven-twenty."

"You're sure it was him?"

"I had his picture next to the window. He had a big hat on, but I had a good look at him. That was the guy."

"We'll be right there. We appreciate your call, Mr. Gagliotta."

Peter had taken the train to the Reading Terminal in Philadelphia and then walked out onto Market Street. He'd bought a large-brimmed hat on Market Street in a store that sold cheap men's wear. It wasn't much of a disguise, but he could keep the brim down over his face and it gave him some protection. He'd walked out Market Street to the Pennsylvania Railroad Station across the Schuylkill and had bought a ticket to New Brunswick. The Abwehr training program had taught him never to buy a ticket to the station he wanted to go to, but instead to spend a little more for insurance. New Brunswick was the station after Princeton Junction.

And then, he didn't take the next train. He walked across Market Street and up toward *The Bulletin.* There was a nice homey bar there, a newspaperman's hangout just across the street. He sat at the bar in Cavanaugh's and had a few beers, waiting for the train at 12:10. He had a roast beef sandwich at the bar, a third beer, and went back to the railroad station where he browsed in a bookstore until just before train time. He caught the train and rode as far as Trenton, where he got off because he didn't like the way the conductors seemed to be peering at everyone. Paranoia, but what was there to lose? It was proper procedure. He caught a bus from Trenton that went right into Princeton, right onto Nassau Street across from the university. He left the hat on the bus.

He went into a drugstore on Nassau Street, looked up Albert Einstein's address and telephone number, and was surprised to find the great physicist listed in the directory. He jotted the listing down and went into the phone booth to try the number.

"Yes?" a woman's voice answered.

"Is Professor Einstein at home?"

"No, I'm sorry. He's at the Institute."

"To whom am I speaking?" Peter asked.

"This is the housekeeper."

"Can you tell me when the professor will be home?"

"This afternoon, late, I expect. Who is calling please?"

"This is Professor King," he said. "I'll try him at the Institute."

"Very well."

He looked up the Institute for Advanced Studies and tried that number, but the receptionist would not put him through. "The professor is in conference," she said. Peter didn't want to push too hard. He didn't want to turn into a minor nuisance Einstein might try to avoid. He had to warn the man.

He asked at the counter where Mercer Street was. Einstein's address was 112 Mercer.

"Just walk on down Nassau Street until the fork, and then bear left. That's Mercer."

"Thanks," Peter said. It was the main road to Trenton. It was right out there in the open. He'd passed it on the bus on the way into town.

He went back to the phone booth and called the New York number once more, trying to reach Trumbull. There was no answer. He had no more choices left. He called the FBI in Trenton, and told the Bureau's switchboard operator, "This is Peter King, the fugitive from the German submarine. You can confirm this with an agent named Dunbar in New York City, or with a Major John Trumbull with G-2, also in New York. I'm calling to give them the message that Karl's target is Albert Einstein and the probable time is this weekend, during the Princeton reunions. You got that?"

"What number are you calling from?"

"Never mind. Just pass on the message," Peter said. And he hung up.

Now the question was whether the guy would believe him or not.

The other question was how they were going to find Karl

without having any idea what the man looked like. Only Peter knew that.

All they knew was what Peter looked like.

Ed Wilson, of the class of '17, was no relation to Edmund. In the ordinary course of things, he'd have been unaware of the other, more famous Edmund Wilson. Ed wasn't the kind of man to read the *New Republic* or keep up with literary celebrities from New York. But because he shared the name and had gone to Princeton, he got asked all the time whether he was *the* Edmund Wilson, which was a pain in the ass. Finally, he found out that the other Edmund Wilson's friends actually called the critic and novelist Bunny. Edmund Wilson, the electrical supplies distributor from Dover, Delaware, learned to answer that, yes, indeed, he was *the* Edmund Wilson, and that the other one was Bunny Wilson, the writer.

Not that he was so formal as to use the whole Edmund most of the time. Mostly he was just Ed, or—to his old Princeton buddies—Itchy, after the time he'd mixed itching powder with the glitter that was thrown on the cotillion leaders of the junior prom, back in 1916. There wasn't any real harm in it—the itching powder was only ground-up human hair from the barbershop—but there had been some stuffy disapproval and some talk about "conduct unbecoming a gentleman," which you could actually get thrown out for.

Ed Wilson thought that there'd been altogether too much talk about Edmund Wilson and F. Scott Fitzgerald, as if those younger literary guys owned the damned place. And clearly they didn't. Princeton was for doctors and lawyers and businessmen, for people who were going to run the country. Those literary types were on the sidelines, jumping up and down, but the real action was out on the field—where you needed a program or some knowledge of the game to know what was going on. The tiger suit, then, was a way of claiming the place as his own, proclaiming that he was Princeton rather than those loudmouth lightweights.

The reunion was always a great time. Ed Wilson had gone to his tenth, had missed his fifteenth, but had gone to his twentieth, and they were really wonderful, with lots of food, more booze than you could imagine drinking, and good times with old friends. It was all stag, until Sunday when some of the fellows had their wives come for the last picnic that traditionally closed the weekend. Until then, it was a kind of endless fraternity party, a long happy carouse, where you found out what had happened to classmates you liked and to classmates you never knew, and even, from time to time, to classmates you hated.

Wilson had come away from his twentieth convinced that the admissions office in 1913 had done a pretty fine job of it. A bunch of decent, likable, intelligent guys. A number of them had been killed in the Great War. A few more had taken the big dive out of lofty windows on Wall Street during the crash. Some of them had become drunks, some had found solace in the company of young women—but those weren't the ones who showed up for reunions. The spirit of the twentieth had been one of mutual congratulations just for having survived. Now, for the twenty-fifth, it was going to be a bigger blast than ever. With another war on and the times as dark as any of them could remember, they owed it to themselves and to each other.

For all those reasons, then, the tiger suit. And to keep it as a surprise was part of the fun. Ed Wilson had it stowed in the trunk of his car which he'd parked in the big lot behind the eating clubs. He'd come back for it later on, maybe Friday night if the mood seemed right, or maybe even earlier. He didn't even want to have it with him in the dorm lest somebody should see it in the closet. He could, if he chose, stop being Ed Wilson and actually be the tiger, go from reunion to reunion, wander from one tent to another, from one class to another, do a little dance now and then, have a drink—you could drink if you sipped through a straw stuck through one of the breathing holes.

Ed Wilson went to register, was assigned a room, got a handsome orange-and-black duffel bag for his free sample of toiletries (one of his classmates worked for an advertising agency that represented a cosmetics company) and his orange-and-black-striped blazer, the traditional uniform for twenty-fifth-year classes. It was an extravagance, but the joke was that if they watched their diets, the blazers would still fit in five years. They could all wear them again, as some of the old guard always did.

The rooms were smaller than he remembered them. And cleaner. There was a plain metal bedstead with a thin mattress that had been made up with linen and a blanket. There was a dresser, and a desk and a desk lamp. Otherwise, the walls and floor were all bare—so that he felt as though he were coming back as a freshman, starting out . . .

"Itchy! Hey, how are you doin'? What a great thing! You're looking good, old friend!" It was Barth.

"Bob, how are you? Good to see you!"

"Stow your gear and we'll go downstairs. They've already got one bar set up."

He didn't feel like a freshman anymore.

The more he thought about it, the clearer his answer became. He couldn't just leave. He wanted to, was sorely tempted, but couldn't run from Karl. It was what he owed America, what he owed Elfreda, and most of all, what he owed himself. If he ran now, then the rest of his life, that life he might save, would be not only worthless but an intolerable burden. Besides, it wasn't such a hopeless task after all. He knew that Einstein was at the Institute for Advanced Studies and would be there until late in the afternoon. If the FBI showed up by the end of the day, then the physicist would be safe enough. And Karl was unlikely to make his move before then.

Not only that, Peter had a fair idea where Karl would try to hide himself. He'd be in among the reuniting alumni one way or another. That was the point of the blazer. So, for Peter, too, that was where to go. He crossed Nassau Street, passed through the stone gate and onto the campus, and remembered his old resentment, as a Rutgers man, of these privileged fellows at Princeton. The campus was an odd collection of Gothic, Spanish, and Georgian buildings, scattered at random. It hadn't ever been planned, having instead evolved with the negligence of wealth and privilege, indulging its whims of the moment. Here and there on the campus were huge green-and-white-striped tents that had been set up as bars for the reuniting classes. There were signs in the Princeton colors indicating to which group each tent belonged. All the classes ended in 2 or 7. The class of '17, back for its twenty-fifth, had the largest and most elaborate installation, their tent sporting two huge plaster tigers rearing to form a kind of gateway. Inside, Peter could see workmen still setting up folding tables and chairs they carried from large carts. Other men were setting up bars at both ends of the tent. Still others were trying to coax a somewhat battered upright piano across the lawn on a dolly—but the dolly's wheels kept bogging down into the turf.

Peter went up to one of the workmen and asked him, "Say, buddy, can you tell me where the employment office is?"

"We're out of New Brunswick," the man said. "They hire there."

"You don't work for the university?"

The man shook his head. "They contract all this out."

"There's got to be some kind of office here, though."

"Just a supervisor over at the Commons. Down that way. It says Madison Hall. But I'm telling you, they hire out of New Brunswick."

"Appreciate it," Peter said.

It wasn't great news but it wasn't the world's worst, either. Peter had gone to Rutgers and so he could say, if he was pressed, that he was from New Brunswick.

A couple of young men passed by, wheeling a smaller cart full of mixers. Obviously, they were bartenders. They had big white aprons around their waists and they wore orange-and-black-striped sport shirts and imitation straw boaters with orange-and-black bands.

That was how to do it.

He walked over to Madison Hall and stood there for a while, watching people go in and out. He walked around the building. There was a side entrance to the basement. He tried the door. It wasn't locked.

He wandered around inside, looking until he found the changing room. After all, he wasn't worried about getting paid. He just wanted to work. And the caterers weren't going to be expecting that. He found a room with a couple of trestle tables and a pile of aprons and a box of those hats. And in another carton, behind the tables, there were those sport shirts. He grabbed a shirt, a hat, and an apron and put them on. He adjusted the hat to a nice rakish angle and walked back out to the quadrangle.

Roeder also arrived by bus, but his bus came from the other direction, from New York. And he went into the same drugstore on Nassau Street, and he looked up Einstein's address in the same phone book Peter had used. He had already called Information, from New York, to make sure that Einstein was listed in the directory. He asked where Mercer Street was, and he got the same instructions from the druggist. He walked down Nassau Street on the north side, across from the campus. Where the campus ended, he crossed the street, first south and then west, and started down Mercer. It was a comfortable suburban street with the houses set well back from the road and protected with hedges and handsome old shade trees. Behind some of the older and larger houses there were outbuildings—not barns, but stables and carriage houses. What Roeder was looking for were guards, policemen, security people. But the old man watching his sprinkler as it swung a fine spray of water back and forth didn't seem to belong in any of those categories.

So far, so good. His conclusion was either that nobody was guarding Einstein or that Einstein wasn't home. Possibly—probably—both of those propositions were true. He walked back along Nassau Street to the Nassau Inn. There was a pay phone in the lobby from which he called Einstein's number.

A housekeeper answered. The professor, she said, was at the Institute. He would not return home until late in the afternoon or early in the evening. He could be reached at the Institute for Advanced Studies until then.

Roeder thanked her.

"You're not the one who called before, are you?"

"No, no."

"Well, you try the Institute, then. Okay?"

"Okay."

There was a bar and taproom in the basement of the inn. That was a possible place to sit and wait, wasting a few hours in relative safety. But he could always come back there. He needed to go out and walk around, scout the terrain, be ready for what was all but certain to surprise him as the time of action neared.

He crossed the street and walked through the campus, passing some of the older men with their striped blazers. There were younger alumni, some of them wearing T-shirts with a tiger printed on the front and their '32 numerals on the back. The fifteenth reunion class had French sailor hats with orange-and-black pompons on the top. There were green striped tents with bars set up in them. None of this had anything much to do with Einstein. It was just something else going on, something to make the traffic a little heavier in town.

Roeder went up Washington Street, past the eating clubs on Prospect, and down the hill to the gymnasium and Palmer Stadium. He turned around and walked back toward Nassau Street. There was a movie theater on Nassau Street with a Humphrey Bogart double feature. Roeder had a sandwich in a coffee shop a couple of doors down from the movie house, and then he went to sit in the theater, not quite watching the films but not oblivious to them.

Dusk. That would be in his favor. And the reunion made it just a little less unlikely that some stranger might come to the door, not quite drunk maybe but not absolutely sober, asking for an autograph. That was all Roeder needed. Just for the door to be opened.

It was late in the afternoon when he came out of the theater. He took another stroll through the campus, watching the alumni, listening to the occasional sound of a piano player or a Dixieland band. He could not understand their passion for funny hats. These were the aristocrats of the United States, weren't they? At the University of Berlin or Heidelberg, there was no such foolishness.

And then he saw the man in a tiger suit, coming out of the parking lot. It was almost as good as being invisible, he realized. A useful thing.

"Excuse me, sir, can you tell me which way to Ivy Lane?" he asked. He'd passed Ivy Lane only moments before.

The man in the tiger suit paused, pointed, then looked at Roeder. Roeder could feel his gaze, could feel its motion, could bask in it the way women do, as it moved downward from Roeder's face to his hand and then settled on the blued metal of his automatic Smith and Wesson .38.

"You're out of your mind, you know?"

"If that were true, and if I were in your position, I'd worry more rather than less," Roeder said. "Turn around. Go toward those cars. I'm right behind you. The pistol is in my pocket, but not so deep I can't pull it back out."

"This isn't very funny, you know? This is really going too far!"

"Take it off."

"I can't do that. I'm wearing nothing but underwear underneath it . . ."

Roeder hit him a glancing blow on the elbow, using the gun

as a bludgeon. "Take it off or I'll put a hole in it. You understand? Now!"

Ed Wilson took the tiger head off. He put it down on the ground. Roeder had Wilson step back a few paces. Roeder picked up the head. He looked around. He saw the parking lot a couple of hundred yards up the street. "That way. To those cars," he said. The two men walked back to the cars, Wilson in front and Roeder, gun in one hand and tiger head in the other, following. When they got to the cars, Roeder ordered Wilson to look for a car that was unlocked. Wilson tried one after another until he found one that wasn't locked.

"Take off the suit," Roeder commanded. Wilson did so.

"Now, the underwear."

"The underwear?"

"The underwear! What are you, some kind of idiot? Do what I tell you. In five seconds, or you're a dead man!"

With a reluctant alacrity, Wilson took off his underwear. All the while, he glared at Roeder. Roeder's gun barrel glared back.

"Into the car," Roeder said.

Wilson got inside. Roeder picked up the tiger suit's body and the underwear too.

Wilson suddenly understood. This was the crazy man's way of keeping him there. It was a lot quicker than trying to tie him up. Sitting in the car—not his own car but a roomy DeSoto no more than fifty feet from his car—stark naked, he watched the man with the gun and the tiger suit and the underwear disappear around a corner.

What the hell! Then he began thinking. The glove compartment. There had to be maps in there. Unfolded, they could make a kind of skirt.

EIGHTEEN

Peter was working the bar at the '27 tent, having simply presented himself there, saying, "They told me to come over here and help out." The activity was frantic. Peter stationed himself behind a beer keg and started filling the big paper cups that were thrust at him by a mob of thirsty alumni. What he planned to do was stand there and work, looking around whenever he could for Roeder or Dunbar or Trumbull. But it was so busy, he hardly had time to look up. And he wasn't confident about his ability to move around. He kept thinking that he was wasting his time. What were his chances, really, of finding Roeder this way?"

He saw a couple of men sauntering through the tent who were obviously not Princeton alumni. They were security people of one kind or another. They were leaner and their eyes were different. They flicked glances from side to side the way only cops can. They were looking and they hadn't found what they were looking for.

Peter went down on his knees and pretended to fiddle with the beer keg. He was frightened. His heart pounded as he fought the panicky thought that Dunbar and his crew were after him. He'd called them, himself. They'd responded.

He could go up to one of them now, identify himself, and hope for the best. He could do that, he told himself. But he didn't trust them. He didn't like them. He couldn't just jump off the roof and into the net they were holding, because Trumbull had warned him against them and then had disappeared. He'd still be better off with Karl, with Karl's damned head on a silver salver. And he knew what Karl looked like. They didn't.

He got up and forced himself to resume his work, pouring beers into the big paper cups or into the large glass pitchers that some of the men were bringing from their tables. It was a matter of four or five minutes of concentrated and demanding effort, pretending to be perfectly at ease, trying not to show any signs of worry, waiting for them to leave the tent, while he stood there like a fool pouring beer.

They'd left. But he couldn't afford to relax. They hadn't found Karl. The chances were that they'd be back. It was important for Peter to be able to move around with more freedom. He was thinking about that when one of the men in tiger suits came in, jumped up on the stage, waved his paws, and started dancing to "Tiger Rag," doing a little time step and kick. He got applause and cheers from the alumni, and then hopped down from the stage and came over to Peter's station for a beer.

He took his head off. It was a Princeton maintenance man who had found the suit some years back, lost or abandoned in the confusion of some other reunion, and who had realized it was a key to all the booze and all the food a man could want, if he was willing to sweat for it. The plush suit was awfully hot.

He put the head of the tiger suit on a chair at the side of the bar. He opened up the zipper but the heat was still terrific, so he took the suit off and put it on the chair too. He had a beer, then another, and then got into a conversation with one of the banjo players from the band, a fellow from town he'd known for years.

Peter, meanwhile, kept his eye on the maintenance man. And on the tiger suit. There was a gurgling noise and then a hiss of gas. The keg had run out. He went to get another from the cart outside the tent. He lifted the tent flap, pulled the chair with the tiger outfit outside and put it behind the cart. He carried the fresh keg in and set it up. Then he went back with the empty one, grabbed the tiger suit, and ran.

There were dormitory entrances that had been left open to allow people access to the bathrooms. Peter ducked into one of them, changed into the tiger suit, and sauntered out again, swinging his tail and looking festive.

Roeder looked as though he lived on the block. He was carrying a big paper bag as though he'd come from the grocery store. But there were other suggestions too—in the way he walked, for instance. He seemed to know where he was going, to be perfectly confident and open about his progress. There wasn't anything sneaky about him.

Special Agent Horner had been out there for about two hours, mowing the lawn. He'd finished the lawn in the first twenty minutes or so and then he'd raked the clippings and gone over the same little patch of turf, stopping at the end of each row to rest and look around. Special Agent Wood had been washing a car, using maybe a thousand gallons of water and rubbing the damned thing with wax until it gleamed. Now they were on a verandah, sharing a pitcher of lemonade, the generous offering of the lady who lived inside the house and who was grateful to have had her lawn mowed so nicely. The agents watched Roeder come down the block. Neither of them thought to alert the other or even to voice any suspicions of his own. And their job was to be suspicious of just about anybody.

It was only when Roeder put down his bag and stopped to tie his shoe that Horner put down his glass and leaned forward. Wood's gaze was on the guy too, but he didn't move. Not until Roeder rose and walked briskly away from the paper bag . . .

Why was he leaving his groceries? What was he doing?

"Christ! He's going for the house," Wood said. He was up and had bounded down the four steps in one leap. Horner was right behind him. They both had their guns out by the time they reached the sidewalk, and there was already another team charging up the street from one of the other posts.

Roeder was already on Einstein's porch. He was ringing the bell. He hadn't run. But he'd managed to move pretty fast, just the same.

"Hold it! Hold it right there! This is the FBI."

"You're serious?" Roeder asked.

"Dead serious," Wood said, holding the gun against his left forearm and crouching in the ready position. "Just back off, there. Down the steps. Nice and slow."

"I came to get an autograph. There's a law against that?"

"There is today," Horner said.

"You've got to be crazy. This is America. What are you, a couple of Fascists?"

"Just back down the steps there," Wood told him.

But Roeder didn't. He turned. He rang the bell again.

Horner looked at Wood. Was Wood going to fire? Or wasn't he? Horner ran up the steps to keep the physicist from opening the door. To wrestle the man to the ground.

He never made it. Roeder turned, produced a gun from somewhere, squeezed off a shot, and dropped Horner. He squeezed off another that was aimed at Wood but missed. He bounded over the side railing of Einstein's porch.

There were shots from behind. Wood had hit the turf, but he managed to look behind him and he saw the other team, Kerwin and Brannagan, both of them firing.

"And what is going on?"

Jesus! It was Einstein. He'd come to his front door and had opened it up.

"Get back, Professor! Get inside!" Wood was up, had reached the porch, was trying to interpose his own body to keep Einstein from the line of fire . . .

Einstein slammed the door.

Brannagan ran up. "Horner's down. Einstein all right?"

"Yeah, he's all right," Wood said.

From inside, they heard the sound of chamber music as Einstein and his guests resumed their practice.

"Kerwin's gone after him, and there are two more guys down at the end of the block . . ."

"Call for an ambulance, will you?" Wood asked.

"They're doing that. But it's not going to help. He's gone."

Inside, Einstein and his guests were playing Haydn.

Roeder had known it would be a long shot, that he would need some luck. Up until the moment he'd reached Einstein's porch, the luck had held. The bag had been his passport and had worked well. But the police across the street had been quicker off the mark, more graceful, more adept than Roeder had bargained for. He'd been counting on just a few more seconds. Had Einstein or anyone at all opened the door, he'd have gone in, turned it into a suicide run, and done the kill. But the two men had come on very fast. And Roeder had had no idea how many locks, chains, or bolts there might be holding the door, whether it was the wood that it looked to be or steel painted to look that way. He had a split-second decision to make and he chose to flee. He could try again, another time.

He was already over the rail, down into a crouch, and zigzagging as fast as he could, around forsythia bushes and over a low privet hedge. He heard shots in front of him, and he cut right, retrieved the bag, and ran up the driveway and through the backyard of one of the houses, through the backyard of the house on Alexander Street, and then stopped suddenly. There was an open garage. The car was gone. There was a lawn mower, a barbecue grill, a length of hose coiled on the wall . . . He closed the doors. Inside, in the near darkness, he felt, for the first time, the pain in his upper left arm. He'd been shot.

He took off his shirt. There was a shelf in the garage with a few garden tools, a hand cultivator, a trowel, a pruner. He took the pruner and cut into his shirt so he could tear it into strips. Slowly and clumsily, he managed to bandage the arm, holding the end of the strip with his chin and pulling the knots secure with his right hand. It was hurting worse all the time.

From the bag, he pulled out the tiger suit. He put it on, zipped it up, and then put on the tiger head. Cautiously, he opened the garage doors. Nobody there.

From time to time, when the wind was right, strains of music came drifting over from the campus.

The arm hurt. To distract himself, he began to whistle. The whistling resonated in a peculiar loudness inside the tiger head. The song was *"Gaudeamus, igitur . . .,"* which is what they sang at universities in both countries. He'd never learned the words.

Peter was able to move around easily enough, but there were a few obstacles he hadn't quite expected. He could wander in and out of the different class tents, but he couldn't simply look around and leave. He was given drinks. If there was a band, the band leader would stop, give him a fanfare, and go into some Princeton song. Peter would then be required to dance to it in a comic shuffle. The first tent he'd visited had initiated him into this routine, with the classmates physically thrusting him up onto a trestle table. He'd done the dance, unable to think of any way of avoiding it. And then there'd been cheers and a little laughter, and then they had gone back to their other, more serious entertainments: drinking and catching up on old times.

It wasn't a bad way to look over a tent full of people. From the platform or bandstand or table, he had an unobstructed view of things. And in fifteen minutes or less, he was out of the place.

There were risks. For one thing, the man from whom he'd stolen the suit would be after him. It wasn't exactly inconspicuous. But for the short term, it seemed better than going around in his own persona, with his own face hanging out for Dunbar and the others to see.

It was in the tent of the class of '12 that the trouble started. He was up there, doing his dance, going along to "Tiger Rag," when another tiger showed up.

Peter's first thought was that this was probably a real alumnus. Peter extended a paw, inviting the other tiger up to the little stage. The other tiger shook his head, and sat down on one of the folding chairs. Peter wondered why the other tiger was reluctant. Not that reluctance served the other tiger any better than it had served Peter. The alumni pulled and shoved the other tiger up onto the platform next to Peter. The band did a couple of chords, and when the music started again, the two tigers danced together, Peter on the left, the other tiger to his right.

Then Peter noticed the blood. The man's arm was bleeding. Was it Karl? If a tiger costume was a good place for Peter to hide, it was good for Karl, too.

Peter grabbed the other tiger and tried to pull off the headpiece. The other tiger struggled. The men of the class of '12 laughed. It was a battle of the tigers. The bandleader quickened the tempo of "Tiger Rag" and the trombone player was going like mad. *Eeyah!* Hold that tiger. *Eeyah!* Hold that tiger . . .

The two tigers struggled on the little stage. Karl tripped Peter, but Peter held onto Karl as he fell so that he pulled Karl down with him. They hit in such a way as to bang Karl's wounded arm. He grunted. The alumni laughed. The band played.

"What are you doing here?" Karl asked.

"I came to stop you."

"To save your own skin, you mean!"

"No. They're after me, too."

Karl laughed, then kicked out savagely, catching Peter in the side and sending a searing pain along his ribs. "You're a fool," Karl said. And he shot. But from inside the tiger suit it was hard to aim. The bullet went wild. Peter lunged at Karl, enraged, grabbing him, trying to throttle him. Karl struggled, but Peter held on tightly. Karl managed to wriggle out of Peter's grasp, leaving him with the empty tiger head of Karl's suit. Peter threw it into the crowd, some of whom were still laughing. But the men toward the front had noticed the blood that was dripping steadily from the right arm of one of the tigers. They weren't laughing anymore. The trombone player had stopped, but the pianist, oblivious, was still going strong.

Peter grabbed a bottle of whiskey from the bar, held it by the neck, and smashed it against the edge of the stage. He lunged at Karl. He felt the satisfactory impact as he hit him. And then he felt a greater impact as he was hit, thrown backward by the bullet at close range.

Nobody was laughing now. The alumni were scrambling to get out of the way, out of the line of fire. Karl sensed their movement. It was his last hope, that crowd of people and the reluctance the cops would feel about firing into such a group. He was badly cut, where Peter's broken bottle had struck him in the chest. But he could still stand, could see, could move. And the gun in his right hand now poked through the hole his first bullet had made. He was circling to his left, toward an open place in the tent side, when Ed Wilson came rushing in. He was out of breath. He hadn't been able to run as fast as the campus police and Major Trumbull, both of whom had taken off pretty fast when they'd heard the shots. Wilson had come to find the bastard who'd stolen his suit.

And some crazy son of a bitch was about to shoot him?

"No, no. Don't shoot. He can have the damned thing!" Wilson called out.

There was a loud report as Roeder fired.

And a louder report as Dunbar and Trumbull fired together. With better result.

Roeder crumpled and collapsed, like a balloon with the air let out of it. The other tiger, with its head still in place, lay motionless on the dirt below the platform.

"It's absolutely incredible," Wilson said, breaking the silence. He sat down on a folding chair, his elbows on his knees and his face in his palms.

"I think you'd better clear the tent," Dunbar suggested.

The FBI man in the campus policeman's uniform got up on a chair and called out, "Everyone outside, please. Everybody out."

The other agent had already gone for the meat wagon.

EPILOGUE

The following day, the newspapers and radio carried the story of the FBI's triumph over the German sabotage team. There were photographs of J. Edgar Hoover congratulating Donald Dunbar, as well as mug shots of Horst Lempe, Willi Morath, and Kurt Engermann, all of whom were in custody. The others—the stories did not specify how many there were, but they mentioned Peter King as being among them—were all dead.

The director was delighted. As General Armistead explained to Major Trumbull, this was good news. It meant that the next time, there would be better cooperation between the military and the Bureau. As for Major John Trumbull, there was a commendation in his record and a recommendation from General Armistead to Colonel William Donovan that Trumbull would be a good man for the Office of Strategic Services that Donovan was setting up. The recommendation was enthusiastic and turned out to be accurate. Trumbull joined the OSS and stayed with it after the war when it turned into the CIA.

One factor in his decision to transfer into the OSS was the smoothly efficient way they were able to handle diverting the ambulance from Princeton to nearby Fort Dix. And the autopsy report they provided of Peter King was absolutely convincing. Peter Prince—King, but born again—also joined the OSS as a civilian employee and was posted back to Switzerland, where he resumed his job in the cocoa-trading concern and also worked liaison with the French resistance.

Lempe, Morath, and Engermann were all tried by a specially convened court-martial in Washington, D.C., and found guilty of espionage and sabotage—despite the fact that none of them had committed any overt act against the United States, and despite the fact that Morath and Engermann had turned themselves in. That last consideration did bear on the sentences. Morath and Engermann received life at hard labor, which President Truman commuted to deportation in 1948. They were sent back to Bremerhaven on a military transport.

Horst Lempe claimed to have telephoned the FBI the day before he was apprehended, but there was no record of any such call having been received. He was sentenced to death, electrocuted in the District of Columbia jail at noon, August 8, 1942, and buried in potter's field.

Rudi Muller's parents were released, but the money their son had been given by the Abwehr was confiscated by the Department of Justice and turned over to the United States Treasury.

In Germany, the report of the disaster had several consequences. For one thing, no such operation was ever again attempted. For another, Reichsführer-SS Heydrich found himself unable to use the Abwehr admiral's embellishment of Hitler's order as a weapon either against the Abwehr or against Canaris himself. There was an appearance of complicity that made it too dangerous for Heydrich to attempt such a thing. Piekenbrock and Canaris had withstood a little longer the assaults of Heydrich and his chief, Himmler.

When Heydrich was assassinated in Prague in June of 1942, Colonel Piekenbrock came to tell his chief the news. "We have outlasted him, excellency. It is confirmed. Heydrich died this morning."

The admiral did not look happy. "We must send flowers. And I must write Lina Heydrich a letter of condolence."

"Assuredly, excellency. But could we not perhaps indulge ourselves? Does the occasion not deserve a bottle of champagne?"

"Heydrich's death doesn't help us, I'm afraid," the admiral replied. "The question is who will replace him? Himmler is still there. The new man may be more clever and therefore more dangerous."

The new man was Ernst Kaltenbrunner.

During the course of the next three years, the Abwehr was diminished in its power and authority, its functions increasingly turned over to the Gestapo.

For his complicity in the plot to kill Hitler, Admiral Wilhelm Canaris, at the age of fifty-eight, was hanged at Flossenburg concentration camp, shortly after 6:00 A.M. on April 9, 1945.

Albert Einstein died in his bed in 1955. He had had very little to do with the creation of the atomic bomb, having spent his years at Princeton trying to work out a unified field theory, which was of no interest at all to the German Reich and would never have been a threat to anyone—even if he had succeeded.